# Gabriel Hawke Novels

*Murder of Ravens*
*Mouse Trail Ends*
*Rattlesnake Brother*
*Chattering Blue Jay*
*Fox Goes Hunting*
*Turkey's Fiery Demise*
*Stolen Butterfly*
*Churlish Badger*
*Owl's Silent Strike*
*Bear Stalker*
*Damning Firefly*
*Cougar's Cache*
*Wolverine Instincts*

# Wolf Moon

A Gabriel Hawke Novel
Book 14

Paty Jager

Windtree Press
Corvallis, OR

This is a work of fiction. Names, characters, places, and incidents either are the product of the author's imagination or are used fictitiously, and any resemblance to actual persons living or dead, business establishments, events, or locales is entirely coincidental.

WOLF MOON



Contact Information: info@windtreepress.com

Windtree Press
Corvallis, Oregon
https://windtreepress.com

Cover Art by Covers by Karen
Photo by Randy Greenshields

PUBLISHING HISTORY
Published in the United States of America

ISBN  978-1943601-72-1

**Special thanks** to Dona Miller, Lynnie Appleton, Josh Kesecker, and Randy Greenshield. Race Marshal and volunteers from the Eagle Cap Extreme Sled Dog Race. I enjoyed my visits with them and learning more about sled dogs and the race. All of their information brought my story to life in my head. I hope you enjoy my deadly version of the race.

# Prologue

Bobbi reluctantly crawled out of her sleeping bag, shoved her feet into her boots, and made her way to the outhouse. She had only been asleep for a couple of hours at the Ollokot checkpoint. She'd stopped for the mandatory 4-hour layover, where the dogs were tended and she'd get something to eat.

After tending to her dogs and filling her stomach, she'd had some time to catch a couple of hours sleep before getting back on the trail. This was the year she was going to win the 100-mile. She had her best team yet and had been training hard. After the trip to the outhouse, she'd gear up and get the team ready to get back on the trail. She was surprised she'd gotten any sleep since she'd consumed too much hot chocolate and water while chatting with the other mushers and waiting for someone to leave the tent.

All day, she'd felt as though someone or something was watching her. Even her team seemed more distracted than usual. The rookie musher, Justine, had checked in with Bobbi when she'd arrived at the musher camp, lovingly called Ollokot Hilton, an hour later than she had. Bobbi considered asking the other woman, whom she had trained with a few times, to run with her. Then she cursed herself for letting a dream about her ex affect her. It frustrated her that she was allowing the dream to ruin this run. But then the hair on the back of her neck stood up, recalling how she thought she had seen him at the start of the race.

Every day since the divorce was settled, she'd wondered how she could have married a man who was so sadistic. All the signs were there, but she'd been so surprised he was infatuated with her, she'd missed all of them.

Rather than deal with putting on her coat and rousing her team, she'd only pulled on her hat with the headlight. Still wearing everything but her insulated overalls, coat, and gloves, she walked the twenty yards to the park outhouses. Her breath created icy clouds in front of her as she breathed. The snow crunched and skritched under her boots. Glancing over her shoulder toward the tents, small headlamps bobbed around as volunteers welcomed and sent off mushers. The string of lights on the Hilton tent made her smile. It was as if a party were going on inside the tent.

The cold, crisp air meant the snow would be hard and fast. Just the way she liked it when she and the dogs ventured out into the wilderness. Right now, it made her need to use the outhouse a priority.

As she reached for the handle on the door, a hand clamped over her mouth. She kicked backwards and tried to use her fists as a weapon. But whoever grabbed her wasn't about to let go. As the arm around her neck squeezed tighter and tighter, pee warmed the inside of her legs and the world went black.

Chapter One

Justine Bartley's watch beeped, waking her up. She glanced toward the spot where Bobbi had camped with her dogs. The area was empty. She'd met the woman the previous year at this sled dog race. The experienced musher had kindly helped harness the dogs and offered tips. After the race, they had met several times to run together. They were close in age and had bonded over their shared singleness and love of mushing.

She pulled the hand warmers out of her boots and slid her feet in. The one thing she hated about mushing was cold feet. As she pulled on her parka, she heard snowmobiles revving up outside of Ollokot. She'd slept two hours after taking care of her dogs. They were getting a good five hours of downtime because she wasn't out to win this race, just have the experience of a long race.

The darkness of two in the morning and the waning light of the Wolf Moon made the erratic and frenzied bobbing of the volunteers' headlights stand out. When she'd slid into her sleeping bag, there had been an orderly movement even with mushers and their teams coming and going all night long. Several excited teams barking had awakened her about an hour after she'd lain down. She'd glanced around and saw the usual lights bobbing around as teams came and went and some really close, oddly moving lights by the outhouse, but she'd closed her eyes and fallen back asleep from the exhaustion that led up to the race and the first leg.

Walking down the line of her dogs, she patted each one on the head and talked to them, keeping an eye on the hurried movements. Something was wrong. She could tell by the people rushing into the comms tent. Curious, she hurried over. She heard someone talking as she approached the tent.

"We found a sled and team but no musher," a voice said. "We were following the last of the two hundred sleds and found a sled on the side of the trail. Ivan is out there looking for her and keeping an eye on the dogs."

"Whose team?" The Race Marshal, Cam Elston, asked.

"Bobbi Whitby."

Justine walked into the tent. "What happened to Bobbi?"

Cam turned to her. "We're trying to determine that."

"What about her dogs and sled?" Justine, having bred bird dogs before switching to sled dogs, always cared about the well-being of the animal first.

"Someone will need to go up and bring them back." The marshal peered around at the half a dozen people in the tent.

"I'll do it. I know the team. Let me get someone to take care of my dogs." Justine knew she could handle Bobbi's team, and she wanted to see where the woman had become separated from her sled and dogs.

"You'll ruin any chance of finishing in the top teams," Cam said.

"The race doesn't matter. We have to find Bobbi and take care of her dogs." Justine left the tent and went over to the Hilton tent. The canvas tent had a wood stove and chairs where the mushers could get warm drinks and food at any time. They could also hang out in the tent to warm up and visit. The volunteers hung out in the Hilton between teams arriving and leaving.

She found Neal Preston, a volunteer handler, sipping coffee. "Neal, could you please feed my dogs and keep an eye on them? I need to go bring back Bobbi's team."

He set down his cup, splashing coffee on the table, and stood. "Why? Is she hurt?"

Justine had noticed a connection between Neal and Bobbi at the vet checks in Prairie Creek and then again at the start of the race. She'd thought at the time that Bobbi might not be single for much longer.

"No one knows. The sweeper snowmobile found her team and sled on the side of the trail and are looking for Bobbi. I'll bring back the team while people continue to look." Then she remembered that her friend Hawke, a Fish and Wildlife State Trooper with the Oregon State Police, was instructing a Search and Rescue group in the area this weekend. She'd tell the race marshal about it and see if he could get the group here quickly to pick up Bobbi's trail.

She and Neal hurried back to the comms tent. As

they walked in, Justine heard the volunteer on the radio calling the authorities.

"State Trooper Hawke is at the SAR training out by Salt Creek this weekend. You could radio Salt Creek and have someone go there and tell them. If anyone can find Bobbi, it will be him," Justine told the people in the tent.

"We'll do a sweep of the area. If we can't find her, then we'll call in the Search and Rescue."

"That could be too late if she's hurt," Justine insisted.

"Go get ready to retrieve her team, and let me worry about finding Bobbi." Cam turned to one of the vets, dismissing Justine.

"Come on," she said to Neal and walked to her camp. The dogs started howling and barking for food and to run the trail. "Settle down, you'll have to wait until I bring Bobbi's crew back. Then we'll see what has been learned before we return to the race."

Justine instructed Neal where to find the food and how much to give the dogs before she put on layers and grabbed her gloves, hat, and goggles. "Thank you. When I bring Bobbi's dogs back, I'd appreciate help caring for them."

"No problem, I hope they find her and she isn't hurt," Neal said, pulling the dog dishes out of her sled.

"Me, too."

On the snowmobile ride up the trail, Justine kept envisioning them getting there and finding the team and Bobbi back on the trail. But she saw the sled off in the four feet of deep snow to the side of the trail and her heart squeezed. What could have happened to her friend?

The dogs hopped up from where they'd been lying and started barking and tugging on the sled. The snub line was fastened to a tree. It looked as if Bobbi had left her team here for a reason. But why did she stop and leave the sled and the team in the deep snow like this? Even if she had to pee, she would have left the team on the groomed trail.

The snowmobile stopped, and she realized there were two more machines up the trail a little farther. As the sound of the machine faded, she heard voices calling Bobbi's name. That could have been why the dogs were so animated. They all stood in indentations in the snow where they had made beds.

Justine climbed off the snowmobile and walked over to the sled. "I'm going to need help getting the sled back on the trail and the dogs turned around," she said to the volunteer who brought her on the snowmobile.

He nodded, not taking his helmet off, and together they released the snub line and grabbed hold of the sled as the dogs tried to take off when there wasn't anything holding them.

"Whoa!" Justine jumped onto the brake to hold the dogs from going deeper into the snow. "Grab the lead dog and bring them to the trail!" she called over their barking and yipping. The volunteer grasped Bongo, the lead dog, and pulled him to the trail. The other dogs followed, and Justine pushed the sled out of the deep snow.

Once the dogs were aimed in the direction of Ollokot, Justine shouted, "Hike!" Bongo tugged at the harness and the lines, catching the other dogs' attention, and the sled lurched forward with all eight dogs pointed forward pulling on their lines and starting the sled in motion.

The dogs were slow to respond to her commands, but didn't balk as they would if she hadn't worked with them before. By the time they arrived back at Ollokot, the dogs were listening to her. She brought the team to a stop, stepping on the brake. A volunteer grasped Bongo, holding the team as a vet and Cam approached.

"Did you have any trouble with them?" Cam asked.

"A little bit at first, but I've run them before when Bobbi gave me pointers." Justine shoved the parka hood off, stomped on the hook to set it, and continued standing on the brake. "Have you heard anything?"

"No. What did you see?" Cam asked.

"The team and sled were in the deep snow on the side of the trail with the snub line around a tree. It was as if she left them there to go look at something." Then she thought of Hawke and that perhaps their moving the sled and dogs hadn't been the right thing to do. He might have learned something from the way the sled was in the snow.

"Have you called in Search and Rescue yet?"

Cam nodded. "We need to find her. There's a storm coming in."

"Cam, over here!" came a shout from a volunteer working with a vet.

Cam walked away, and the vet who had been waiting with Cam stepped up. "My tech will help you get the dogs settled, and I'll come by and check them out."

Chapter Two

Hawke snuggled into his sleeping bag, wishing he were home, curled up against Dani, instead of near Salt Creek station, instructing Search and Rescue members how to track in snow and survive with little to no supplies.

He'd signed up to be an instructor this year because he was taking time off next month to go somewhere warm with Dani. She was encouraging him to explore places she had been during her military service. He had plenty of vacation time to use and figured that now he had someone to share it with, he might as well.

"Hawke!" A voice called from somewhere near the tent that was being used as a command center for the weekend activities.

"Might as well get up," he said to no one but himself. The other members participating in the event were spread out in the forest, sleeping in snow caves they made just before dark. Since he wasn't the one instructing them on that particular thing, he'd stayed near the command center and set up a tent with a propane heater.

"Hey, Hawke!" His tent shook.

"Yeah. I'm awake," he said, throwing back the top of his sleeping bag and placing his feet on the cold ground beside the cot.

"A musher is missing between Ollokot and McGraw. And there's a storm going to hit in about four hours."

"Shit! Round up a snowmobile to get me to Ollokot, and then get the rest of the SAR members rounded up and over. I'll meet them there to give them instructions." He pulled his pants and wool shirt over his long johns and then put on his waterproof and windproof pants, coat, and cap with earflaps. After shoving his feet into waterproof boots, he picked up his daypack and leaned over to step out of the tent opening.

The man who'd delivered the message disappeared into the command tent as Hawke started walking that direction. Another person hurried out of the tent, and a snowmobile revved to life.

By the time he'd crossed the distance between the two tents, Blakley stepped out. "Ollokot knows you're coming. Pete has the snowmobile ready to go."

"Thanks." Hawke walked to where the snowmobile was purring and stepped over the seat behind Pete, who held up a helmet. Hawke replaced his cap with the helmet and sat. Tapping Pete on the shoulder, Hawke let the man know he was ready.

They took off across the snow using the headlights as they flew through the trees at forty miles per hour, under the stars and full moon. Hawke hoped it wasn't his friend Justine who was missing. The last time he'd been in the Rusty Nail, she'd told him how she'd taken time off to participate in the Eagle Cap Extreme Sled Dog Race. He knew she'd moved from bird dogs to sled dogs, but he hadn't known she was participating in races.

Hawke arrived at Ollokot twenty minutes after leaving Salt Creek. He liked when places where his ancestors had lived were named after them, but he also felt anger that the area wasn't called by the name his ancestors called it. Ollokot was young Chief Joseph's brother who died during the battles that ensued when the cavalry chased their band of Nez Perce to Montana. This area was where Ollokot and his band of Nez Perce had camped.

Before disembarking from the snowmobile, he sent out a silent prayer to his ancestors. He stepped over the snowmobile, handed the helmet he'd been wearing to Pete, and strode toward the Comms tent. He'd been to the Ollokot check-point ten years ago when he'd been sent up to arrest a volunteer who had been caught stealing. The place hadn't changed much. A few more individual tents, but the layout was pretty much the same.

"Hawke!" a female voice called.

He spun around and found Justine hurrying toward him.

When she stood in front of him, she said, "I tried to get them to call you sooner. It took a storm coming in for them to do it."

"I'm glad it isn't you I'm looking for. Let me get the information from the race marshal, and then I'll talk to you." He patted her on the shoulder and headed to the Comms tent. He heard Justine following him.

At the tent, he pushed through the flap and stood inside the door, taking in the radio equipment and a large map with little colored flags with numbers following red lines.

"State Trooper Hawke here to help with the missing musher," he said, making heads turn his direction. "Where's the Race Marshal?"

"He's out with a vet," said a man with a red beard and overalls standing in the corner. "I'm Lance. Cam told me to take you on the snowmobile to where we found the sled."

"Is the sled still there?" Hawke asked.

"No. I brought it back," Justine said. "The Race Marshal wanted it brought back so the dogs could be taken care of."

Hawke studied Justine. "What did you see when you picked it up?"

"It was off the groomed trail, sitting in four feet of snow. The dogs had made beds in the snow but were standing and barking at the people out calling Bobbi's name. The snub line was around a tree to keep the dogs from running away with the sled. They were all off the groomed trail in the snow, like someone put it there."

"What about footprints? Did you see them going in any direction?" Hawke wondered why a musher would leave their team off the trail and wander off.

"I didn't look for footprints. My priority was getting the dogs and sled back here safely." Justine's face reddened. "I wondered on the way back if it would have been better to have left it there."

"Has anyone touched the sled?" Hawke asked,

thinking there might be something on the sled to
indicate what might have happened.

"We, Neal, a handler, and I, took dog food out of it
to feed the dogs," Justine said.

"Did you notice anything different about the sled or
the contents?" He watched as his friend stared at him as
she ran through what she'd seen.

"No, not that I could see. I've trained with Bobbi a
few times, and her equipment looked like usual."

"Does Lance know the exact spot where the sled
was found?" He glanced at the man waiting for him.

"I do. I was with Ivan when we found the sled and
dogs and I took Justine up to get the sled." Lance
handed a helmet to Hawke. "It's only about a ten-
minute ride by snowmobile."

Hawke grabbed the helmet and said, "Let's go." As
he walked by Justine, he said, "Make sure no one
messes with the dogs or the sled, please."

She nodded, and he walked out of the Comms tent
and followed Lance to a snowmobile. He was getting
his fill of riding on the machines today. His favorite
form of transportation, any time of year, was by
horseback.

Lance was right. It took them only ten minutes to
follow the groomed trail that veered to the left shortly
after leaving Ollokot. It had been a fairly straight run
along the bottom of a canyon, then it was a climb up to
the top of a ridge. Then the trail had curves and the
snowmobile slowed as the sun sent a glow over the tops
of the Seven Devils in the distance.

Lance stopped the machine in the groomed trail.
He pointed and said in a muffled voice, "That's where
we found the sled."

Hawke stepped off the machine, took off the helmet, placed it where he'd been sitting, and pulled a flashlight out of his pack. He advanced to the indentations in the snow where the sled had sat and the upheaval of snow from the removal of the sled.

He shone the light outside of the tracks, looking for footprints. He found two sets heading down the side of the ridge. "Who made those?" he asked.

Lance stood beside him, his helmet under his arm. "That's where Ivan and I walked out and called to Bobbi. We knew whose sled it was and started calling for her. When we couldn't get an answer or find her, I came back and drove to Ollokot and told them what we found. Then I brought Justine back, and we could still hear Ivan calling for Bobbi. I helped her get the sled loose and then called Ivan back. Cam, the race marshal, told me to bring him back, and we'd send out a full crew. But then we heard about the storm coming in, Cam decided we needed people with more training. That's when they called Search and Rescue."

Hawke walked into the middle of where the sled sat and shone the beam of his flashlight slowly around all sides of the sled. "There is nothing here that shows anyone walking away from the sled. He looked back at the groomed surface. "Where does this go?"

"It's only about a half mile to where the trail goes left to PO Saddle, the next checkpoint, and then the sleds come back, and instead of turning to follow this trail back, they go straight and make a loop back to Ollokot." Lance nodded his head back the way they'd ridden.

"Has anyone checked the trail between here and PO Saddle? She could be walking in the groomed trail."

He shone his light on the eight indentations from the dogs. But why go on foot when you had a team of dogs to pull you? "Take me back to Ollokot."

Hawke turned off his flashlight and walked over to the snowmobile. He pulled the helmet onto his head, and as Lance settled onto the machine, he said, "Go slower on the way back. I want to see if anyone walked off the trail." He swung his leg over and held on as the snowmobile turned and they moved at half the speed they had on the way out.

## Chapter Three

Back at Ollokot, Hawke found the SAR members who had been at Salt Creek. He gathered them in the Hilton tent and told them what he'd seen and what he suspected. "She must have stepped back onto the groomed trail and walked somewhere. I'm going to contact the state police and have them run her name and see if anything pops up that might make this a kidnapping or her wanting to vanish. In the meantime, half of you need to go to the site where the sled and team were left, and in case I'm wrong, spread out and see if you can find anything that shows she went down the ridge on either side. The other half need to follow the trail and see if any tracks are leading off the trail."

The person in command of the SAR members started calling out names and telling them which job they had.

Justine walked up to him. "Cam is in the Comms tent waiting to hear what you discovered. And no one has gone near Bobbi's sled or team."

"Good. Keep an eye on it." He started to walk away when Justine tugged on his sleeve.

"I heard what you said about kidnapping. Her ex has a really mean, nasty streak. She told me about some of the things he did when they were married. You might want to find out where he is."

Hawke stopped and studied his friend. "Does he have a record? What's his name?"

"I think his first name is Mark or Marcus. But I don't know the last name. I know she took back her maiden name when she divorced him." Justine shrugged. "That's all I know. She didn't talk much about him. She said he was the past and she was moving her life forward."

"This is good information. If you think of anything else, let me know." Hawke continued across to the Comms tent. The muted sun was beginning to shine through the clouds gathering over the canyon.

"Trooper Hawke, I'm sorry I wasn't here to greet you when you first arrived," a man in his fifties said, stepping forward and holding out a hand.

Hawke shook hands. "You must be Cam Elston, the race marshal. I'll catch you up on what we're doing." Hawke told him about what he saw, suspected, and what he had the SAR members doing to look for the missing musher.

"Your people need to be aware not to get in the way of the sled teams." The race marshal seemed to puff up like a mating ruffed grouse.

"They know to stay out of the way of the racers." Hawke faced the woman sitting at the ham radio. "I need to contact the state police in Wallowa County. Can you do that?"

She shot a glance at Cam and waited for him to nod before saying, "Yeah."

"I'd like to get in contact with Sergeant Spruel at the Winslow State Police Office. If it's easier, I can talk to someone out of La Grande." Hawke pulled up a chair and sat beside the radio operator. There was a small wood stove heating the tent. He unzipped his coat and slid his arms out. He was overdressed for anything other than a ride on a snowmobile.

The woman spoke call letters into the radio and asked for the Prairie Creek Command Center.

A voice on the other end said, "This is the Prairie Creek Command Center."

"In regards to the email Cam sent, we—"

Hawke put a hand on her shoulder. "You have a way I can send an email to my superior?"

She nodded.

"Then disregard putting this out on the radio."

She relayed the disregard message and handed him a laptop. "It should be logged in already."

Hawke opened the computer and found it was logged in and showing the real-time stats of the racers. "Can you get me on an email service?"

She clicked out of the map and into a mail service.

Hawke composed an email to Sergeant Spruel explaining about the missing woman. "What's Bobbi's last name?" he asked.

The woman told him, and he typed the last name and the first names that Justine thought were her ex's name. Then he told him that it was possibly a kidnapping. *Please do a background check on the woman and the ex-husband.* At the bottom, he added, *I may be up here longer than the weekend if we don't find the woman.*

He sent the email and asked the radio operator if she would let him know when the sergeant replied.

The race marshal stood inside the Comms tent waiting for him. "What do we do now?"

"I want to know the times when Bobbi arrived at Ollokot and when she left and talk to everyone she talked to while she was here." Hawke watched as the man shook his head.

"We can get you the times she came and went, but as for talking to everyone she did, most of them are out on the trail racing. They'll be coming back in to either check in or rest."

"Get the list of people she saw, and I want to talk to them when they come back through here." Hawke didn't wait for the man to say that wouldn't work. He walked over to where Justine stood, petting a dog.

"Is this your team or Bobbi's?" he asked.

"Mine. Bobbi's team and sled are over there." She pointed to a sled and eight dogs, three camps away from hers.

"You should get back into the race, keep your mind on other things," Hawke said.

"No. I want to help find her. She was good to me when I started mushing. She was the only one who stopped and helped me when I was confused or unsure if I was doing things right. We built a friendship from our love of dogs and mushing." Justine looked up from the dog she petted and peered into Hawke's eyes. "She was as close a friend to me as you and Dani."

He understood her need to help find her friend. He had a driving need to help anyone who was in trouble.

And a friend made his desire to help even more crucial. "Let's go through her sled and see if you see anything amiss."

They walked over to the sled. As they approached, the dogs all started barking and yipping as if they thought they were going on a run. All but one.

Hawke studied the dog on the end. He wasn't interested in them. He kept sniffing the air. "That dog. How long has Bobbi had him?"

Justine followed his pointing finger with her gaze. "That's Bongo. He's her lead dog. She's had him about five years."

"Longer than the rest?" Hawke asked, walking toward the dog.

"Yeah. She got him when he was a pup and trained him to be the lead dog."

"What was he doing when you found the sled?" Hawke held his hand out to the dog, let him sniff, then scratched the animal behind the ears. "Hey Bongo, what do you know that has you on alert?"

"The others were barking in the direction where the snowmobile operator was calling Bobbi's name. But Bongo was looking back down the trail." Justine walked up to them. "Do you think he knows which direction Bobbi went?"

"Maybe. Can you find a leash so I can let him sniff around?" Hawke wasn't sure what the dog might be able to help them with, but he had always trusted Dog, his canine companion.

Justine dug in Bobbi's sled and came up with a leash.

Hawke took the lead, clasping it to Bongo's collar before unhooking the neckline from the gangline.

Bongo pulled on the lead, digging his feet into the snow, pulling Hawke toward the outhouse.

He thought it was odd the dog was pulling him toward the building, but when the animal put his nose in a patch of yellow snow with flattened and disturbed snow around it, he handed the leash to Justine. "Hold him over there."

Standing still and twisting his body to see the pattern of the disturbed snow, he judged that there had been a struggle here. The footprints to the disturbed area had one set coming from the musher camps, and two sets, deeply indented in the snow, coming from the side of the building. He stopped and studied the two sets of deeper prints that went round the back of the tents.

Hawke took Bongo's lead back from Justine. He followed the prints leading Bongo to the large signboard that designated this as Ollokot Campground. A sled with boxes sat at the base of the sign.

Bongo sniffed the air and whined. Hawke led him toward the sled. "What is that sled for?"

"That's what they use to haul injured or tired dogs back to Prairie Creek Command Center where the mushers pick up their injured dogs when they finish the race." Justine grasped Hawke's sleeve. "You don't think—"

"You stay here," he told Justine and let Bongo lead him over to the sled. The dog put his nose to one of the kennels and sat down, whimpering.

Hawke patted the dog on the head. "You know she's in there, don't you?" Sighing heavily, Hawke led the dog back to Justine. "Take him back and tie him up, then get the Race Marshal and have Sheriff Lindsey radioed to come back to Ollokot."

Justine studied him. "You think she's in one of those boxes? But then how did her team and sled end up out on the trail?"

"That's what I'll have to find out. Go." He watched until the woman and dog were almost to the line of dogs yipping and tugging on their lines. Hawke walked over to the sled and knelt in front of the kennel Bongo had indicated. Peering through the mesh door, he saw clothing and long dark hair. "Shit!" He sat back on his haunches and studied the two sets of prints in the snow. One set went off through the trees and the other headed to the camping area. Two people had shoved the victim's body into the kennel and then went about their business as if nothing had happened.

## Chapter Four

The Race Marshal nearly lost his last meal when Hawke told him what he believed. By the time the sheriff arrived, Hawke had chased several people away from the crime scene. Luckily, he'd taken photos and mapped out the footprints he'd spotted before they were obliterated by all the people wanting to know what was going on.

He was glad Justine was taking care of her dogs as well as the victim's. It gave her something to do and would keep her away when the medical examiner finally arrived and they took the body out of the kennel.

"You're telling me the woman we've been looking for is stuffed in there?" Rafe asked as he stood beside Hawke, staring at the sled with kennels.

"Keep your voice down, I've had to chase nearly everyone in this camp away once the word got out that I was guarding the sled," Hawke said, barely loud enough for the sheriff's ears only.

"Sorry. I'm just thinking about how they did it." Rafe pulled out a cell phone. "Want me to call Gwendolyn?"

"She should be showing up any minute. I asked the Race Marshal to contact her and send a snowmobile out to pick her up."

"It's not going to be pretty getting the body out of there." Rafe said what had been on Hawke's mind.

"No, it's not." Hawke had a thought. He pulled out his walkie-talkie and contacted the relay person at the SAR communications tent. "SAR Com Salt Creek, this is Hawke. Over."

"This is SAR Com Salt Creek, go ahead, Hawke. Over."

"Have someone bring the tallest tent that's at least eight by ten feet to Ollokot, please. Over."

"Copy. Over."

Hawke turned to Rafe. "When they get here with the tent, we'll set it up over the sled so no one will see how the body is removed."

"Good idea. Want me to take over keeping an eye on it, while you get out of the cold and get some coffee?" Rafe zipped his coat up to his neck.

"Thanks, I'll do that. Have someone come get me if I'm not back by the time the tent or Dr. Vance arrives."

"Will do." Rafe leaned against the sign at the front end of the sled.

Hawke walked over to Justine's camp. "Come get some coffee with me. I want to warm up and see if anyone in the Hilton talked to Bobbi last night."

Justine nodded, gave the dog one last pat, and followed him. "Is that really Bobbi in the box?" she asked in a quiet voice.

"Does she have dark hair?" he asked, knowing it had to be the woman because the dog had detected her scent, and it explained why they hadn't found her near her sled and dogs.

"Yeah. About the same length as mine."

He watched from the corner of his eye as Justine swiped at her eyes. "I'm sorry. I wish I could say it was someone else, but it would still be a horrible crime, and it needs to be solved." He held the flap back on the Hilton tent. Justine walked in ahead of him.

The murmuring stopped. He counted eight people inside. Three appeared to be mushers and the others were volunteers. Hawke followed Justine over to the large pot of coffee and picked up a paper cup, filling it.

When he turned, all eyes were on him. *No time like the present.* "Were any of you in here last night when Bobbi Whitby arrived?"

"Is that who you've been looking for?" one of the mushers asked.

Hawke glanced around at the faces. Some knew who they'd been looking for and others appeared to be just learning about it. "Yes. Her sled and dogs were found about five miles up the trail. However, her body was found here in camp."

"Oh no!" one of the women volunteers cried.

"You're sure it's Bobbi?" asked a man who'd nodded to Justine when they'd entered.

"We'll know for sure when the medical examiner gets here. Now, to my question, were any of you in here last night when Bobbi arrived?"

The woman who'd cried out nodded. "I was. We talked a bit. She said she had a good first leg and was excited to get bedded down to get out quick from the mandatory layover here." The woman tapped a finger against her lips and said, "But then, for talking about getting to bed and getting off before the others, she hung around in the tent a while after she ate."

"She was walking to her camp with Neal—" Justine motioned to the man she'd nodded to when they entered— "when I arrived. She came over and helped me secure the team, and we talked a minute or two before she went to her camp, checked her dogs, and slipped into her sleeping bag," Justine said. "I grabbed a quick bite after I took care of my dogs, and then I crashed."

Hawke nodded at his friend and then speared the man, Neal, with a stare. "You walked her out. How do you two know each other?"

"I helped her get her dogs to her camp area when she arrived, then I had to go help with the next team that came in. Then I walked her from here to her camp later. She seemed edgy. She said it was just nerves about the race, but when she said it, I didn't think she sounded sincere. Walking to her camp, she kept staring at everyone who walked by, like she expected to see someone."

"Neal, why didn't you say something sooner?" Justine jammed her hands on her hips. "You know that she worries about her ex retaliating."

Hawke glanced at Justine and then at Neal. The man's face was growing redder by the second. "How do you know about her ex-husband?"

"We've been friends through this event for a few years. She told me about how difficult her divorce was and that her ex-husband had threatened her when the papers were delivered to him." Neal shrugged. "But that was four or five years ago. He should have cooled off by now."

"In my line of work, I've learned some people never cool off." Hawke pulled out a notebook and pen. "What's the name of her ex-husband?"

Neal shrugged again. "She only called him Marcus. I assumed his last name was Whitby."

"No, she took back her maiden name, but she never told me her married name either," Justine said.

Hawke glanced around the tent. "Anyone else notice Bobbi acting differently?"

One volunteer nodded. "She did hang out in the tent longer than usual. In other years, she'd come in, grab food and something hot to drink, and go back to her camp to eat."

The picture that everyone was painting showed a woman who was anxious about being alone. That would have made her hours of solitude while mushing hard to endure if she was worried about someone around every bend and tree.

"Do you know if there was anyone at this race who she's had problems with?" Hawke asked.

They all shook their heads.

"She was always the first one to help another musher and never talked bad about anyone," said the woman who had first commented.

The others agreed.

Hawke thanked them for visiting with him, then he asked Neal and Justine to follow him out of the tent.

"You two seem to be the two closest to the victim." Justine flinched at his use of the word victim. He'd have to watch how he talked about her friend. "I have someone at the State Police looking into her ex-husband. Is there anyone else that you can think of who would want to cause her harm?"

They both shook their heads. "If you think of anything she might have said about anyone, come find me and tell me." He looked both of them in the eyes before he walked back toward the sign and dog box.

He scanned the encampment searching for anyone who appeared overly interested in the happenings. No one seemed to stand out. There had been two people who committed the homicide and concealed the body. That was why he hadn't found footprints leading away from the sled. Someone drove the sled from here and left it alongside the trail. Then the second suspect picked them up. Another musher who followed behind or someone on a snowmobile?

"Just received word that Gwendolyn will be here in twenty minutes. And here comes the tent. Perfect timing," Rafe said, pointing to a snowmobile swishing through the trees with a loaded basket fishtailing behind.

Rafe went down to meet the person who brought the tent. It turned out to be one of his deputies. That would help with policing the area until the body was removed. The two county officers packed the tent over to the sled with boxes.

"Hey, Hawke," said Deputy Calvin Cochran before he headed back to the snowmobile and basket for the poles.

When he returned, the three of them started putting up the poles and then the canvas tent over the frame. By the time they had it in place, the sound of another snowmobile announced the medical examiner's arrival.

This machine drove right up to the tent. Hawke couldn't see who the driver was through the helmet he wore.

Dr. Gwendolyn Vance sat behind the driver. She stood and swung her leg over the seat, removed her helmet, and thanked the man for the ride. He nodded and handed her what looked like a large purse.

"Hawke, we have to stop meeting like this. You know how I feel about the wilderness." She said this with a smile and a twinkle in her eyes.

Hawke smiled back. "I applaud you coming out here on a snowmobile. Was it as fun as a horse?" The doctor didn't like riding horses and had expressed it to him on several occasions.

"I much preferred the snowmobile." She studied the tent. "What have you found this time?"

"Let's step inside and I'll show you." Hawke held the flap back.

Dr. Vance and Rafe entered. Hawke motioned for the deputy to stand guard, and he followed.

"I don't see a body?" Dr. Vance said as she pointed to the sled. "Are you telling me it's in there?"

"I'm afraid so," Hawke said.

"What is this world coming to?" she said, setting down the bag and pulling out latex gloves. She handed them each a set. "I'm not going to be able to do this myself."

Hawke opened the kennel door and a hand fell out.

"You know some bones may have been broken just putting her in here," Dr. Vance said, her head shaking. "You poor child. I'll be as considerate as I can be."

Hawke stood back, peeling the latex gloves off as Dr. Vance did a preliminary examination of the body now laid out on a tarp. In the time it had taken them to unfold and get the body out of the kennel, a forensic team had arrived along with SAR members and a body bag.

"I'd say given there are no external wounds and the bruising and trauma on her neck, along with the petechial hemorrhaging, I'd say she was strangled. But the neck is also at an odd angle. I'll know more when I get her on an examination table." Dr. Vance held out a hand, and Hawke helped her to her feet.

"What kind of strength would it take to possibly snap her neck while strangling her?" Rafe asked.

"She's small. Anyone who knows how to snap a neck could have done it easily without much of a struggle. But with the signs of strangulation, I'd say she fought and the person doing it wasn't experienced." Sadness filled her eyes. "Why do people do these things to each other?"

"I'm afraid we'll never know." Hawke nodded to forensics to move in and get what evidence they could find from the body before it was moved. "From the footprints I found, two people carried her over here and put her in the kennel."

Rafe stared at him. "You're saying we're looking for two suspects?"

"At the least, the killer and the accomplice." Hawke crossed his arms. "I've learned that she had a nasty ex-husband. I've asked Sergeant Spruel to see what he can dig up. You can go down with the body and make sure it gets sent to the state pathologist after Dr. Vance does a more thorough examination. I plan to stay up here until the volunteers leave and talk to as many people as I can."

"Calvin can stay and keep people away while forensics does their thing and then assist you in questioning," Rafe said.

"Thanks." Hawke opened the flap and held it for Rafe and Dr. Vance.

Justine stood behind the line of crime scene tape Deputy Cochran had put up.

Hawke walked over to her. "Do you know Bobbi's next of kin by any chance?"

"No. I think she has a sister. Her parents are dead." Justine shook her head. "This is all so senseless."

"Murder always is," Hawke said. "Finish your race and I'll catch up to you back down in the valley."

"No. I'm going to take care of Bobbi's dogs until they transport them to Race Central. Cam has someone taking care of her sled. I'll take my team down when the volunteers start tearing down the camp. I can help you get information from people until then." Justine crossed her arms as if to emphasize her stubbornness.

"Where did Bobbi live?" Hawke asked, deciding to just let the woman feed him information and help him talk to the volunteers and mushers.

"Stanley, Idaho. You can get all the information from Cam or one of the judges." Justine fell into step beside him.

"I suppose Stanley is a good place to train sled dogs," Hawke said, stopping to watch as a musher and team arrived at Ollokot. He watched as a volunteer ran out and held the lead dog, while another volunteer with a clipboard talked to the musher, counted dogs, and wrote on a card, handing it to the musher.

"What's that all about?" Hawke asked.

"That musher just arrived from the second leg of the hundred mile. They stayed the mandatory hours here last night, took off early morning, and headed to

PO Saddle. Now they can either keep going or stop to rest, but they can ask for a vet check of their dogs if they want one before they head to the finish line." Justine glanced at him. "Do you want to talk to that musher?"

"Yeah. But why is the person with the clipboard digging through the sled contents?" Hawke wondered if the race marshal had asked to have each sled checked for a weapon.

"Each sled has to have safety equipment or the musher is penalized. At each checkpoint, the volunteers check for the equipment and mark down whether or not a musher wants a vet to check an animal and to write down the time the team arrived." Justine waved her hand. "Now, a handler, what Neal does, is helping take the team to the musher's designated parking area."

Hawke was learning there was more to sled dog racing than hooking dogs up to a sled and yelling, 'Hike!' "What about when a team leaves, do they just harness up the team and take off?"

"No. The teams are not unharnessed while they're resting. The dogs learn to sleep in their harnesses. When a team first arrives, their safety gear is checked, and they stay here for a mandatory rest for the dogs of three hours for a hundred miler and four hours for a two hundred miler. It's to rest, feed the dogs, take care of any needs they have. It could be massaging cream into their feet, massaging a sore leg, whatever the dogs need to keep them healthy, and give the vets time to check the dogs."

"Let's talk to that musher and then go find out what time the impostor Bobbi left last night and find out why no one realized it wasn't her."

## Chapter Five

Hawke walked over to where the musher was securing his team between two trees. "Excuse me. I'd like to talk to you for a few minutes."

The man, clearly older than Hawke, by the silver beard and cloudy eyes, studied him a moment and went back to what he was doing.

"Sir, I'm State Trooper Hawke and I'm asking questions about the body we found—"

The man swung around. "Body? What body? Where?"

"A musher. Her name was Bobbi—"

"Little Bobbi girl?" the man interrupted, his eyes glistening with tears. He swiped his coat sleeve across his eyes, before regaining his surliness. "What happened?"

"That's what we're trying to find out. Do you know if her team left here last night before you did?" Hawke pulled out the small notepad he'd dug out of his backpack earlier.

"No, she'd just pulled her team up to the departure line when I told my team to go. I wondered why she didn't catch up to me. Her team is fast. She usually goes around me at some point. Good little musher."

"What time did you leave here?" Hawke asked, writing down everything the man said.

"It was one-thirteen. That's the earliest my time card said I could leave. I made sure I was up and waiting for the volunteer to check my things in plenty of time to get out on the dot." The man nodded his head. "Did Bobbi have an accident on the trail?"

"No, that wasn't her with her team." Hawke watched the man as he stared at the dog at his feet.

"That makes sense. I wondered why she didn't reply when I told her good luck. Usually, she'd laugh and tell me I needed the luck to beat her." He smiled. "She was a good kid. Loved the sport."

"Can you think of anyone who had it out for her?" Hawke figured there wouldn't be anyone since everyone considered the woman a friend.

"You could ask Unity. She was complaining last night when Neal walked Bobbi out of the Hilton that he'd be smart to look for a woman with seasoning rather than money."

Hawke latched on to the last word. "Money? Did Bobbi have money?"

"Yeah, she told me once that she could spend all her time training dogs and racing because she inherited the family legacy from her grandmother when she passed." The man shrugged. "You would have never known she had money or that she came from it. Bobbi was as down-to-earth as you could get. I think that's why Neal was drawn to her. Now that Unity…She'd be high maintenance. Never did understand why she mushed. Might break one of her fancy nails."

Hawke asked for the man's name and added it to

the bottom of the information. When they were out of hearing of the man, Hawke asked, "Do you know Unity?"

"I've heard of her, but I don't think I've met her. She's been mushing a while and she doesn't hang out with the women." Justine made a face.

Hawke wasn't sure what the face was about. "Let's go find out who checked the Bobbi imposter out last night and see if we can find out where Unity is."

"The Comms tent is where we'll find out both." Justine led the way to the tent with the tall antennae behind it.

Cam spun around as they entered the tent. "How are things going?"

"Forensics should be gone soon, as well as the body." Hawke flipped open his notepad. "Can you tell me who would have been the one to check out the person impersonating Bobbi last night after one-thirteen?"

"That's a hectic time with the two hundreds arriving and the one hundreds leaving." He grabbed a clipboard. "Looks like it was Earl Anton as the time keeper and Jasmine Axel as the handler. It's Earl's first time at Ollokot, he's helped at Salt Creek the past two years. And this is Jasmine's first year."

"How well did Earl know Bobbi?" Hawke asked.

"Just to see her mush in, drop her number in the box, and mush out. At Salt Creek, they just mark down the musher's number and count the dogs as well as note the time. The mushers don't stop for any reason unless they have an injured dog or something like that." Cam narrowed his eyes. "Why are you asking these questions?"

"It's pretty obvious that Bobbi was dead when her sled and team left here last night. I want to know how no one noticed it wasn't Bobbi on her sled." Hawke let his glance slide to the man at the radio and back to Cam.

"Like I said, mushers are coming and going that time of night. Everyone is in a hurry to leave or take care of their dogs. As cold as it was last night, the person was probably wearing a ski cap and or a neck gaiter. The only way to know who it was would be by the bib number and the dogs."

And that was how they got away with stalling the discovery of the body. By misdirection. "Where can I find Earl and Jasmine?" Hawke asked.

"Either the Hilton or sleeping." Cam motioned to Justine. "She knows which tents."

Hawke nodded. "And I need to know where Unity is and her last name. Also, do you have any information on the next of kin for Bobbi?"

"Why Unity?" Cam asked, typing on a laptop. A map appeared on the monitor and Cam pointed to a red dot. "That's where you'll find Unity. She's headed here for the final check-in."

"Do you have a time estimate of when she'll get here?" Hawke asked.

"In about thirty minutes, give or take."

"Thanks. What's her last name?"

Cam glanced up from the monitor. "Allard."

"And the address for Bobbi's next of kin?" Hawke reminded the race marshal.

"Yeah. Tom, email Cassandra at Central and get the next of kin information on Bobbi, please." Cam headed to the tent opening. "I promised Dr. McPherson I'd catch up to him in case he had dogs to pull from teams." The man disappeared from the tent.

Hawke focused on Tom. "How long do you think it will take you to get a response?"

"Hard to say. Depends on whether Cassandra's alone or has someone helping her."

Hawke handed him a piece of paper with his email. "Can you send it on to me at this address?"

"I can."

"Come on." Hawke led Justine out of the tent. "Do you know Earl and Jasmine?"

"I met him at the Musher Banquet last year, and I think I know who Jasmine might be. There are only a few unfamiliar people and most of them are men." She headed toward the Hilton.

Hawke glanced at the sign board and saw that the SAR snowmobile carrying the body to a road was gone, and Deputy Cochran, along with another person, were taking down the tent. He didn't see any sign of the forensic team; they must have left as well. His stomach grumbled.

Twisting his hand, he checked his watch. It was almost two o'clock. He had jumped out of his sleeping bag in the early morning hours and hadn't eaten anything since last night. That's what tended to happen when he worked a case: he forgot to eat until his stomach complained.

Entering the Hilton, the aroma of warm bread, onion, and spices made his stomach growl again. "Let's eat," he said to Justine, figuring she hadn't had anything either.

She didn't say a word, just walked over to a table with several crockpots.

Hawke read the labels in front of the pots. Chicken Gumbo. Chili. Loaded Potato. He put a ladle of chili and the potato in a bowl and picked up two warm rolls. He knew they couldn't have baked rolls here, but their warmth and aroma made his mouth water.

They sat in chairs not far from the table of food. Once he had eaten one roll and was dunking the second one in his soup, Hawke scanned the interior of the tent. Close to a dozen people were hanging out. Some were eating, some sipping drinks, and others were just talking. He was beginning to notice the difference between the mushers and the volunteers. The mushers had on boots that would deal with the coldest weather, while most of the volunteers had on good-quality winter boots. The mushers also had thicker overalls and coats. Many had red, wind-burned cheeks and noses.

Hawke cleared his throat loudly.

The chatter stopped and everyone stared at him.

"I'm State Trooper Hawke. I'm here investigating the death of Bobbi Whitby."

Several people gasped or murmured.

"If any of you talked to her during this event, I'd like to talk to you to try and see what her frame of mind was like and if she might have mentioned problems with anyone." His gaze traveled around the room. He noticed a couple of women whispering in the corner. "I also would like to speak to Earl Anton and Jasmine Axel. If either of you are in here, please see me before leaving the tent."

Justine leaned toward him. "There are two female mushers in the corner whispering. I'm going to go have a chat with them."

Hawke nodded as a middle-aged man with a red

beard and round build walked up to him. "I'm Earl. I'm guessing you want to talk to me about what state Bobbi was in when she left here last night with her team."

Hawke motioned for Earl to take the seat Justine vacated. "Yes, what can you tell me about her as she was waiting to leave?"

"I haven't really dealt with her before, other than seeing her drop her number in the box at Salt Creek and write down her time and dogs. But she kept pulling her gaiter up to cover her face, which I thought was odd since she needed to answer my questions on the check sheet."

"It's because it wasn't Bobbi. It was someone wanting you to think it was her." Hawke watched the man's face go from surprised to thoughtful.

"That makes a lot more sense about how she was acting. She only gave one-word answers, kind of soft, to where I could barely hear them. Then when Ferdie said something to her, you could tell he was hurt that she barely noticed him." Earl sat back in his chair. "Damn shame, she was a really good musher and good human being."

"Do you know where I could find Jasmine?" Hawke asked.

"She's been spending a lot of her free time around the vet tent. I think she wants to be a vet tech and is trying to see if it's what she'd like to do." Earl rose as Justine returned. "I hope you find the creep that did this." He walked away, and Justine sat down.

"He said Jasmine spends her off time around the vet tent," Hawke said.

"Those two mushers overheard Unity saying she'd turn Neal's head to her instead of that drab Bobbi. That doesn't mean she killed Bobbi, but she did have a beef with her over Neal." Justine picked up her soup and finished eating while Hawke helped himself to another bowl.

When he returned, another volunteer was talking to Justine.

"Hawke, this is Opal. She's a judge and knows a bit about Bobbi."

He rescued another chair and placed it beside Justine. The woman sat and stared into the cup she held.

"What can you tell us about Bobbi? Anything would help. Especially if you know anything about her next of kin." Hawke spooned soup into his mouth and then pulled out his notepad and pen.

"She has a sister who lives in Seattle. They are complete opposites. Bobbi used her inheritance to train, raise, and mush dogs, like her great-great-grandfather. Her twin sister, Beverly, used her inheritance to set up an art gallery in Seattle. They weren't close considering they were twins, but they did stay in touch."

"Do you know the name of the gallery?" Hawke asked.

"Distinction Gallery. It's well known." Opal sipped her drink. "Marcus Radburn is the one mistake Bobbi made in life. That man was horrible. If she hadn't been divorced from him before she came into her inheritance, I'm sure he would have killed her for it."

"Did he know about the inheritance when they were married?" Hawke wondered if there had been a loophole somewhere in the paperwork.

"No. It was a complete surprise to both girls. It was a surprise to the whole family, actually." Opal sipped again.

## Chapter Six

"How so?" Hawke asked.

"There were four cousins. Bobbi and her sister and then a brother and sister from their dad's sister. From what Bobbi said, none of the cousins expected to get anything. They thought it would go to their parents. But Bobbi and Beverly's parents died in an airplane crash about fifteen years ago. I think that's when the grandmother must have changed her will to benefit the two who lost their parents. Anyway, Bobbi said her cousins and their parents contested the will, but only wasted money. The grandmother had left them all a small sum and household items."

"Thank you. This is all good information." Hawke had scribbled all the information in his notepad. He now had a next of kin and more suspects.

"I'm so sorry to see such a bright light snuffed out. She would have gone on to the Iditarod and made us all proud." Opal pulled a tissue out of her pocket and blew her nose.

Justine hugged the woman and peered at him.

Hawke picked up his soup and finished it. By then, the woman had moved on. "I'm ready to talk to Jasmine," he said as Justine dropped her spoon in the empty bowl.

"Me, too." She took his bowl, cup, and spoon and dropped them all in a garbage can as they exited the tent.

"Let's check the vet tent. If she's not there, I'll go into the women's volunteer tent and see if she's there." Justine tromped through the large snowflakes that fell from the sky.

Hawke pulled the collar of his coat up around his ears as the wind howled through the trees. "I think that storm they were worried about has hit."

"Yeah, I'm kind of glad I'm not out mushing in this. It would be hard to see the trail," Justine said over her shoulder.

Whining could be heard over the barking of the dog teams as they neared the tent. Hawke grabbed the zipper as it started moving. He stepped back as a man and a woman stepped out.

"Can I help you?" the man asked.

Hawke had on his Oregon State Police cap. "I'm State Trooper Hawke. I'm investigating the death of Bobbi Whitby and wondered if I could have a chat with you, and if Jasmine is here, I'd like to talk to her."

"I'm Dr. McPherson. This is Sheri Nichols, she's a vet tech. I'm not sure what we can tell you. Bobbi's dogs, as usual, were healthy and fit every time I checked them. She took pride in her animals."

"Did anyone check them before the team left last night?" Hawke asked.

"No, they were checked when she arrived. There was no need to recheck before she left. All the dogs were healthy." Dr. McPherson glanced at his watch. "Is there anything else? I need to get a team inspected."

"Is Jasmine in there?" Hawke asked.

"No, I think she went to lie down for a while," Sheri said.

"Thank you." Hawke walked away with Justine following.

When they were out of earshot of the two, Justine said, "He's never praised how I care for my dogs. It's just as good as Bobbi. And he was being so formal and dry. Usually, he jokes a bit. I found him too unemotional."

Hawke stopped and studied her. "What are you saying without saying it?"

"I've always thought he had a bit of a crush on Bobbi. Nothing creepy, just if she had given him the okay, he'd have been asking her out." Justine motioned for him to stay put. "That's the women volunteers' tent. I'll be right back."

Hawke pondered what Justine had said, waiting for her to return with Jasmine.

Justine returned alone.

"She's not in there. But I did get a photo of her." Justine showed Hawke a photo of a young woman with dark hair and a cheek and nose ring.

He nodded. "She'll stick out around all these older people."

"I'll check the women's restroom," Justine said.

"I'll check the Hilton again." Hawke walked in the opposite direction of Justine, thankful there was a generator purring in the background of the barking dogs. The lights on the Hilton tent made it easy to find in the ever-thickening, blowing snow. He hoped Justine could find her way back here from the restrooms.

He stomped his feet before pulling the flap back and walking in. It appeared everyone who was in camp had migrated to the Hilton. The tent was full of people sitting and standing. The voices were muffled and loud. He stood inside the door, no one paying any attention to him as he scanned the room for Jasmine.

Hawke spotted her as the flap behind him moved and Justine stepped in beside him. He pointed to the corner where the young woman was talking to two older women.

Moving through the people, he managed to stop a couple of feet from Jasmine. He touched the brim of his cap and nodded to the two older women. He recognized them as the volunteers who had spoken up about Bobbi in his first visit to this tent.

He faced Jasmine. "I'm State Trooper Hawke. I'm here investigating the death of Bobbi Whitby, and I'd like to ask you some questions."

The young woman's eyes widened, and her mouth formed an O as she stared at him. "I don't think I'll be much help. This is my first year, and I don't even know if I met her."

"I learned that you were the handler for her team when it left here last night. After one A.M.," he added to jog her memory.

"The woman after Ferdie left?" she asked.

"Yes, that's the one." Hawke pulled out his notepad.

"When I was walking away from holding Ferdie's lead dog, she asked me to hold for her. Since I was already dressed for the cold and didn't see anyone else around, I did."

"Did she say anything else to you? Or did you get a look at her?" Hawke asked.

"She only asked me to hold. I didn't see much of her. She had a gaiter covering all of her face that her goggles and stocking cap didn't." Jasmine tapped her cheek ring with an index finger.

"Why would she need goggles at night?" Hawke asked, thinking it was one more way to hide the person's identity.

"I wondered the same thing. But you know how athletes have rituals. I thought maybe it was hers," Jasmine replied.

"How tall was the person?" Justine asked.

Hawke smiled at his friend. That was going to be his next question.

"My height, maybe a little taller." She stared at them. "Shouldn't you know what she looks like?"

"That wasn't Bobbi, it was someone impersonating her," Hawke said.

Jasmine's face lit up. "That's why the dogs didn't respond to her at first. She shouted, 'Let's Go' and they all stopped hopping and looked over their shoulders at her. Then she shouted 'Hike' and they took off. But the lead dog kept looking back toward camp until they were out of sight."

The height of the musher and the dogs not responding would have been a giveaway that the musher wasn't the right one. How had the impersonator been lucky enough to have two new people who didn't know Bobbi as the people to send them off?

"Thank you," Hawke said and drew Justine back to

the tent opening as the flap opened. Deputy Cochran walked in with the race marshal. Calvin nodded toward the outside and Hawke followed him out.

"Forensics found a few things that might help with the investigation. And as soon as the tent came down, the race marshal had the return dogs loaded into the sled to take to Command Central." Calvin stood in the flurry of snow only a foot from Hawke, but he was hard to see even in the beam from the string of lights on the tent. "Cam just gave the order that the mushers who are here, must stay. It would be too hard to see the trail at night with just a headlamp."

"That's a smart idea. I've learned more about the victim and have several leads for people who might have wanted her dead. However, most people say she was well-liked." Hawke watched as the snow piled up on Calvin's cap and shoulders.

"We're stuck here tonight," Calvin said. "The race marshal said we could sleep in the volunteers' tent, but I took the liberty of setting the tent we used to cover the removal of the body up behind the Comms tent."

"I like that idea better," Hawke said.

"We won't have heat, but we'll have our own space." Calvin stared at the Hilton. "I'm going to grab something to eat and then go to bed."

"I'll be right behind you. I have one more person to talk to." Knowing that the mushers who arrived weren't allowed to leave, Hawke had a feeling Unity was either in the tent or with her team.

He stomped and shook the snow off before following Calvin into the Hilton. Justine raised a hand and waved. He walked through the people to her.

"That's Unity." She pointed to a woman in her 50s

with bleached blonde hair, makeup, and long flashy nails.

"She's a musher?" he asked, not believing someone that made up would lift a finger to tether dogs and hook them to rigging.

"Yep. And she likes men." Justine gave him a push toward the woman.

Hawke scowled at Justine over his shoulder, then walked up to the flamboyant musher.

"Well, hello," she said when he stopped in front of her. "You must be a new volunteer."

"No, Ma'am, I'm State Trooper Hawke. I'm here investigating the death of Bobbi Whitby."

The woman's eyes snapped at the name, but the smarmy smile remained on her lips. "I see. And why would you want to talk to me?"

"I'm questioning everyone who might have come into contact with Bobbi during the race." Hawke pulled out his notepad. "Please give me your full name and how you knew Bobbi."

"Unity Love Allard. I've raced with Bobbi in several different events. As for this race, I saw her and Neal laughing and talking at the vet check-in at Prairie Creek, and then when the two of them walked out of the Hilton last night." She made an exaggerated surprised expression and then said, "You don't think Neal had anything to do with…" She waved a long, brightly colored nail back and forth, "you know."

"Those were the only times you saw Bobbi? Did you speak to her?"

Unity leaned back and studied him. "If I said I only saw her from a distance, how in the world would I speak to her?"

Hawke shrugged. "I thought you might have spoken to her when she wasn't with Neal."

The woman's eyes narrowed. "Are you trying to say I killed her?"

"No, Ma'am, I'm just trying to get to the truth." Hawke had a feeling this woman did speak to Bobbi. She was being too antagonistic not to be hiding something.

"I only saw her the two times." Unity turned away from him and shoved people out of her way as she walked over to the hot drinks.

Hawke decided to call it a night. He didn't see Justine and figured she'd gone to check on the dogs.

Stepping out into the wind and snow, it felt like he was on another planet. Small white lights bobbed around in the distance and close by. Without a light for himself, Hawke realized he'd have a hard time finding the tent Calvin had set up for them. It also made it difficult to figure out where the dogs were. It was eerily quiet. The dogs must have bedded down to sleep out the storm. Not a bark or yip sliced through the wall of snow falling from the sky. He hoped Justine found her team and Bobbi's and had a warm, dry place to sleep.

A light shone from behind him.

"What are you doing standing here gathering snow?"

## Chapter Seven

Hawke turned and a bright light blinded him.

"Sorry, shoulda said, want me to light your way to wherever you're going?"

Hawke recognized the voice. It was Ferdie.

Turning so the light wasn't directly in his eyes, Hawke asked, "Could you take me to Bobbi's dogs and then Justine's? I'd like to make sure they are all bedded down okay. Then I have a tent behind the Comms tent."

"How about I take you to your tent, and I'll check on the dogs and Justine. That way I don't have to trudge out to the dogs, back to here, and then out to my camp in this mess."

Hawke knew it made more sense, but he wanted to make sure his friend was okay. "That works, but if you'll wait for me to get a flashlight, I'll walk to the dogs and Justine with you."

"Suit yourself."

They continued to the Comms tent and then behind

it in silence. Hawke opened the flap and looked around for his backpack. It was sitting in a corner with his cot, sleeping bag, and duffel. He dug in the side pocket and came up with a flashlight. "I'm ready. Lead the way to the dogs."

Back out in the blizzard, Hawke pulled the hood of his coat up over the top of his cap and shivered as snow melted down his neck.

"Bobbi's dogs should not be too far. She always tries to camp near this tree." Ferdie tipped his head, running the beam of his headlight across the snow. A bump in the snow moved. A dog stuck its head out of the snow where it was curled up.

"Should we take them in somewhere?" Hawke asked, thinking about Dog cuddled up in front of a fire at Dani's feet.

"They're used to this. The snow insulates them from the wind, and I'm pretty sure whoever is taking care of the dogs covered them with the blankets Bobbi always used." Ferdie walked along and asked, "Where is your friend from here?"

"She was three camps down." Hawke shone the beam of his flashlight ahead and spotted Justine's sled. He continued forward, trying to see if she was sleeping in the sled or had gone to the musher's tent.

A dog growled and Hawke stopped.

Ferdie made a kissy sound. "It's okay, we're just checkin' on you and your musher," he said.

"I'm fine," Justine's voice came from behind the sled. That's when Hawke spotted her head and that of two dogs. "We bedded down here out of the wind."

"Did you bed down Bobbi's dogs?" Ferdie asked.

"Yeah, they each had their blanket. But I could tell

they didn't understand why I was putting them to bed instead of Bobbi. They'll be even more confused when I load them up and take them to my place. I told Cam to let Bobbi's sister know I have them. She can decide if she wants them or wants me to find homes for them." She yawned. "I'm going back to sleep. You two need to find your beds and wait out the storm."

"Night," Hawke said. He faced Ferdie. "Are you going to be able to find the way to your camp?"

"It's just over yonder. I'm more worried about you getting back to your tent."

"I'll be fine. I know where it is now. Thanks." Hawke watched the man until he could no longer see his headlight bobbing. The wind had picked up and so had the size and quantity of snowflakes falling.

He stomped the snow where he was standing as he tried to catch one last glimpse of the musher, then pivoted, located the faint flare of lights on the Hilton tent in between wind gusts, and walked back down his barely discernible tracks to the tent Calvin had set up for them. When he entered, he found the deputy already snuggled into his sleeping bag.

"Thanks for grabbing my gear out of my tent," Hawke said, as a gust of wind struck the side of the tent like a giant hand.

"I have earplugs if you need them to shut out the sounds of the storm." Calvin held up a small bag with earplugs.

"No thanks. I enjoy the sound of nature in all its forms." Hawke found his cot and set it up, then the pad, and finally his down sleeping bag that would keep him nice and toasty all night. Once he was down to his long johns, he slid into the sleeping bag and listened to the wind howl and tree branches creak.

Barking and the revving of snowmobiles pulled Hawke's head out of his sleeping bag. The camp had come to life. He glanced over and saw Calvin listening, too.

"Sounds like we need to get up and see what's going on," Hawke said, shoving his sleeping bag to his knees and shivering. He quickly dressed, donned his parka, and pulled on a stocking cap before tucking gloves in his coat pocket.

He reached down and untied the tent flaps and found three feet of snow piled up against the tent. Snow tumbled onto the tarp floor. "Great. I wonder if this is a drift or if we'll be battling three feet of snow all day."

Calvin was dressed and standing beside him, staring out at the sunny world. "Looks like it put several feet down overnight. The snowmobiles with the groomers are moving around the middle of camp and I see a couple of them headed out to the trail."

"I imagine once the groomers get the trail cleared, the mushers will be allowed to leave." Hawke wasn't sure if he was happy to get away from here or needed more time talking to the people who were at the camp when the victim was killed.

"We can get back to the valley and start digging into everyone's background." Calvin sniffed. "Smells like there might be some breakfast in the hospitality tent."

"Let's go see and maybe learn what's going on." Hawke's gaze traveled to the trees where the mushers and dogs spent the night. The dogs were hopping around, yipping, barking, and howling. It seemed the snowy night didn't dampen their desire to pull a sled. If Justine wasn't in the Hilton, he'd go check on her before he grabbed something to eat.

Ferdie was coming out of the tent as they approached. "Mornin' officer. Looks like your friend and Bobbi's dogs had a good night. Nothing to worry about. If a person can't stand a stormy winter night, they have no business mushing." He walked away from the tent.

"Who was that?" Calvin asked.

"A veteran musher." Hawke moved the tent flap aside and stepped into a warm, delicious-smelling environment. He spotted Justine talking to Neal. Rather than barge in on their conversation, he went to the table with rolls, meats, cheeses, and soups. Hawke grabbed two rolls and slapped turkey on one and ham on the other, along with a couple of different cheeses. Then he grabbed a cup of coffee, smiling at the woman who was filling cups, and sat in a chair where he could watch the people.

Unity entered the tent, and while everyone noted her arrival, it was Justine and Neal who strode across the tent to stop her by the door.

They both lit into her. Hawke decided he'd better intervene and see what was going on.

"You have no business being a musher," Justine said as Hawke stepped beside her.

"What right do you have to tell me that?" Unity asked, poking a finger in Justine's chest.

Neal stepped between the two women. "If everyone else in the tent knew how you cared for your dogs, they'd all be telling you the same thing."

"Hey, what's going on here?" Hawke asked,

moving beside Neal, to block Unity's view of Justine.

"This has nothing to do with you," Unity said between clenched teeth. "Keep it down," she added to Neal.

"Unity didn't check her dogs before going to the musher tent to sleep last night," Justine said, glaring at the woman. "A true musher would have put their dogs' well-being over their own."

Several other mushers crowded around.

"Is that true?" someone asked.

"I know she wasn't with her dogs, and they were whining towards morning. I'd say they were cold," another one said.

"What's going on here?" Cam asked, pushing through the crowd that had gathered around.

"I want you to take a vet and check Unity's dogs," Justine said, defiance in her tone. Her expression was hard as stone as she stared narrow-eyed, her gaze remaining on Unity.

"They don't need to be checked! They were checked when I came into Ollokot." Unity's voice was now a shrill plea.

"I believe you should check her dogs. While you do that, I'd like to have another conversation with her." Hawke took Unity by the arm. "Deputy Cochran, would you bring me a cup of coffee to our tent and stay to take notes?"

Calvin nodded, understanding the woman could make accusations that would be hard to disprove if Hawke questioned her alone.

"I don't understand why we have to leave this tent," Unity said, digging her heels in.

"I'm pretty sure you don't want everyone at this

camp to hear the questions I have for you or possibly your answers." Hawke raised an eyebrow.

She must have understood, because she started walking.

Once they were outside, he released her arm. "Follow me."

She glared at him but followed him to the tent Calvin had set up.

Hawke motioned to his cot. "Sit."

Calvin pushed through the flaps with three cups of coffee. He handed one to Hawke and one to Unity.

"I still don't understand why you think you need to talk to me again," Unity sipped the coffee and made a face. "I use cream and sugar."

Calvin dug into his pocket and produced packets of creamer and sugar. She plucked them from his hand and tore them open, adding all of them to her cup. The deputy then offered her a spoon, which he produced from the same pocket.

While she stirred her coffee, Hawke asked, "Why did you neglect your dogs last night?"

Her head tipped back as she stared up at him. "That's none of your business."

"It is when there was a body found here less the twenty-four hours ago. And your name popped up when we asked if anyone had a grudge with the victim."

"Who said that?" she shrieked. "I bet it was one of those prune-faced volunteers. They think I use mushing to be able to hang out with men." She sat up straight and pushed up her boobs with an arm. "Look at these. And do you see any lines on my face? No, you don't. I take care of myself and men appreciate that."

"What man appreciated it last night?" Hawke

asked. Glad that he'd fallen for Dani, a no-nonsense, no make-up kind of woman.

"I don't kiss and tell." She made as if to zip her lips shut and took a sip of her coffee.

"I think it would be in your best—"

The flap to the tent flew open, and Justine stood there out of breath. "Hawke, you need to come see this." Her gaze shot to Unity. Hawke saw the rage boiling in his friend's eyes.

Chapter Eight

"What is it?" Hawke started toward the door.

In a whisper, Justine said, "Bobbi's coat was in her sled."

Hawke nodded. "Deputy Cochran, keep Ms. Allard here until I get back." Then he thought about the woman and stepped out the door. He spotted one of the women volunteers. "Ma'am!" he called out to her.

She changed direction and walked over to them. "Yes?"

"If you aren't busy at the moment, could you wait in this tent with Deputy Cochran? I don't want to leave him alone with Unity Allard. I don't trust her not to try to use a harassment charge against the deputy."

The woman smiled. "That is good thinking on your part, I agree. I can wait here until you return." The woman entered the tent and gave her name to Calvin.

"Okay, now we can go." Hawke fell in step beside Justine. "How do you know it's Bobbi's coat?"

"It's the parka she wears when she's mushing. It has her kennel name on it, and I saw the spot where she had to get it patched after a problem dog bit her. Why would she have Bobbi's coat unless Unity helped whoever killed her?"

It was a fair question and assumption. But he'd check at the Comms tent to see if Unity could have been in the camp at the time the imposter left with Bobbi's sled and team. Maybe she picked up the person and dropped them off somewhere to be picked up by someone else.

Justine stopped at a sled that had Cam, Dr. McPherson, and Neal all standing around as if they'd had an argument and were only there to see what he had to say.

Hawke nodded to the men and stepped up to the sled. A parka was lying across the handle of the sled. "Where did you find it?" He directed his question to Justine.

"Neal and I were digging through the sled to find food for the dogs and he pulled it out, thinking Unity had an extra. I noticed the kennel logo and looked at the spot where I knew it had been patched." Tears glistened in Justine's eyes. "That's Bobbi's. The one she had on when she started the race."

"Unity has had it out for Bobbi ever since they both started attending the same races," Cam said.

Hawke glanced at the veterinarian and the volunteer. They both had their heads down, staring at the snow at their feet. He had a pretty good suspicion Unity had coveted the two men and they only had eyes for Bobbi. It wouldn't be the first time jealousy had been the motive behind murder, but the timeline didn't fit. At least that's what he thought.

"Neal, go to the hospitality tent and see if you can get a clean garbage bag. I'll bag the coat and have it sent to forensics. Maybe we can get some DNA or something off of it."

Neal nodded and jogged toward the Hilton.

Hawke pulled back the top flap on the sled. "Justine, do you see anything else in here that looks like Bobbi's?"

She stepped closer to the sled and peered in. "No, I don't see anything that stands out."

He nodded and faced Cam. "I need to know where Unity was from the time Bobbi arrived at Ollokot until an hour after the imposter left here with Bobbi's team."

Cam stared at him.

"You should know that because of the trackers on the sleds," Hawke said. He snapped his fingers. "When the sweepers found Bobbi's sled, did you know it had stopped?"

Cam shook his head. "No. The tracker was still moving when they found the sled."

"On the trail?" Hawke asked.

"I'm sure it was or someone would have noticed." Cam shook himself. "I'll go look into all of that."

Hawke turned to Dr. McPherson. "Did Unity's dogs seem extra tired when she arrived here before the storm?"

"No. They seemed the same as always. She was distracted."

"What do you mean?" Hawke studied the man.

He blushed. "She didn't flirt with me. I wasn't in the mood after learning bout Bobbi and then she didn't rub up against me or even make a comment about meeting up with me to stay warm."

Hawke played the vet's comment over in his mind. The woman must have already known her competition was dead and didn't feel the need to press her intentions.

Neal arrived with the bag. Hawke had Justine pick the coat up and place it in the bag, since she had already touched it. He twisted the top of the bag. "Keep this to yourselves. I'm going to question Unity about it now."

Hawke walked back to the tent and entered to find Calvin and the volunteer visiting and Unity sitting on the cot, pouting.

"Thank you for your time," Hawke said to the woman and held the tent flap open.

The woman smiled, nodded, and exited.

Hawke walked over to Unity and opened the bag. "This was found in your sled when Dr. McPherson ordered your dogs to be fed."

Unity peered into the bag and looked up at him with a puzzled expression. "I don't know what that is."

"It's been identified as Bobbi Whitby's parka. How did it end up in your sled?" Hawke twisted the top of the bag and knotted it. Then he placed it on Calvin's cot.

"How should I know how it got there. Someone must have put it there last night when I was sleeping in the musher tent." She started picking at the edge of the paper cup.

"Who was sleeping in the tent besides you?" Hawke asked.

"I don't know, I just took my sleeping bag in there because it was warm. I didn't do bed checks." Her voice was strong, but her flushed cheeks made him think she did do a bed check, perhaps looking for a sleeping partner.

"How many people were in there?" Hawke picked up his coffee and sipped. It was cold, but it gave him something to do as he waited for her answer.

"Just me and Sean Tucker." She didn't look at him.

"Did he acknowledge you when you entered the tent?" Hawke asked.

"Yes."

"And you stayed in the tent all night?"

"Yeah, why wouldn't I? We weren't allowed to leave camp with the storm." Her gaze flew up to his. Anger flashed in her eyes.

"Did Sean stay in the tent all night?" Hawke watched as her cheeks flushed.

"Yes."

"Did anyone else enter?"

"No."

"What about the night before? When did you come into camp and when did you leave?" Hawke watched as the woman studied the cup in her hands. She was either trying to remember the times or trying to figure out how not to incriminate herself.

"I arrived first at about six. I grabbed a sandwich, watered my dogs, and we took off on the second leg of the race." Unity said.

"When did you return from that?" Hawke watched as she mulled this around.

"I believe it was about two. I took care of my dogs, and went into the Hilton to get something to eat and get warm." She glanced up. "You know you could ask them to pull up my times."

Hawke nodded. "The race marshal is doing that. But it's quicker to get the information from you."

She seemed to take that as she was helping and gave him a smile. "After I ate and warmed up, I grabbed my sleeping bag and went into the musher's tent. There were only a couple of people in there.

Mostly hundred milers getting ready to take off. I found a corner and went to sleep."

"What time did you get up?" Hawke asked, wondering why she hadn't gotten up and out of the camp before the race was halted due to the storm.

"Seven, I think. When I went to the Hilton, everyone was talking about Bobbi being missing. I figured I'd stick around and see what was going on." She studied her hands as she stated the last part.

Hawke wondered if she'd stuck around to keep tabs on the investigation. That made sense if she was in on the deception of making people think Bobbi was lost somewhere other than where her body was hidden.

A thought came to him. He needed to talk to the race marshal. "You can go. But give your information to Deputy Cochran in case I have more questions." Hawke exited the tent and headed to the Comms tent.

When he stepped inside, someone was speaking on the radio.

"Ollokot, the trail is groomed to the finish."

"Copy. We'll start sending out the mushers," the radio person replied.

Hawke walked over to where the race marshal sat, flipping through pages attached to a clipboard.

"How often do dogs get put in the kennel sled to be transported?" he asked.

Cam looked up at him and blinked. It was clear his mind had been on the papers. "The box sled?" He ran a hand over his face and said, "It depends on how many dogs become injured or too tired to continue. Once we get enough to fill the boxes, it is delivered to Race Central, where the dogs are taken out and handed over to someone to care for them until their musher finishes the race."

"How many dogs did you have when we found the body?" Hawke asked.

"I think six. A couple more and we would have loaded the sled."

"And found the body unless someone who takes the sled to Race Central knew there was a body in it and loaded one less dog." Hawke was talking out loud.

Cam's gaze flew up to Hawke's face. "That would mean that person was in on the murder."

"Who was taking the box sled down to Race Central?" Hawke asked.

"One of the volunteer snowmobilers. It could have been anyone who was waiting around for a job to do. There isn't anyone set to do that job." Cam shook his head. "I don't see that person as being in on the murder. Because it is a random job."

Hawke nodded in agreement. But it had to be someone who hadn't planned on the body being found so soon. Otherwise, there would have been no reason for the misdirection.

Cam handed him a piece of paper. "Here are the times Bobbi checked in and out and the times Unity checked in and out."

Hawke noticed an overlap of time when the two were in the camp together, but by Justine's accounts and what Unity said, they didn't meet up.

"Can I get a list of names and contact information for all the mushers and the volunteers. I understand they will all be heading back to their homes by tomorrow, and I want to be able to contact them if I have more questions." Hawke folded the paper with the times and put it in his pocket.

"I can have them print it out at Race Central. You can pick it up there," Cam said.

"Okay. I'll talk to a couple more people and then I'll be heading out. Sorry the homicide and weather messed up the event." Hawke shook hands with Cam and left the tent.

He found Calvin over at Justine's camp talking with her. Hawke wandered over. "I'm done here. You don't need to stick around until everyone is gone." he said.

"I'll stick around here until the last team takes off." Justine was dismantling Bobbi's sled.

"What are you going to do with Bobbi's team and sled?" They would have to let the family know where the dogs and sled were.

"I'll contact the sister and see what she wants me to do with them." Justine shrugged. "I'm guessing that is what Bobbi would want me to do."

Hawke nodded. "What time do you think you'll be showing up at the finish line?"

"I'm hoping mid-morning." Justine smiled. "That's a beautiful time to be mushing."

"Call me or Dani when you get to the finish," Hawke said.

"I will. I'm glad you're going to look into Bobbi's death. It's such a waste. She was a good person who didn't deserve to die like she did." Tears glistened in her eyes.

"No one deserves to die before they are ready." He put a hand on her shoulder. "See you in the valley." He walked away, motioning for Calvin to follow. "Let's take down our tent, gather our stuff, and head out of here. I need to do background checks."

## Chapter Nine

Hawke helped load the tent and their belongings onto the sled behind the snowmobile. After they traveled from Ollokot back to Salt Creek and loaded their vehicles in the parking lot, it would be late by the time he arrived home. He might as well relax and start digging into the backgrounds of the people he found suspicious in the morning.

He drove home and parked his truck in the driveway, thankful there was only four inches of snow down here and most of it had melted off the roads. Contemplating whether to unload his gear, he sat in the vehicle staring into the darkness beyond the barn. Everyone had sung praises for the victim. That would make it harder to find out what had caused someone to strangle her.

The ex-husband sounded violent. He was the first person Hawke planned to check up on.

A burst of light turned his attention to the front door. Dani stood backlit from the lights in the house, and Dog ran to the vehicle.

Hawke stepped out and decided to wait until morning to unload. He grabbed his duffel bag as Dog jumped up, putting his front paws on Hawke. He scratched the dog's ears. "Okay, that's enough, let's get in the house before Dani fills it with cold air."

Dog dropped to his paws and trotted ahead of him to the house.

"How was the training?" Dani asked, closing the door behind him as he dropped his duffel bag on the floor.

"It turned into a missing musher and finding a homicide victim." He opened his arms and Dani walked into them. This was something he hadn't known he needed the two decades after his divorce and before he met Dani. Having someone to share his day with and having human companionship.

"You're kidding me?" She leaned back to look into his face.

"Nope. And it was one of Justine's friends." That was what would drive him harder to find the killer. Justine had been through more grief than most people, and yet she kept a sunny disposition. He wanted to bring justice for Bobbi to help his friend.

"Should I call her?" Dani and Justine had become friends since he and Dani became a couple.

"I'd wait until tomorrow. She's waiting to come out until the last musher leaves. I don't think she'll get home until late. She's taking her friend's dogs to her kennel. She'll have to deal with the extra dogs." He'd always known Justine was loyal to those who treated her well. She'd not been treated kindly by her sister and father and had helped him prove they were murderers.

"I'll call her in the morning and offer to come help her since I'm sure you will be working to track down the person who did it." Dani stepped away from him and walked to the kitchen. "I have a pot of soup, and Darlene brought some of her rolls this afternoon."

"I smelled the soup when I entered. It all sounds good." Hawke shed his coat, draping it over the back of a chair, and followed her into the kitchen. It was nice to come home to something besides microwaved food. He thought about the nearly two decades he'd lived over the Trembley's arena, with only a hot plate, microwave, and coffeemaker to cook with.

Dani dished up the soup. "Would I know the person who died?"

"I don't think so. Bobbi Whitby. She's from Idaho." Hawke grabbed a roll from the basket and dipped it into his soup.

"Oh, that's the woman Justine has trained with a few times. That's awful. But why? From what she's said, the woman was kind and generous." Dani sat down beside him at the counter.

"Yeah, everyone I've talked to thought that about her. But she does have an angry ex-husband. I'm looking into him first. The people I talked to said she was acting as if scared of something."

"It has to be the ex, then." Dani pulled her roll apart and spread butter on it.

"That is the logical suspect. There is also a jealous musher. I don't know if she killed her, but I think she might have been an accomplice. The timing works, and she seems petty enough to cooperate to get a rival out of the way." Hawke couldn't stop thinking about Unity's jealousy and need to upstage others.

"I'm sure you'll have this figured out in no time."

Hawke shrugged. He hoped it was as easy as discovering where the ex-husband was on Thursday night.

The next morning, Hawke went early to the State Police Office. He wasn't on duty and should have still been up at Salt Creek helping with the SAR training, but he felt the homicide investigation was more important than his showing the trainees how to track. There were other knowledgeable people still up there.

He opened his computer and found an email from Sergeant Spruel with the information he'd discovered about Bobbi's ex. Marcus Radburn had been arrested three times for assault. One of the victims had been Bobbi Whitby.

Hawke wrote the man's home address and work address in his notepad. He lived in Idaho. Having Idaho State Police talk to him made sense - time and money-wise, but it wouldn't give him a good idea about the man. He'd have to ask for permission to question the man himself.

He put in Unity Allard's name and wasn't surprised to see the list of misdemeanors she had. While she had a record for stalking men, she didn't have anything violent on her record.

Just to be thorough, he put in Neal Preston. He was a local. Married, three children. He worked at the feed store in Prairie Creek. Hawke wrote down his residence and the place where he worked. Then he wrote *married* and circled the word. Had his wife become jealous of Bobbi? He'd have to see the woman to decide if she was strong enough to strangle another woman.

Then there was Cam Elston, the race marshal. He'd given Hawke a weird vibe. He wondered if Bobbi had spurned the race marshal's advances. Digging into the information on the race marshal, he was married, had two grown children, lived in Washington, and officiated at a number of races each year. Hawke wrote down the races and would look up contacts to see what they had to say about the man.

Last on his list was Dr. McPherson. He seemed to have a hard-on for Bobbi as well. It made Hawke wonder why people hadn't said she slept around or worse. But then he had no evidence that she did. Only that several men were interested in her. She could have been one of those women who didn't know men were attracted to them. He made a note to ask Justine about this.

He put in Ronald McPherson DVM into Google because he hadn't asked where the man was from. He hadn't become a suspect until Hawke had seen how he reacted to the death, and later the mention of Bobbi. Three veterinarians appeared. Luckily, they had photos, and he found the one he was looking for. McPherson resided in Montana with his wife and four kids. Hawke was beginning to wonder if these men traveled around to these events to hook up. Unity would be more than happy to be the hook up, but from the stalker charges, it also appeared that she didn't like letting go.

Hawke shoved away from the computer and pulled out his phone, scrolling for his superior's number. He found it, hit dial, and waited as the phone rang.

"Hawke, hold a minute," he answered.

"Sure." Hawke put the phone on speaker, and he opened up an email that had just popped up on his screen. It was from Dr. Vance.

*My initial observation was incorrect. The victim's neck wasn't broken. She was asphyxiated by an arm around her neck. It was a struggle because of all the bruising. Internal injuries in the neck are consistent with strangulation. I didn't find any skin under her nails, but the State Pathologist might be able to find something.*

"Hawke, are you still there?" Spruel asked.

"Yeah, must have been a call from a family member," Hawke said, knowing Nathan's kids were in college.

"I wish. No, it was Major Lowell apprising me of the changes coming. It's always the smaller offices that get hit the worst when there are budget cuts."

Hawke knew this was a bad time to ask about making the trip to Idaho. But it was important to the investigation. "This is poor timing," Hawke said and continued, "I'd like to go to Council, Idaho, and question the ex-husband of our victim."

Nathan was quiet for a few seconds. "Why do you need to go?"

"I want to see his reactions when he's asked where he was this past weekend and when he last saw his ex-wife." Hawke didn't wait for Spruel to tell him no. "He is our strongest suspect. He's been violent to her before."

"If you can find someone who saw him here, then I'll allow you to travel to Idaho to talk to him. There's no sense in wasting money if he wasn't even here. Have Idaho troopers ask his work and friends if he was there, and you see if you can find someone who saw him here."

Hawke was glad he and Nathan had worked together long enough that they respected each other's decisions.

"And Hawke, aren't you supposed to be at Salt Creek teaching tracking in the snow today?" Nathan said it in a tone that wasn't a reproach but as if he knew Hawke would call.

"I felt getting on the investigation was more important."

"It is. Let me know if you need anything else from me."

"I will." Hawke ended the call and printed out the email from Dr. Vance and a photo of the victim's ex. Since it had been a struggle, the attacker could have been a woman. He imagined Bobbi had been strong from lugging food and water to her dogs and caring for them.

As he walked out to his work vehicle, he wondered how he would be able to show a photo of Marcus Radburn to people who were part of the event but were scattering.

<><><<>>

Hawke called Justine to see if she'd made it back.

"Hello, Hawke. I just finished talking with Dani," Justine said by way of answering.

"Hey. Thought I should make sure you made it home. And I have a question. Is there any way I can get some of the mushers and volunteers together to flash a photo of Bobbi's ex?" Hawke figured it was a long shot.

"You're in luck. Because the race was held up by the storm, they're having the Awards Reception tonight at the community center in Prairie Creek. Starts at six.

A good number of people will be there. Some already headed for home because of the delay."

Hawke grinned. He hoped to find someone tonight who had seen Marcus. "That's good to hear. I'll see you there."

"Bring Dani. She can be my plus one. I could use her common sense to get through tonight. There's going to be a vigil for Bobbi afterwards." The tremor in her voice told him she needed Dani's support.

"I'll do that. See you then." He ended the call and immediately texted Dani that they were going to the Awards Reception tonight.

She replied, *Sounds good.*

Chapter Ten

Hawke parked his pickup in the full parking lot of the Prairie Creek Community Center. Several of the vehicles were loaded with dogs. The barking and howling weren't as excited as at the race. These were more mournful, ready to go home howling.

He and Dani walked up to the building, and Hawke opened the door. The room was full of people. He found where the speaker would stand behind the podium and directed Dani to the right of the entrance.

Several of the people he'd talked to at Ollokot spotted him and made their way over.

"Have you learned anything?" one of the women volunteers asked.

"No, but I have a photo of someone that I'd like you to take a look at." He showed her and the people around him the photo. "Did you see this man anytime during the race?"

They all shook their heads.

"Did he do it?" another person asked.

"I won't know until I determine he was here and talk to him." Hawke moved further into the group. Dani split off from him. He glanced in the direction she was headed and spotted Justine. As he continued through the crowd, he asked if anyone had seen the man in the photo.

Ferdie stepped in front of him. "Didn't expect to see you here tonight. Did you come for Bobbi's vigil?"

"Yes and no. Did you happen to see this man anytime during the race events?"

The man took the paper from Hawke's grasp and studied it. "I did. It was during vet checks in Alder. He was standing kind of behind my truck, looking up the street."

This was the news he needed to make a trip to Idaho. "What was up the street where he was looking?"

Ferdie handed the paper back and rubbed the silver stubble on his chin. "I was at the tail end of the line of mushers waiting for vet checks. I think it was three woman mushers. Bobbi, that new girl you know, and Unity, and then Ralph, Trent, and me in that block."

"Thank you. Can you point out Ralph and Trent to me?" Hawke would see if either of the men had seen Marcus. Then he'd show it to Unity and Justine. Though…he stretched his neck and peered around the room. He didn't see Unity anywhere.

"That's Ralph, and over there in the corner with his family is Trent." Ferdie narrowed his eyes. "Is this Bobbi's ex?"

"I can't divulge who he is. Just a person of interest." Hawke didn't need Ferdie, or anyone else who had liked Bobbi, going after Marcus.

He made his way to Ralph and showed him the photo. By the way the man studied the photo, moving it closer and then farther away from his eyes as if trying to focus, Hawke had a feeling the man didn't see very well. "Thanks," he said when Ralph shook his head.

He walked to the corner of the room where Ferdie had indicated Trent.

The man glanced over the head of the child he held in his arms. "You're the Trooper who was at Ollokot, aren't you?"

"Yeah." Hawke held up the photo. "Have you seen this man around the race events?"

Trent studied the photo. "I can't be positive, but he looks like a guy I saw standing at the corner of Race Central when Bobbi and I were moving toward the start. She was ahead of me as we moved to the starting line. I noticed him step away from the building as she went by. Her head swiveled around, and then she looked forward and didn't look back. I thought it was odd the guy didn't shout 'Good luck' or anything. Just stood there."

Hawke nodded. "Did he look like he was intimidating her?"

"Could be. I know she was fumbling around with her hook and drag brake, like she was flustered while she waited for the signal to go." Trent glanced down at the child in his lap and said quietly, "You think this guy, you know?"

"Now that I have confirmation he was here, I'm going to ask him. Thanks." Hawke scanned the room, found Dani and Justine. He walked over to them as the announcer stepped up to the podium.

"I found what I needed," he said as the announcer

shouted out the winner of the 31-mile race.

"What were you doing talking to Trent?" Justine asked.

Hawke showed her the photo of Marcus.

"Who is this? I saw him watching Bobbi and Neal during the vet checks." Justine's eyes widened, and she asked, "This is him, isn't it? The ex?"

"Yes, and I had enough people confirm they saw him here that I can go question him tomorrow."

Tears glistened in Justine's eyes. "Do you think Bobbi saw him and that's why she was so nervous?"

"According to Trent, she saw him just before she started the race." Hawke watched as Dani moved closer to Justine.

"Why didn't she tell someone? She could still be alive if she'd told us. We would have never let her go anywhere alone." Justine's voice was filled with remorse.

"Maybe she thought she was seeing things. Did she mention anything about feeling like he was stalking her?" Hawke asked as the announcer continued to call out the winners, and the room around them exploded in clapping and cheers.

"No, she didn't really talk like she thought he would actually hurt her. She said he'd wanted his freedom from her as much as she'd wanted it from him." Justine wiped at her nose and stopped with the tissue resting against her nose. "She did mention that when she received the inheritance from her grandmother, he started coming around asking for handouts. Maybe she thought he was there to ask for money?"

The announcer finished calling out the first,

second, and third-place winners of the various races. "Now let's all bow our heads and in the silence think good thoughts about Bobbi Whitby."

Everyone bowed their heads but Hawke. He searched the room to see if anyone else wasn't paying respect to the murder victim. Everyone in the building seemed to be genuinely moved by the passing of Bobbi Whitby.

"Thank you all for coming." Cam Elston said, getting everyone's attention. "I know having to stop the race for the storm set you all back a day."

The announcer nodded and said, "We look forward to seeing you all next year. If you want to hang around, we'll be lighting some candles for Bobbi and telling stories about how we know her."

Hawke hadn't noticed Elston earlier. Where had he come from? He turned to Justine.
"Has the race marshal been here the whole time?"

She glanced at the man in the front of the room and shrugged. "I don't remember seeing him earlier, but there are a lot of people in this room."

Some people began moving to the doors, while a small group hung back and Opal handed out candles.

Justine seemed hesitant to walk over and join the group.

"Let's go get a drink at High Mountain," Dani said, linking her arm in Justine's. "I bet you could use a drink and some downtime."

"That sounds good. But just one. I need to be up early tomorrow to get all the dogs taken care of before I go to work." Justine and Dani walked out of the building arm in arm with Hawke following.

He caught up to them at Justine's car. "You two go

on ahead in Justine's car. I'll be behind you."

Dani studied him. "You learned something in there tonight, didn't you?"

"Yeah. I'll be talking on my phone to Spruel on the drive to Alder. You might as well have a good conversation with Justine." He knew she saw through it. But at that moment, he spotted Elston and strode toward the man, reaching him as he grabbed the car handle of his fancy SUV.

"Excuse me. I'd like to ask you a question," Hawke said, as the man opened the vehicle door and the interior lit up. A young woman sat in the passenger seat.

Elston closed the door and spun around to face him. "Trooper Hawke, I've told you all I know about Bobbi."

Hawke unfolded the photo. "Have you ever seen this man?" he asked, holding up his phone with the flashlight on so Elston could see the photo more clearly.

"He looks a bit familiar. But I'm not sure where I've seen him. Why?" Elston peered up at Hawke.

"Think. Was it where you work, live, or at a race?" Hawke wanted to see if Elston might have been part of what happened to Bobbi. He'd been acting as if he had something to hide, and after seeing the woman in his vehicle, Hawke had a feeling he might have been edgy because he had this woman waiting for him when he was done officiating.

"I-" He glanced back at the car and then sighed. "I remember seeing him at a race last year and a couple this year."

"Were they races that Bobbi participated in?" Hawke asked.

Elston stared down at the paper and nodded his

head. "Yes. Bobbi was at all of them. Is this the man you think killed her?" His gaze shot to Hawke's face.

"It is her ex-husband. I've also received confirmation he was here this past weekend. Did you see him then?" Hawke watched the man. He seemed to be surprised.

"Here? This weekend? No, I didn't see him. Was he at Ollokot?" Fear tightened the man's face and his voice was shriller.

"That's what several people have told me," Hawke said, not explaining the man was only seen at the race start. "Thank you for helping me with the investigation." Hawke pulled the paper from the man's fingers and walked to his pickup.

On the way to Alder to meet Dani and Justine, he called Spruel and told him about witnesses seeing Marcus Radburn in Wallowa County, specifically at the race.

"You can take tomorrow and talk to him, but check in with the local police and have one of them go along with you or bring him into the local office to question him." Spruel was a stickler for protocol, which Hawke appreciated. But there were times when the sergeant had looked the other way when Hawke had not gone by the book to get the information needed to catch a murderer.

He walked into the High Mountain Brewery feeling good about the investigation so far. He spotted Dani and Justine at a tall table near the window.

"I ordered you an iced tea since you're driving and will be on the road early in the morning," Dani said, raising one eyebrow.

Hawke smiled. "You're right. I'll be headed to

Idaho tomorrow to have a talk with Marcus Radburn."

Justine's eyes lit with anger. "You don't let him tell you he wasn't here. And find out why he'd want to kill someone as sweet as Bobbi."

"Don't worry, if he killed her, I'll arrest him." Hawke just hoped they could come up with some solid evidence against the man if he didn't confess. So far, there had been little to go on, but he'd sure like to know who the accomplice was who drove away from Ollokot on Bobbi's sled.

## Chapter Eleven

Hawke was up bright and early Monday morning, driving down I-84 toward Idaho. He had a four-hour trip and aimed to arrive at the Adams County Sheriff's Office by ten. Sergeant Spruel would call to confirm that Hawke was checking in and would need a deputy to assist him in questioning Marcus Radburn.

He stopped at a truck stop about three hours from home along I-84 and the Snake River to stretch his legs and buy a cup of coffee. From there, he continued down the freeway another three miles and turned off toward Weiser, Idaho. At Weiser, he turned onto Highway 95 and continued another forty-five minutes.

The small town of Council was easy to navigate. He found the Sheriff's Office and County Jail on the north end of town. Parking his work vehicle, he put his Oregon State Trooper hat on and stepped out of the pickup.

A deputy walked out of the building. He held his

hand out. "Deputy Ted Chin. You must be Trooper Hawke."

Hawke shook hands. "Yes. My sergeant must have contacted you."

"He did. Sheriff LaMott felt it would be best to bring Radburn to the office for questioning. I've verified he's at work. Want to ride along with me or wait here?" The deputy motioned to his vehicle parked not far from the building.

"I'll come along. You never know what could happen. Where does he work?" Hawke asked, lowering into the deputy's car.

"Martin's Automotive Repair. The owner is a friend. I asked him not to say we were coming." Deputy Chin started his car. They drove out of the parking lot headed back toward town.

"Has Radburn been in trouble besides his violence against women?" Hawke asked.

"His temper has gotten him thrown in jail for assault a time or two. He's a hothead and he's big. Makes him dangerous to anyone who slights him." Chin parked as close as he could get to a building surrounded by vehicles of varying makes, models, and ages.

They exited the county car and walked toward the open roll-up doors. Hawke spotted Radburn before Chin. "He's at the far corner of the building, heading to the back." Hawke jogged to the end of the building.

Chin was looking around the corner by the time Hawke stopped. "He's getting into a truck. Not sure if it's his or he's bringing it around to work on it."

"Is he coming this way?" Hawke asked.

"Yeah."

Hawke walked out and stood, waiting for the truck to stop in front of him. The vehicle slowed and the engine revved, but when Hawke didn't budge, the man stopped and leaned out the window.

"Get out of the way! I got a job to do!" Radburn shouted.

"I need to talk to you. Get out of the vehicle and come have a chat with me." Hawke motioned to the vehicle and kept a friendly expression on his face.

"What's this about?" the man called, not moving out of the vehicle.

"Come talk to me and you'll find out." Hawke waved for the man to come to him.

The engine revved, and Chin popped out from behind the corner.

"Marcus, just come along peacefully. Trooper Hawke just wants to ask you some questions." The deputy started walking toward the vehicle. "John knows we're here to talk to you. He won't get upset."

The engine died, and Radburn stepped out of the truck. Chin hadn't been kidding about the man being big. He stood a good six feet, six inches and close to 250 pounds of solid muscle. Hawke couldn't imagine Bobbi's small body taking a beating from this man.

"Well, start talking," Radburn said, crossing his arms and leaning against the front of the truck.

Hawke decided he'd get more out of the man by talking to him here rather than ask him to come to the county station. He walked over and pulled out his notebook. "Were you in Wallowa County this past weekend?"

"Maybe, what of it?" Radburn's face remained a statue of disdain.

"Why were you there?" Hawke asked.

"Is that bitch of an ex-wife saying I was stalking her? Well, I wasn't. I just wanted to talk to her about an investment."

"When she turned you down, did you kill her?" Hawke asked.

Radburn uncrossed his arms and stood straight in front of him, leaning just a bit toward Hawke. "What are you talking about? I never got a chance to talk to her. And what do you mean, kill her? Is she dead?"

Hawke studied the man. He seemed to be genuinely surprised. "She was strangled at the Ollokot base camp during the sled dog race Thursday night. Where were you Thursday night?"

Radburn ran a hand over his crewcut hair and started pacing. "She can't be dead. I needed her—"

"Answer my question. Where were you Thursday night?"

"Thursday night? I was here, in Council. After I saw Bobbi take off from the start line on Thursday, I climbed in my truck and headed back here. I watched a football game at Ace, and went home about ten."

"Does anyone live with you to verify you were home?" Hawke asked.

The man's red face scrunched up. "I didn't kill her. I needed her to give me some money to pay off a debt. I know I'm not in her will, so her death wouldn't help me. I needed her alive to get anything out of her."

"Maybe she refused and you blew up on her, just like you're doing with me, and grabbed her, just trying to get her to agree to give you money, and you squeezed too hard." Hawke watched the man.

The color drained from his face and he shook his

head. "I didn't kill her. I regret the times I did get mad at her and lashed out, but I wouldn't kill her."

Hawke glanced at Deputy Chin. He seemed to believe the man. "Don't leave town. We're going to check out your alibis, and if you were here, I'll have some more questions for you."

Hawke spun around, and Chin followed. When they were out of earshot, he said, "Let's talk to his boss, the bar, and his neighbors."

"You don't think he did it either," Chin said.

"No, I think he needed her money in a big way, but he didn't kill her. Like he said, he doesn't get anything by her death, but he could probably scare her into giving him money. Which was why he was probably stalking her. To make her scared so she would give him whatever he wanted to leave her alone."

They walked into the building and Chin walked up to a man about his age. They shook hands. "John, this is Trooper Hawke from Oregon. We'd like to know if Marcus was here on Friday? And if you know of any of his activities the night before."

"Why are you interested in him?" John asked.

"His ex-wife was murdered. He was seen at the race start on Thursday," Hawke said.

John stared at him. "Bobbi's dead? That's a damn shame. She was a good person. Thought she could change Marcus. He's too set in his anger to change." He shook his head and said, "Marcus was here working on Friday. I think he and Rich…" John motioned to a man in the far corner working on a sedan, "…met at Ace Thursday night to watch a football game."

"How did Marcus act on Friday?" Hawke asked.

"Same as usual. Maybe a little grumpier. He took

Wednesday and Thursday off to take care of business, he said. But whatever he went to take care of didn't seem to make him happy. Because he took the two days off, I had him work on Saturday. It's not usually his day, but I needed some cars finished and out of here."

"You have any idea what the business was he needed to do?" Hawke asked.

"No. He doesn't talk to me more than to find out about a job and ask for time off." John searched the inside of the building and nodded to a young man wiping down tools. "Henry hangs on Marcus's every word. You could ask him; he might know."

"Thanks." Hawke walked over to Henry. "Hi, I'd like to ask you some questions about Marcus."

The young man, in his early twenties, stared at him. "You really a Oregon State Trooper?" Henry asked.

Hawke motioned with his hands down his body to draw attention to his uniform. "Yes, I am. Did Marcus ever say anything to you about why he needed to take Wednesday and Thursday off?" He pulled out his notebook and poised his pen.

"Not really. But I heard him saying he'd have money for whoever he was talking to when he came back to work on Friday." Henry studied him. "Why are you asking me this when you were talking to him?"

"We wanted your view of things. Did you go to Ace on Thursday night with Marcus and Rich?" Hawke asked.

"No. I don't get invited to the bar with them." The young man set his gaze on Chin. "Why are you letting someone from Or-ee-gun, ask the questions?"

Hawke didn't like how Henry made fun of the state

name. "Because it is my homicide case." He pivoted and headed to the far corner to talk to Rich. Chin said something to Henry, but Hawke didn't hear it. He was already halfway across the garage.

Rich was a guy in his 50s. He glanced up and turned off the machine he was using. "Can I help you, Officer?"

"I would like to ask you about Thursday night. I understand you and Marcus went to the Ace and watched a football game." Hawke pulled his notebook and pen out of his pocket.

"Yeah. Marcus called me when he got back into town. We grabbed a burger and beer, and watched the game. Probably had about six beers by the end of the game. So we stayed about an hour after the game finished to sober up with a cup of coffee. I had to drive home and face my wife. Marcus is lucky he didn't have to worry about anyone getting in his face for not coming home right after work."

"What time did you leave the bar?" Hawke asked as Chin joined them.

"I think it was about ten. I arrived home at ten-thirty, so it must have been ten. It takes about thirty minutes to drive to my house. My wife was pissed. That I remember clearly." Rich shook his head. "She is not a pretty woman when she's mad."

Chin made a sound, and Hawke glared at him.

"Did Marcus leave when you did?" Hawke asked.

"Yeah, pretty much. He left a few minutes before I did. Shoot, he was probably home before I walked out of the can."

"Thank you." Hawke closed his notebook, shoved it in his pocket, and walked out of the garage.

Chin hurried by him and over to his vehicle. "Sorry for being rude in there. But if you saw Rich's wife, you'd know there was nothing pretty about her ever. She is the sourest woman I've ever met."

"Probably because her husband goes to the bar rather than coming home." Hawke pulled out his notebook. "I want to talk to the people at the Ace Bar and then Radburn's neighbors."

"That's what I figured." Chin put the car in gear and they headed to the center of town. He parked in front of a small grassy square with trees and two steam engines. They crossed the street to a large old brick building with a wooden front. The sign on the corner of the building said Ace Saloon.

Chin opened the door. Hawke stepped inside, standing to the right of the door, allowing his eyes to adjust to the dimly lit interior. It smelled of stale smoke, body odor, and yeast. The establishment was old. The tables and chairs looked like something from the 50s and 60s. There were two faded pool tables and a long bar with both fixed and movable stools along the side of the narrow, elongated room.

Chin walked up to the bar, removing his sunglasses, and asked, "Cheryl, could you go tell Mel we'd like to talk to him?"

The woman in her forties with dyed black hair, three studs in one ear, and one in her cheek, said, "Sure thing. Is he in trouble?"

"Nope, just need to ask him about an alibi for someone else." Chin smiled and turned to Hawke. "She's the Sheriff's daughter."

Hawke nodded.

A man in his sixties slowly walked out of a room in

the back, wiping his hands on an apron tied under his protruding belly. His gaze flicked over Hawke and landed on Chin. "What can I help you with, Ted?"

"We need to know when Marcus Radburn arrived here on Thursday night and when he left." Deputy Chin said in a low voice.

Mel glanced at Cheryl. "Marcus came in with Rich right after work, didn't they?"

"No. Marcus was here first and then Rich showed up. They watched the football game. The one with the fish and the hawks. Kind of funny, really. Hawks like to eat fish." She smiled.

"When did they leave?" Hawke asked.

"Marcus left shortly after the game finished," Mel said. "Rich had another drink, and then he left about ten."

Hawke noted that Rich didn't tell them the truth. He must have been buzzed and didn't want the cops to know he'd been driving drunk. "Do you know if Marcus left with anyone?"

"You mean a woman?" Mel asked.

Hawke nodded, noting the flush on Cheryl's cheeks.

"Naw, he never leaves here with a woman. I think his marriage breaking up soured him on women." Mel dropped the apron he'd been drying his hands on. "Anything else? I'm trying to replace a keg."

"That's all. Thanks, Mel," Chin said, heading for the door.

Hawke hung back and leaned on the counter near Cheryl. "Did you spend the night with Marcus?"

She stared at him.

"I won't tell anyone. But if he was home all night, I

need to know. His ex-wife was murdered on Thursday night, and if you know he was here and didn't do it, I won't pull him in for questioning."

She glanced over her shoulder and leaned close. "I've been spending most of my nights at his place. He went home from here Thursday night about nine-thirty and was there when I arrived after my shift at two a.m. We spent the rest of the night together before he had to go to work. I slept through the morning, leaving his house about noon."

"Thank you." Hawke walked toward the door when it opened and Chin stuck his head in.

"Are you coming?"

"Yeah, I just had a couple more questions. Let's go talk to the neighbors."

# Chapter Twelve

It was one o'clock by the time they finished talking to the neighbors on each side of Radburn's house and across the street. The older woman across the street said she saw Marcus arrive home about 9:40 Thursday night after being gone for a couple of days. She also saw a woman sneaking into the house about 2 a.m. The neighbor had been up letting her dog out and saw the woman creeping along the side of the house. She saw Marcus leave at 8 a.m. on Friday. She wasn't sure when the woman left.

Hawke and Chin sat in the Seven Devils Café eating lunch and discussing what they'd learned.

"He didn't kill his ex-wife. Too many people saw him here." Hawke's stomach, though hungry, wasn't being satisfied by the burger. If it wasn't the ex-husband, then who could it be? There didn't seem to be anyone else with a motive, except Unity, who felt Bobbi was cozying up with some of the men.

He quickly finished up and asked Deputy Chin to take him back to the county office.

At the sheriff's office, Hawke climbed into his vehicle. He'd barely driven out of Council's city limits when he called Justine.

"Hey, Hawke, did you find out anything?" she answered.

"Yeah, he didn't do it. He has multiple people here who saw him, and I don't think any of them are covering for him. I have a question for you. Bobbi seemed to have several men interested in her. Was she someone who slept around?" He knew that was a touchy subject, but he needed to know the truth.

Justine laughed and then said, "No, she didn't sleep around. That was what caused her divorce: Marcus sleeping with other women and hurting her physically when she accused him. I don't think she actually caught on that the men were interested in her that way. She called everyone a friend, including the men who hovered."

"So, there would be no reason for a jealous wife or girlfriend to want to hurt Bobbi?" he asked.

"Not unless they didn't do their due diligence and follow their husband. They'd know he and Bobbi never slept together or kissed." Justine said something about 'that goes to table seven,' before her voice was clear and she said, "You need to look for some reason other than a love interest because she didn't have any. She was only in love with training and mushing sled dogs. I have to go. The café is busy today."

The call ended, and Hawke continued down Highway 95 toward home. If it wasn't her ex or a jealous woman, that left money. He'd put in a call to her sister tomorrow morning.

Hawke helped with a traffic accident on I-84, making his return home later than he'd planned. He found Dani, Herb, and Darlene sitting at the dining room table. The aroma of lasagna hung in the air. The three, his partner and their neighbors, were relaxing in the chairs, visiting.

"Sorry, I'm late. A crash happened right ahead of me. I controlled the scene until others arrived." He sat down at his spot at the table with a clean plate. Then he dished up a large portion of the lasagna that remained in the middle of the table. He added salad and crusty garlic bread to his plate.

"Did you find your murderer?" Dani asked.

He shook his head, wiped his face with a napkin, and said, "He didn't do it. We ran down all his alibis. He was in Idaho, not in these mountains."

"This about the woman who was killed during the sled dog races?" Herb asked.

Dani answered for him. "Yes. She was a friend of Justine's."

"Oh, how is she doing?" Darlene asked.

"I talked to her today. She was at work and busy. She didn't say much other than she hoped Hawke could pin the death on the woman's ex-husband."

Hawke finished chewing a mouthful of lasagna and said, "I wish I could. But it's not going to be that easy. I talked to Justine about all the men who seemed to be enamored with the woman, but she said Bobbi wasn't looking for a man and didn't even notice the attention they were giving her. She was focused on sled dog training and racing."

Dani held up her fingers. "The motives of revenge and jealousy are gone. What does that leave?"

Hawke shook his head. "There is still one jealousy. A woman musher felt Bobbi was getting too much attention from some of the men. And she had the victim's coat in her sled, though she says she didn't know it was there. I'm going to have a chat with her tomorrow and with the victim's twin sister. The sisters inherited from their grandmother. I want to find out how much it was and if there is anyone else who might be named to inherit it."

Dani started gathering the dirty dishes. "Money would be a strong motive, I'd think."

"Who are these two? Anyone we would know?" Darlene asked.

Hawke thought it was unlikely that the Trembleys would know the Whitby girls. "I doubt it. I don't think they have any connection to Wallowa County other than Bobbi coming here to race."

"What's their names?" Darlene insisted.

"Beverly and Bobbi Whitby. They're close to Justine's age." He finished off the lasagna and salad. Leaning back in his chair, he crunched on the bread.

"Whitby? Wasn't there a family who lived in Alder when we were kids?" Darlene said to Herb.

He nodded. "The father worked for the mill in Prairie Creek. There were two kids, a boy and a girl."

"James and Brenda," Darlene said. "I remember them. They were in swim lessons when my siblings and I were."

"It's probably not the same family," Hawke said. He'd yet to dig into the family history and didn't know the father's name.

"If it is, let us know," Darlene said, taking dishes to the sink and helping Dani put them in the dishwasher.

Herb leaned across the table. "Yeah, I can talk to some friends and see what I can find out about the family. If I remember right, Chuck Sampson lived next door to them before they moved."

Hawke reached for the iced tea Darlene placed in front of him, and wondered, not for the first time, how this couple knew everyone who lived or had lived in Wallowa County.

Tuesday, Hawke pulled into the State Police Office in Winslow and went straight to his desk.

"How's it going?" Ivy Bisset, the newest OSP officer, asked.

"Hoping today will shed some light on a motive for a woman's murder." He glanced up from the computer. Ivy wasn't wearing a uniform. "What are you doing in here on your day off?"

Her cheeks flushed. "Looking at the vacation calendar. Bryce and I are engaged. I need to see when we can schedule a wedding."

Hawke rose out of his chair and hugged the young woman. "That's good news. Dani and I will get an invite, won't we?"

"Of course! If not for Dani believing in me and bringing me to help you and Bryce, we wouldn't have met. I hadn't planned on marrying before I'd been on this job for at least five years, but as Bryce said, 'we aren't getting any younger.'"

Hawke thought that was true of Bryce, but Ivy was ten years younger. However, he had seen the connection between the two of them when they were trying to capture a killer who was trapping wolverines illegally.

"What's all the noise in here?" Spruel asked, walking into the open area where the troopers had access to computers and wrote up their reports.

"Ivy and Bryce Hendrix are getting married," Hawke said, feeling good inside that she'd found someone who made her happy. And who would protect her. Bryce had been in the military and came home with scars, inside and out. Ivy had seen past the external scars to the man who lay beneath. He was a good man. One who Hawke was proud to call a friend.

He sat back down as Nathan led Ivy to his office to figure out the vacation schedule. The first thing Hawke entered was Beverly Whitby and the name of her gallery. The website was impressive. Some of the art he thought looked like a grade school child could make. But then, he liked realistic forms of art.

He found the phone number for the gallery and dialed.

"Distinction Gallery, this is Janelle, how may I help you?" a crisp and proper woman's voice answered.

"Hi Janelle, this is Oregon State Trooper Hawke. I'd like to speak to Beverly. It's about her sister."

"One moment, let me see if she has time to talk."

Soft classical music played as he waited.

A song ended in the middle, and a soft voice said, "Hello? This is Beverly Whitby."

"Ms. Whitby, I'm Oregon State Trooper Hawke. I found your sister's body at the Ollokot camp during the Eagle Cap Extreme Sled Dog race. I wondered if I could ask you some questions?" The report had said the woman was contacted about her sister's death. Her intake of breath surprised him.

"Thank you for contacting me. I've been wondering how she died." The woman had regained her composure. The words were spoken without inflection of emotion.

"It was murder."

Again, the intake of breath. "Violence?" she said quietly into the phone.

"Yes, what had you thought?" he asked, wishing he were sitting in the room with her to see her true emotions.

"I thought it was a sledding accident. She'd told me of some harrowing runs she'd made, and I feared she'd end her life racing. That's why when the call came, it was easy to take in that she was gone and had gone doing what she loved. That was my consolation. But now…you say she's been murdered? How? Why?"

"I can tell you the how, but I'm hoping you can shed some light on the why." He told her about the victim being strangled and how someone had taken her dogs and sled and left them in a remote area as a decoy. The body was found in the camp by her lead dog.

"That's so awful. I know that her friend Justine has the dogs and sled. I told her to keep them or do whatever is best for the dogs. That's what Bobbi would have wanted."

He heard a sniff, and the woman cleared her throat.

"I was wondering if you knew who would benefit from your sister's death. Did she make out a will? And what is she worth?" He didn't like to be so callous talking about money, but it had to be the reason behind the murder.

"You heard we inherited a large sum of money from our grandmother." The woman said it as if it were a bad thing.

"Yes. I know you opened up your gallery, which is doing well, and Bobbi started raising and training sled dogs."

"Have you looked into where Marcus, Bobbi's ex-husband, was when she was killed?" Pure hatred echoed in her words.

"He was my first suspect and he has been cleared. He has solid alibis for the time of her death." He flipped open his notebook and said, "What can you tell me about your cousins who didn't inherit from your grandmother?"

"Ivan and Raina? They received stocks and one hundred thousand each. If they invested it wisely, they wouldn't have any need for my sister's money. Since Grandmother didn't leave more than that to them, I'm sure Bobbi wouldn't have left them anything, so why would they want her dead?"

"What are their last names and where do they live?" Hawke wrote the names down in his book.

"Ivan is Tabor, like his father. He lives in Wallowa County on his family's farm in Promise. His mother is my father's sister. Their names were James and Brenda. Raina has been through three marriages that I know of. I'm not sure what her last name is." Beverly sighed. "After seeing my cousin's poor marriages and seeing what marriage did to Bobbi, I'm not planning on letting a man make a fool of me."

Hawke could hear Darlene. *I told you they used to live in Wallowa County.*

"Do you happen to know who your sister's attorney is? I'd like to see her will."

Beverly gave him the name of an attorney in Boise,

Idaho.

"Thank you. If you can think of anything else that might help me find the person who did this, I'd appreciate the information."

"I'll let you know if I think of anything. Please find out who did this and lock them up. Bobbi wasn't one to care about the finer things, but she loved animals and people. She had a big heart. I'll miss her."

"I'll do my best to find the person responsible." Hawke ended the call and immediately dialed Darlene.

## Chapter Thirteen

"Good morning," Darlene answered.

"This is me eating crow. You were right. The Whitbys were in Wallowa County, and apparently, the daughter, Brenda, married a man named Tabor who lives out in the Promise area. They had a son and daughter, Ivan and Raina." Hawke waited. Darlene wasn't one to gloat. However, he knew she'd remind him of this the next time he said she didn't know his suspect.

"Ahh, that's right. I forgot about Brenda marrying Jack Tabor. She left him when the kids were small. She took Raina and left Ivan with his dad."

"Do you have anyone who can find out where either Brenda or Raina lives?" If he could find where they lived, he could look up info on them.

"I'm sure someone from Promise would know. I have a fair meeting tonight and will ask Mildred Fleming."

"Don't say why you're interested. We don't have any leads and wouldn't want to tip off the wrong person." He knew that Darlene was crafty in getting information from people, but he didn't want to be called to her homicide one day and discover she'd been digging up information for him.

"I know not to let on I'm helping the police. You can find Jack Tabor on his property. He doesn't leave the property anymore." She ended the call.

Hawke pulled up Jack Tabor's driver's license info and jotted down the address in his notebook. If luck were on his side, Ivan would be there.

Next, he looked up the phone number for the attorney in Boise and made the call. He waited, listening to 80s rock n' roll, until an associate of the law firm asked him the reason for his call and took down his name, title, and badge number.

"I'll see if Mr. Stevens is available to help you."

The music returned, and Hawke put the phone on speaker so he could use both hands to type the information he'd received from the sister into the report as he waited.

The music stopped, and a gravelly voice said, "Mr. Stevens, here. How may I help you?"

Hawke went through who he was, that he was investigating Bobbi Whitby's homicide, and could Mr. Stevens give him information about who would benefit from her death.

"Oh, my! This is the first I've heard of this. Homicide, you say. That's not good, not good at all. Such a violent way for such a sweet young lady to go." From the man's choice of words and gravelly voice, Hawke wondered if the man was past retirement age.

"Did Bobbi have a will made up?" Hawke asked, drawing the man's attention from the death to the legal issues.

"Yes, I suggested it when she divorced her husband. I told her it was a sure way to keep him from trying to get any of her money when she died. Especially, if she remarried and started a family." There was a pause. "But that won't happen now, will it. Damn shame. Such a lovely young woman."

"Mr. Stevens, who are Bobbi's beneficiaries?" Hawke asked.

"Well, her sister Beverly is to get all the family heirlooms and such, her cousins, Ivan and Raina, each get twenty-five thousand, and the rest goes to three different sled dog training kennels." He coughed and said, "She threw her heart and soul into training sled dogs and racing when she divorced Marcus."

"What are the names of the training kennels?" Hawke asked, thinking it was interesting that she died during a sled dog race.

"Let me see here." The sound of pages turning riffled through the phone. Throat clearing was followed by, "Razor Ridge Runners, owned by Cam Elston, Sawtooth Sliders, owned by Russell Nichols, and Wallowa Run Dogs, owned by Justine Bartley."

Hawke's mouth dropped open. He knew in his gut that Justine didn't kill her friend. But then, why didn't she say she was a beneficiary? "Did these people know they were the beneficiaries?"

"Only if Bobbi told them. Beneficiaries are never notified until after the person's death."

Another thought came to him. "Do any of these people use your law office?"

"Not that I'm aware of."

"Could you have someone look through your records and let me know if there is anyone related to the beneficiaries who uses your services?" Hawke gave him his email address and phone number to contact him. "Thank you for your time and information."

"You're sure it wasn't her ex-husband who killed her?" the attorney asked.

"He has several alibis, so I'm certain he didn't do it. Thank you again for speaking with me." Hawke ended the call and circled two of the sled dog training facilities. It looked like he'd need to request help from the local authorities in the jurisdictions of the Razor Ridge Runners and the Sawtooth Sliders. Once he had information about the kennels and the people involved, he'd determine if he needed to make a trip to Washington and Idaho.

Hawke sent his requests and planned to head north to Promise and talk to Ivan Tabor until Spruel walked up behind him and dropped a paper with a report from a concerned citizen on his desk.

"Take a look at this, please. You're the only Fish and Wildlife officer this week."

"After I check it out, I'm going to Promise to talk with Jack Tabor. His son is one of our victims' cousins."

"As long as you follow up on this call." Spruel spun on his heel and disappeared into his office.

Hawke read the report taken the day before from a snowshoer. The person, Audrey Wilkens, called in to report carrion birds flying in circles about two miles south of Ferguson Ridge Ski Area up McCully Basin.

Since the area was near where the sled dog race started and not that far from Salt Creek, his curiosity was piqued.

There hadn't been any shots fired while he was up there. He doubted anyone would be foolish enough to poach during the chaos of the race. But people have little common sense these days. Or maybe an animal could have died of old age. In his line of work, he never knew what he might encounter on any given day.

The drive was smooth since the road to Ferguson had been well-used these past few days. He parked at the ski lift lot.

Getting out of the vehicle, he put on his insulated boots, pulled on his parka, swapped his ball cap for a stocking cap, and strapped on snowshoes. He locked the vehicle, slung his small day pack over his shoulder, and put on gloves. Looking south, he moved through the trees toward McCully Basin.

He walked a quarter of a mile east and came to the creek. He followed McCully Creek for about two miles when he heard birds squawking and the flapping of wings. They were fighting over whatever was dead. He followed the sounds up the west side of Ferguson Ridge. The birds and a coyote were fighting over what appeared to be a human body. There were pieces of clothing scattered around where the creatures were fighting.

Hawke shouted and waved his arms. He hadn't expected to find a body. As he drew near, he put a hand over his mouth and nose and stared at the remains of a female. The only way he knew that much was the long, bleached hair and the one long, flashy nail that hadn't been destroyed by the birds and animals.

He'd seen nails like that before. This was Unity Allard. Shedding his daypack, he zipped it open and pulled out the emergency foil blanket, placing it over the body to keep the birds and critters away. Using rocks, he weighed the corners down and then pulled out his phone to see if he had service here. Barely a bar. He eyed the side of Ferguson Ridge.

If he climbed the ridge, he'd get reception. Now that he knew it was a body and not a dead animal, he needed to remain on the ridge until forensics and Dr. Vance arrived.

Halfway up the side of the ridge, he had two bars. He texted Sergeant Spruel. *I found a body approximately two miles up McCully Creek from Fergie. Sending a pinpoint. Will remain here until a team arrives.*

He sent the pinpoint, and his phone dinged. *Identification?*

*I believe it is one of the mushers from the race. Not much left for facial recognition.*

*I'll contact forensics and Dr. Vance. You could be there overnight waiting for forensics.*

*Send someone up with a tent and sleeping bag.* He hadn't planned to be camping again this January, but he was first on the scene and would make sure the body wasn't destroyed more than it already had been until Dr. Vance examined it.

*Copy. I'll send up a deputy.*

*Copy.*

Hawke walked through the several feet of snow back down to the body. With the blanket over the victim, the birds had vanished. A hungry coyote hung back in the trees, sniffing the air. Hawke hoped nothing larger and meaner than a coyote caught the scent of the decaying body.

He pulled out one of half a dozen granola bars he had in his daypack. While he'd survived on the bars before, it would be nice if whoever brought Dr. Vance up also brought his gear and food. As he sat on a rock, eating his granola bar and drinking water from a bottle he brought, Hawke studied the ground beyond where the animals had fought over the body. There had to be tracks to show how the woman ended up here. Was she dead before she was left? Or had she tried to get away from someone, become disoriented, and froze to death? Or did someone bring her here to kill her?

Finishing the bar, he capped the bottle and shoved to his feet. He walked over to the body and did a full 360° scan of the perimeter. The only indentations in the snow that couldn't be accounted for came down from the top of Ferguson Ridge.

He glanced down at the blanketed body, figured no one would get here for at least two hours, and headed up the side of the ridge, taking photos as he went.

Huffing and wondering if his legs would carry him much longer, he stopped to catch his breath. He'd been climbing up the ridge, the snow growing deeper with each 100 feet in elevation he went. Taking a drink of water, he scanned the white and thought he saw what looked like an odd shadow in the snow.

He shoved the bottle back in his pack and continued up, using the shadow as his guide. Luckily, it was only another 50 feet, and it appeared to be where a snowmobile had been parked, coming in from the east and taking off to the northeast. Snapping photos, he circled the packed snow, getting photos of the snowmobile tracks and the two sets of indentations in the snow that had to be footprints. He wasn't sure how two tracks left the snowmobile and turned into one not far from it. Unless one person stepped in the other person's tracks to make it look like one set and then walked in the same tracks on the way back to the snowmobile. This had been planned out and methodical.

Running the list of suspects through his mind, Hawke tried to envision which one would be this calculating. He didn't know the person who owned the Sawtooth Sliders. Elston had the brains, but did he have the restraint? Hawke didn't think so.

He finished taking photos and headed back down. The doctor and deputy should be showing up soon. They had the shortest travel time. He didn't expect the forensic team for another couple of hours. They were driving from Pendleton.

The downhill travel in the snow was almost as exhausting as the uphill. It was a good thing that it became easier the lower the elevation. He was sitting on a rock, munching on another granola bar, when he heard snowmobiles.

# Chapter Fourteen

The snowmobiles had to be the medical examiner and more law enforcement. The direction they were coming from wasn't a usual route, unless it was someone setting traps along the creek.

The nose of a snowmobile broke through the trees. He stood and waved them to park a safe distance from the victim.

Dr. Vance climbed off the back of the first snowmobile and walked toward him. "I'm thinking about getting a snowmobile. After my rides the last few days, I'm beginning to really like them. And it's an easy way to enjoy the outdoors."

Hawke shook his head. "They make too much noise and scare all the animals. On a horse, you see and hear everything that makes up the forest."

"You won't convert me," Dr. Vance said. "What did you find?"

"A woman. I believe it is one of the mushers from

this past weekend. However, the animals and birds have done a number on her, so we'll have to use other ways of officially identifying her."

He walked the woman over to the silver emergency blanket. "I covered her up to keep the scavengers away." He pulled back the blanket.

"I see what you mean. I don't know if I can determine the cause of death out here. It's going to take a close examination of the body." Dr. Vance knelt by the body. She tugged on latex gloves and stuck her hands in the pockets. She pulled out the lining of the coat pocket. Small brown crumbs fell to the snow. She picked up one and handed it to Hawke.

Holding it close to his nose, he smelled and squeezed it between two fingers. "I think it's crumbs from dog treats."

Dr. Vance held up a piece of paper that she pulled out of the woman's shirt pocket.

Deputy Dave Alden walked up and handed Dr. Vance an evidence bag.

"Good to see you," Hawke said by way of greeting.

"I've been told to stick it out here until forensics is done and to help you." Dave took the bag from the doctor and wrote the time and place on the label. "Want to see it before I seal the bag?"

Hawke took the latex glove Dave offered him and pulled it on. Then he used two fingers to draw the piece of paper out of the evidence bag to read. "It's a receipt for dog food. We should be able to find out who this is by checking the bank card number." He dropped the paper back in the bag and the deputy sealed it up.

Dr. Vance stood. "I didn't find anything else to identify her. And like I said, I can't determine the cause or time of death until an autopsy is completed. I can tell you, she was dead before the animals started dining on her. But I didn't see any large amounts of blood around the body. I don't think she was killed and bled out."

Dave motioned to the person still sitting on a snowmobile. "He'll take you back to your car at Fergie."

"I'll get on this as soon as the body is delivered to me." Dr. Vance nodded to them and walked over to the snowmobile. After she was on board, it revved to life, and they took off back through the trees.

"Have you gathered evidence?" Dave asked.

"Just that this victim didn't come here alone." Hawke showed the deputy the photos he took and explained his thoughts on what might have happened.

"You believe the victim was either tricked to come here or brought here against her will?" Dave asked.

"That's what it looks like." Hawke stared at the emergency blanket covering the body.

"You know who she is. I can tell by the way you're staring at the blanket."

"I'm pretty sure it's one of the mushers. One that was on my suspect list. I think she helped with the misdirection of the missing musher who was found dead at Ollokot. The first victim's coat was found in this victim's sled. I felt like this victim was being evasive when I asked her questions. I think she picked up whoever drove the first victim's sled and dogs out of Ollokot and left the dogs and sled on the side of the trail to make us look there. I believe they had hoped the body would be transported to Prairie Creek before it was found. Giving them more time to return to whatever they were doing before the murder."

"So this is connected to the homicide over the weekend?"

"Yeah, I'm certain it is. And since a snowmobile was used in this crime, I'm wondering if it was someone on a snowmobile who dropped off and picked up the impersonator that night. I hadn't factored in the volunteers with snowmobiles." Hawke made a mental note to ask for the list of snowmobile drivers for the event.

"If you don't think there is any evidence we can find, let's set up camp. I'd like to have it up before dark and that's coming soon." Dave stared up at the sky.

Hawke had noticed the temperature dropping and the sky dimming as the sun set over the mountain tops. "Let's do it."

They had a tent set up, with a propane heater inside, two cots, sleeping bags, and a roaring campfire outside by the time they heard snowmobiles coming from the north.

"They must have followed our trail in," Dave said.

Three snowmobiles, all pulling sleds, appeared out of the trees down by the creek. They headed straight for the campfire and parked. Two of the sleds held battery-powered lights and equipment. The other had a folded body bag in it.

Hawke greeted the State Police forensic team and a SAR member who had come to retrieve the body after the forensic team finished.

Dave offered them coffee to warm up with before they started setting up the spotlights and got to work.

Thirty minutes later, the forensic team pulled back the tarp and started meticulously going over every inch of the body, rolling it to see if anything on the back could be of use to determine the killer or the cause of death. When they were through with the body, Hawke and Dave helped put it in the body bag and strap it down in the empty sled.

"I'll take this back now. Dr. Vance wanted it as soon as possible before the animal desecration deteriorated too much of the flesh," the SAR member said, shoving his helmet on his head.

"Okay. Be careful heading back in the dark," Hawke said, knowing that the sooner they knew the cause of death, they could determine the best way to go about looking for the killer.

Hawke and Dave assisted the forensic team by holding evidence bags and sealing them. It was close to midnight when they had all their gear and the evidence loaded up. They climbed onto the snowmobiles and headed out.

The sound died away and Dave asked, "You want to take down camp and follow them out?"

"No. We're staying the night. In the morning, we're using your snowmobile to see where the one that brought our victim here came from."

"Works for me. We have a nice warm tent, and I don't have to listen to my wife and teenage daughter arguing."

Hawke laughed. He wished he had Dog here to help, but other than that, he was content to spend another day in the wilderness. Especially now that he had a snowmobile to haul him up the side of Ferguson Ridge.

The next morning, Hawke and Dave tore down the camp after a breakfast of sausage, eggs, and muffins.

Once everything was loaded onto the sled, they settled on the snowmobile, and Hawke directed Dave up the side of the ridge to the spot where the snowmobile had parked.

Hawke enjoyed being carried up the mountain in a quarter of the time it took him to walk.

Dave stopped at the packed snow where the snowmobile had been parked. "Is this where you want to start?"

"Yeah." Hawke pointed to the tracks through the snow. "Follow those. I want to see where the machine came from."

Dave nodded, put his visor back down, and revved the snowmobile, causing it to lurch a little as it took off up the incline.

Hawke grasped fistfuls of Dave's coat to keep from going over backward off the snowmobile. It was evident by the trail they followed that the person driving was an accomplished snowmobile driver. His actions had either been trying to scare the other person or show off.

Tapping Dave on the shoulder, Hawke shouted, "You don't have to follow his tracks exactly, unless you can't see them otherwise."

Dave gave him a gloved thumbs-up and stopped swishing back and forth following the tracks.

At the top of Ferguson Ridge, the tracks continued southeast until they came across the groomed trail the mushers used. At that point, they couldn't follow the tracks anymore.

Dave stopped the machine, took off his helmet, and said, "Let's take a break here, and then we'll head back to Fergie and our vehicles."

Hawke nodded, barely hearing what Dave said as his mind raced to determine when the last person would have traveled this trail at the end of the race. He'd have to contact Elston and get the times of the last people to cross the finish line. Ollokot volunteers would have been hauled to Salt Creek to catch rides out to Prairie Creek. Only the mushers would have been on this trail.

A thought zinged through his mind. Did Unity cross the finish line? If so, how did she get back up here, and what happened to her dogs and sled?

"Hawke, get up and move around a bit before we head back," Dave said.

Mechanically, Hawke did as he was told, but his mind was buzzing with all the questions in his head.

## Chapter Fifteen

As soon as Hawke was in his vehicle, he called Dani to explain why he hadn't made it home, then he called Spruel to say he needed more information from the race officials and who he believed the victim was, along with why he believed it wasn't an accidental death.

"You know I'm short-staffed right now. I can't permit you to travel around to gather information. You have to use a counterpart in the states and counties where you need people interviewed."

Hawke knew it had been a lot to ask, but he had to try. "I'll talk to the people I have gathering information for me already. You know I like to see the people when I talk to them."

"Yes, you have keen observation skills, but you'll have to figure out what you need from here."

"I'm headed to the office to see what information has been gathered so far."

"I'm headed out. Our youngest has a basketball game. Keep me updated."

"I will." Hawke ended the call and drove through Prairie Creek, headed to Alder.

Driving through Alder, his stomach growled. The breakfast Dave cooked had worn off. He decided to pop into Olive's café. He hadn't been in since the first of the year and knew she could always use the business.

He parked on the street, locked his vehicle, and sauntered into the small café with Indigenous décor and drum and flute music playing. He took a seat at the short counter left over from the days when this building was a drugstore that sold sodas and ice cream at the counter.

"Haven't seen you since before the holidays," Olive said, pouring a cup of coffee and placing a menu in front of him.

"Everyone but me takes their vacations this time of year. I've been all over this county three times this month." He sipped the bold-flavored coffee. That was the one thing missing from his breakfast. Dave didn't drink coffee and had brought tea. Hawke only liked iced tea, not hot tea. It could never replace the relationship he had with hot, strong coffee.

"Poor you. Be happy you have a job. My Logan just lost his job at the feed store. They said they couldn't afford him anymore." She glanced around the dining area.

Hawke followed her gaze. There were three tables with locals. Their conversations had all lowered in volume once he and Olive started talking.

She must have noticed, too. The Nez Perce mother of three put her hands on her hips and said loudly, "You can all go on with your conversations. We aren't talking about scalping you." Then she laughed and slapped her order pad on the counter.

Hawke grinned and said, "I'll have the Reuben and a salad, please."

"Coming up." Then she leaned closer and said, "Serves them right for listening in."

Hawke would have agreed if her voice hadn't been raised so high when she was angry about her son losing his job, which had caused the conversation to wane at the other tables.

While waiting for his food, he spun his chair and did a more thorough scan of the people eating. He knew they were locals because they were dressed for the weather in well-worn clothing. Out-of-towners always wore shiny boots, fresh-looking coats and hats, or not warm enough clothing.

Olive brought his food out.

"Did you have a good weekend with the sled dog race people here?" he asked.

"Yeah, it was pretty good. It's like a powwow. All the family members come to cheer on the person racing, just like families travel with dancers to support and cheer them on. They can't do anything while their loved ones are racing, but they sit here watching them on their phones and laptops as their loved ones make their way along the trail."

"Really, they sit in here and watch the race?"

"Yeah. There is a map. It shows where each racer is on the course. I heard one person say it's because they have trackers on their sleds. They use the trackers to know where the people are. You know, in case they get in trouble or a storm comes in and they get lost."

Hawke nodded. Anyone could have followed where Bobbi was during the race and known when she was at Ollokot. But how could they have known she would use the outhouse when she did? Had the two been sitting to the side of the building waiting for her?

"You're not listening to me," Olive said. "I might as well go talk to my brother. He listens just as well as you." She disappeared into the kitchen.

Hawke wondered if he could still see the movements of the racers. That would let him know where Unity was when the impostor took off on Bobbi's sled. She had to have been involved in the first homicide to have ended up being the second.

He finished his meal and left the restaurant. He had a lot of emails to read and phone calls to make when he arrived at the office.

Hawke's phone buzzed as he parked in the OSP parking lot. A glance at the screen and he slid his finger to open the call. "Dr. Vance, what did you find out?"

"Are you still at Ferguson Ridge?" she asked.

"No, I just pulled into the Winslow office. Do you know the cause of death?"

"Yes, I'm sure the second victim was killed the same way as the first, strangulation. The hyoid bone was broken in the same way as the first victim. Because you gave me a name you thought it might be, I was able to get dental and medical records, and it is Unity Allard. I made a print of the one finger that wasn't mangled. I figured just one more way to confirm who she was. I sent it to OSP in Pendleton."

"Thank you for being thorough. I discovered how she ended up there, now to figure out who did it."

Hawke had to find the next of kin. That was at the top of his list of things to do.

"I have faith you'll figure it out. You usually do. I'm sending all my findings to you and to the State Forensics. I'll hold the body until they say it's okay to release."

"Thanks. I'm headed in now to notify her next of kin and then go through all the information from the first victim. Enjoy the rest of your day." He ended the call and strode into the back door of the building Oregon State Police shared with the Oregon Department of Fish and Wildlife. Fish and Wildlife had the main floor. OSP had the second floor. Which was fine. They were only in the office to file reports and attend meetings. Otherwise, their vehicle was their work station.

The only sound upstairs was the computers humming and the coffeemaker gurgling. Which was odd. If no one was here, why was it gurgling?

He walked into the conference/breakroom and spotted the sticky note on a freshly brewed pot of coffee. *Thought you might need this. Nathan.*

Hawke smiled. It was good working with people who knew you well. He poured a cup, sipped, grinned, and headed to his desk. He hit the on button for the monitor, and his email inbox appeared.

He had a dozen new emails about the investigation. While he wanted to dive into the information that had been gathered, he needed to contact Unity's next of kin. He first looked at the musher list sent to him from Race Central and discovered that Unity lived in Washington. He went to the Washington DMV site and typed in her name.

Nothing.

He typed in just Allard. Forty-six names came up. He deleted the male names and then went through the female names looking for the address that was on the race information. Nothing came up. Interesting. He put in the address.

Three people with driver's licenses for that address came up. Cameron Elston, Rachel Elston, Melanie Mirsky. Why would Unity be using Cam Elston's address? If she lived there, why hadn't he said anything when questions were being asked?

He looked up Rachel. She appeared to be Cam's wife. Pretty woman. Hawke didn't understand why he had the young woman in his vehicle after the awards ceremony. He opened Melanie's driver's license information. Staring at him was the woman who had been in Cam's vehicle.

He read the woman's description. Her height and weight were comparable to Bobbi's. She could have been the person who drove Bobbi's dogs out of Ollokot and left them alongside the road.

If Cam knew about the will, he could have decided he wanted his share now, not later. But why take the life of a musher that everyone loved? That was risky.

He Googled Cameron Elston and then the sled dog outfit Razor Ridge Runners. There were articles about past wins by the Razor Ridge Runners team at several of the larger sled dog races. But that was ten years earlier. He did notice that Melanie Mirsky was on the website as the kennel manager.

Grabbing the list of mushers, he scanned the page for her name. She hadn't been racing. Then he scanned the page for mushers from that kennel. Unity was the only one. Was that why she'd put down the kennel address and not her own? She had to have moved to Washington recently and had a driver's license in another state. But which one?

Hawke ran a hand over his cropped hair and stared at the screen. He needed to ask Cam, his wife, and Melanie if Unity had mentioned where she came from before joining their kennel.

Picking up the phone on his desk, he dialed the number for the kennel.

"Razor Ridge Kennels, this is Melanie," answered a hurried voice.

"Melanie, just the person I need to talk to. I'm Oregon State Trooper Hawke. We met briefly when I talked to Cam beside his vehicle after the awards ceremony."

She sucked in air.

"That answers whether or not Mrs. Elston knew you were there with Cam." He grinned and continued, "I need to know where Unity Allard lived before she joined your kennel."

"Unity? Why? What has she done?" The belligerent woman he'd witnessed in the vehicle had shown up.

"She's dead, and I'm trying to find her next of kin to let them know."

"Dead? How? That can't be. She was bringing back the C team today." The distress in the woman's voice would have made him sympathetic if she hadn't mentioned the dogs.

"We're still determining that. Could you give me a name or where she lived before so I can find the next of kin?" he pushed.

"I don't know where she came from. She just showed up here asking for work. After proving she knew about mushing and how to care for the dogs, Cam put her to work."

"What did she put down for a name and address on her tax form?" Hawke needed to know where she was from.

There was silence for a long time.

"Are you still there?" Hawke asked.

"We don't take out taxes. Cam pays us in cash."

Hawke wasn't surprised by the information. He could tell Cam had things he didn't want revealed. "Did Unity have any friends that she talked to or might have told about her life?"

"All she talked about when she was here was the men she slept with and how it was liberating to be a single woman. I really have to go. There are dogs that need to be trained and others that need to be tended."

"Thank you for your time." Hawke ended the call and stared at the monitor. How would he find out who she was if the fingerprint came back without a match?

Chapter Sixteen

Hawke jumped to the report from a Washington State Police Detective who dug into Razor Ridge Runners Kennel. It appeared that the kennel was losing money. Elston had a couple of harassment suits against him from female mushers. An influx of cash, like from an inheritance, would help him out considerably. But did Bobbi tell him about the will? He wondered if Justine would know.

Hawke picked up his phone and called Justine.

"Hey, Hawke, how's the investigation going?" she answered.

"Slow. We also have another victim."

"Oh no! Who?"

Since it would be in the news soon and Justine had never divulged anything he'd told her before, he said, "Unity Allard."

"No way! I thought she was a suspect. She had Bobbi's coat." Anger made Justine's voice deeper.

"She was on my list as an accomplice. Now I'm certain of it, and she was killed to keep her from saying who she helped." Hawke took a sip of coffee and asked,

"Did Bobbi ever tell you who she had in her will?"

"No. She did say that she planned to leave a legacy in the sled dog world, but I thought that meant she planned to win the Iditarod many times. I know she had enough money to go after her passion and not have to work while doing it, but I wouldn't think she'd have enough that someone would want to kill her for it."

Hawke wasn't going to disclose all he knew about the will. Better if it came as a surprise. "Did she have a connection with Razor Ridge Runners Kennel?"

Justine huffed and said, "I think she gave them some money to help them buy better dogs. I didn't like it because the race marshal, Cam Elston, owns that kennel. I thought if others found out, they'd think he was letting her get away with things because she gave him money. She said it was a good investment because his new trainer was young and good at what she did."

"Melanie?" Hawke asked.

"Yeah. But I was surprised when she wasn't racing this weekend. I think it might have been because Cam was the race judge and he may not be able to have his dogs in the race."

"But Unity was racing," Hawke said.

"Yeah, those were her dogs."

"Not Cam Elston's C team?" Hawke knew he had heard Melanie right.

"Why would she be racing Cam's dogs?" Justine asked.

"Because she worked for his kennels." Hawke was now wondering why Cam and Unity had kept that a secret.

"Well, if she was working for him, I know for a fact she wasn't racing his dogs. The dogs she had are the same ones she's been racing, give or take one or two, since I started attending races." She paused. "Not unless she's been working for him for three years."

"I don't know how long she's been working there. Did Unity ever say where she was from besides Washington?" Hawke asked, trying to find another state to try and find her in the DMV records.

"I think she mentioned Wyoming once. And I know she has a daughter, but from what I gathered as soon as the daughter left home, Unity started dog racing so she wouldn't be alone at home all the time." Barking sounded on Justine's end of the call. "I have to go, some potential buyers just showed up. I may not have finished the race, but people liked my dogs and suggested them to their friends."

"Good for you. Talk to you later." Hawke ended the call, wondering about the C sled dog team. Where were they? He made a note in his notebook about the team and what Melanie and Justine had told him.

When he finished, he pulled up the Wyoming DMV records. He typed in Unity Allard. Nothing.

This was a dead end.

He went to the race website and discovered finishing times were under Official Race Results. He scanned the list for Unity's name. Found it and moved his eyes across the table and discovered she'd been scratched from the last leg of the race. Who scratched her? Did she scratch herself so she could ride off with the person who killed her? Or was she scratched because she didn't show up at the finish line? Which left him wondering where her dogs and sled were.

He texted Justine. *Were there any dogs or sleds left at Ollokot when you left with yours?* He knew she was busy and wouldn't get a reply right away, but he was curious.

He didn't want to call Elston. He glanced down at the list of mushers. His gaze landed on Ferdie. He picked up his desk phone and dialed the number on the information sheet.

"Hello?" answered the man.

"Ferdie, this is Trooper Hawke. We met at Ollokot."

"Yeah, I remember." There were dogs barking and howling in the background. "What'cha want?"

"Why would a musher be scratched from the last leg of the race?" Hawke asked.

"They would tell the officials that they were scratching because of dog issues. A sick or lame dog, or they may not be feeling well themselves." Ferdie shouted at his dogs. "Quit, I'll be there in a minute!"

"When you left Ollokot for the last leg of the race, did you happen to see if Unity's dogs and sled were still there?" Hawke asked.

"I can't remember. Look at the results. That will tell you when each of us left."

"I did. It said she scratched." Hawke let that sink in.

"She looked just fine when I saw her that morning. In fact, she had a smile like she was expecting to get a little somethin', if you know what I mean. The last time I saw her, she was headed into the maintenance tent. I thought it was strange at the time. Only the maintenance crew uses that tent." The ruckus on his end got louder. "I have to go. Good luck."

The line went quiet, and Hawke put his phone down. Unity scratched herself from the race and went into the maintenance tent.

He pulled up the list of snowmobile volunteers. He wasn't sure if they went in the maintenance tent, but he knew a snowmobile had transported her to her death.

One name stuck out on the list.

Ivan Tabor.

Bobbi's cousin.

It was late afternoon. A good time to see if Ivan was at his father's place in Promise.

After calling Dani to tell her he'd be late coming home, he headed toward Eagle, following Highway 82 through Eagle and on west until he came to Promise Road. He turned right onto the road and continued following the road for forty-five minutes. He was only 25 miles from Eagle, but the road was gravel, rutted, and not plowed.

Using his GPS, he knew that Tabor Ranch was a mile west of the road. He kept going until he saw a pole archway and a sign that read Tabor Ranch. He followed the gravel road for another mile.

His headlights illuminated a 19th-century two-story farmhouse ahead. As he moved closer, a faded gray hay barn with missing shingles sat to the side and behind the house in the distance. Turning onto the driveway, his headlights revealed a gray, worn shed filled with rusty, dull equipment. The only thing that appeared new on the property was a blue Dodge diesel 4x4 pickup truck, shining brightly amid the dull gray buildings.

Hawke parked beside the pickup and walked toward the house. The sun had set as he drove the mile back into the house. One faint light could be seen through the dirty window by the front door. He walked up and knocked on the door.

A dog started barking, a man hollered, and boots tromped toward the front of the house.

Hawke was surprised to see Ivan open the door.

The young man took a step back and stared at him.

"Good evening. I'm Trooper Hawke. I'd like to ask you some questions. I'm conducting the investigation into the deaths of Bobbi Whitby and Unity Allard. Both women were part of the sled dog race that happened over the weekend. I understand you were one of the volunteers."

Ivan shook his head.

"You weren't one of the snowmobile volunteers?" Hawke asked.

"Yes. Yes, I was. You say another body has been found?" he asked, surprise widening his eyes and raising his voice to a sharper pitch.

"Yes. Can you tell me where you were and what you were doing between midnight and three a.m. on Thursday?" Hawke pulled out his notebook.

"Who's there? What do they want?" a man yelled from deep within the house.

"I'm taking care of it, Dad." Ivan waved his hand for Hawke to enter the house. "We'll go to the parlor. The porch light hasn't worked for several years."

Hawke followed Ivan into a room to the right, twelve feet down from the entry. The man flipped a switch on the wall, and a light reluctantly flickered on.

"This place is full of old wiring. One of these days I expect to come home and find it in ashes." Ivan sat on a straight-backed chair.

Hawke sat in the identical one across from it. "Could you tell me where you were at the time and day I mentioned?"

"Yeah, let me think. That would have been while I was following the tail end of the two hundreds. That's when we found Bobbi's sled and dogs on the side of the trail. Lance wanted to call it in, but I figured it shouldn't be put out on the radio and told him to go back to Ollokot. It wasn't that far. Then I started calling for Bobbi and looking around. Then you and Lance came to the spot, and I continued to call for her until the Search and Rescue guys caught up to me and told me they'd take over."

Hawke wrote it all down and then asked, "What were you doing Saturday morning when the last of the mushers headed toward the finish line?"

"I helped pack up things at Ollokot and haul people to Salt Creek. I think I made two trips." He smiled.

Hawke's gut was saying this guy wasn't that squeaky clean as he recounted what he was doing at the time the two women were murdered. It was as if he'd rehearsed what to say. That usually meant he needed an alibi.

"Had you met Bobbi or Unity before?" Hawke asked.

The man's face went still, his gaze fixed on the window to his right. "No. This was the first year I volunteered. I saw the request for more snowmobile volunteers, so I went to a meeting and thought it sounded like a good way to spend the weekend riding my machine, and Dad couldn't complain about it."

"That didn't answer the question I asked. Had you ever met Bobbi or Unity before this past weekend?" Hawke watched him closely.

Ivan slowly moved his gaze to Hawke. "I said no, I hadn't met them before this past weekend."

"You hadn't met either of them? Are you sure?" Hawke waited until the man stared at him with a stiff jaw and narrowed eyes. "Then you're telling me you didn't know that Bobbi Whitby was your cousin? A cousin who received a huge inheritance from your grandmother?"

"Well, I knew my cousin's name was Bobbi Whitby, but I didn't think she'd be a musher with all the money she got. I figured it was someone else." He stared into Hawke's face as he said it, but his shoulders came up as if he were ready for a blow for lying.

Hawke leaned back. "I'm not buying it. You knew she was your cousin. You were angry she received money and you didn't. You took this volunteer job to get close to her. To maybe see if you could sway her to give you some money?" Hawke pointed with the pen to the front of the house. "That's a nice shiny new truck you have out there. How did you pay for it?"

"That's none of your business!" Ivan shouted and shot to his feet. "You can leave now. I told you all you need to know. Get out of my house." He stomped to the front door and opened it before Hawke stood, put his hat on his head, and walked toward the open door.

"If you were involved in either of these deaths, I will find out and I will arrest you." Hawke smiled and walked out of the house. He felt the young man's hatred. It was palpable. But what had he thought he'd get if he killed his cousin?

Hawke stopped at the blue jacked-up truck. He wrote down the dealer and the license plate. He'd find out tomorrow who actually purchased the truck. That might give him a clue as to whether or not Ivan was the killer or the cleanup man.

## Chapter Seventeen

Hawke started Wednesday with a wreck on the highway between Alder and Winslow. On his way to work, he spotted the compact car fishtailing moments before it spun into the path of a delivery truck. There was nothing anyone could do as he watched the impact and hoped the people in the small car survived.

As the first person on the scene, he checked the car's occupants first. It was a car of three women heading to a bible study group. They were all conscious but scared and a few bruises. He checked on the truck driver. He asked about the women in the car.

"I couldn't do anything but hit them," he said. "I couldn't put on my brakes or I'd have been sliding like they were."

"No worries. I saw the whole thing. It will be a no-fault accident. You're sure you're not injured?" Hawke asked.

"I'm fine. Do you need me to help with the ladies?" the trucker asked.

"No, when the EMTs arrive and check them, we'll

get them out of the vehicle. They say they aren't hurt, but I don't want to risk moving them. Neither vehicle will catch on fire. It was a low-impact collision." Hawke asked for the man's driver's license and trip sheet. By the time he had the man's information written down, the EMTs arrived.

"If you could direct traffic until I get the EMTs apprised, that would be helpful," Hawke said.

The trucker nodded and started waving vehicles two at a time around the crash.

Hawke walked toward Roxie Paley and Bonnie Fletcher, EMTs he'd worked with many times.

"What do we have?" Bonnie asked.

"The car spun out of control and hit the truck. The driver is fine, but the three women in the car are shaken up. I'm not sure if any of them are hurt. They said they weren't, but they didn't sound sure. They're all of an age that an impact could snap a bone. I told them to stay put until you arrived to assess them." Hawke walked with the EMTs to the car.

"Hello, ladies. I'm Bonnie. This is my partner, Roxie. We're going to ask questions to make sure you can get out of the car without hurting yourselves. Okay?"

The women's heads bobbed.

Hawke left them to deal with the women while he took over directing traffic. Unfortunately, it was the time of morning when most people were trying to get to work. Some people were considerate and others revved their engines and glared at Hawke when he made them wait their turn to go.

A county car finally pulled in behind the EMT vehicle. Deputy Calvin Corcoran stepped out and walked over. "Looks like you have things under control."

Hawke waved a car through and handed the paddle with STOP on one side and SLOW on the other to the deputy. "This is a good job for you. I need to go catch a killer."

He strode to his car, pulled out in front of the car waiting to go toward Winslow, and when Calvin flashed SLOW, he moved by the crash and headed to the office. Now he'd have to write up this report before he could start digging into more information about his suspects and the victims.

After reading through the rest of the emails from the day before, Hawke decided to call Russell Nichols of the Sawtooth Sliders Kennel in Idaho. He felt it would be a dead end since people from the Razor Ridge Runners had been at the sled dog race and as far as he could tell, other than a vet tech with the same last name, there hadn't been anyone else connected to the Sawtooth Sliders at the race.

"Hello?" answered a man.

"Hi. Is this Sawtooth Sliders Kennel?" Hawke asked.

"Yes, I'm the owner, Russell Nichols. Who are you?"

"I'm Oregon State Trooper Hawke. I'm investigating two deaths that happened during the Eagle Cap Extreme Sled Dog Race in Wallowa County last weekend."

"We didn't run in that race. I'm not sure how I can be of help to you."

The man's rudeness only made Hawke want to dig

deeper. "Do you know Sheri Nichols?"

"She's my wife. She was at the Extreme helping in her capacity as a vet tech. If you want to know anything about the race, you should talk to her."

"I will as soon as I finish talking to you." Hawke tapped his notebook with a pen. "Do you know Bobbi Whitby?"

"Yes. She's an excellent trainer of sled dogs and a good human being. She has been here to teach some of our clients training techniques, and she took one of our problem dogs and made him one of our best lead dogs." His tone softened as he talked about Bobbi.

It was evident he didn't know she was dead. Hawke hated to be the one to break it to him, but it seemed strange his wife hadn't told him. "I'm sorry to inform you that Bobbi Whitby is one of the deaths I'm investigating."

The line was quiet for a long time.

"Mr. Nichols? Are you still there?" Hawke asked after what he felt was a long enough time for the man to digest what he'd said.

"Umm, yeah, I'm here. I just can't… How did she die?" The man was barely keeping it together. His voice shook with emotion.

"She was strangled and then shoved into a dog kennel to hide the body." There was no sense in sugar coating it. He needed everyone who cared about the woman to help him figure out what happened.

"Murder? Who would want—?"

"Do you have any idea who would have gained from Bobbi's death?" Hawke asked.

"Have you checked out her ex-husband? He's one vindictive piece of shit." This was what Hawke wanted.

The man to be so enraged, he'd throw out all the people who might have a squabble with the victim.

"I looked into him first. He has solid alibis. Can you think of anyone else?" He wondered if Mr. Nichols was aware of her will.

The silence dragged on so long, Hawke was about to ask if the man was still there when Nichols asked, "Is there some place I could meet with you?"

"Can you come to Oregon? I could meet you in Ontario, that's about halfway for both of us." Hawke knew he'd have to do it on his next day off, but it would be worth it if this man could come up with some good leads.

"Yeah, I can do that. What's a good day?"

"Saturday. Eleven a.m. at the burger joint off Oregon Street." Hawke knew that would be the same time zone as Nichols and an hour earlier than his time.

"I'll be there." He paused and asked, "Who is the other victim?"

"Unity Allard. Do you know her?"

"I've seen the name somewhere. But I can't place where."

"Maybe at a race? She's a musher," Hawke said to try and jog his memory.

"No, I don't think it was a race. Seems like it was on a piece of paper. Maybe I'll remember when we meet. I have dogs to tend to. Sheri has been busy at the clinic since she returned, and I've been dealing with all the kennel chores. She'll be here Saturday so I can get away." The man's demeanor seemed to lighten a bit. Perhaps helping to solve Bobbi's murder would help him with his grief.

"Can I get your wife's number?" Hawke asked as

he put a reminder on the calendar on his phone about being in Ontario on Saturday. He'd take Dani with him. He'd not been spending much time with her lately.

"Yeah." The man rattled off the number. "She may not answer right away if she's with a patient."

"Thanks." Hawke ended the call and pushed in the number he'd written down for Sheri Nichols.

"I'm busy right now. Leave a name and number. I'll call you back as soon as I'm available." The phone beeped, and Hawke left his name and phone number.

He went back to reading the reports. Ten minutes later his cell phone rang. He glanced at the caller. Herb. "Morning, Herb."

"Hey, Hawke. I'm having lunch with Chuck Sampson at High Mountain. You want to join us in half an hour?" Herb asked.

Hawke flashed through his last conversation with Herb. It came to him. Chuck was a neighbor of the Whitbys when they lived in Wallowa County. "Sure. I can meet you there. Think he'll give me anything to help my case?"

"He is keen on telling me about his neighbors," Herb replied.

"That's good enough for me." Hawke glanced at the list of people he still had to contact. It would have to wait until after lunch. Maybe he'd get lucky and Chuck would have something that could help him learn more about the Whitby family.

He turned off his monitor, rolled his chair back, and headed out, wondering where everyone was today. Usually, at least Nathan was in the office when he came in. Everyone else came and went, writing up reports and checking schedules.

The roads were still slick as he headed toward Alder on Highway 82 out of Winslow. He stayed under the speed limit and was glad to see most of the other drivers doing the same. He didn't want to deal with another wreck caused by the weather. He needed to follow up with Roxie and Bonnie to include what happened to the women in his report. He'd swing by the fire department after finishing lunch.

Hawke parked in his usual spot, in the corner of the lot where only those leaving the parking area would see his state vehicle. He eased his feet over the slick surface and felt relief when he stepped onto the salted sidewalk. The brief warm spell they had melted some of the snow before temperatures dropped again, leaving sheets of ice in parking lots, on sidewalks, and on less-used roads.

He saw Herb's pickup parked near the front of the establishment. Hawke liked the High Mountain Brew Pub. It was family-owned, served good food, and had a welcoming atmosphere.

"Over here!" Herb called and waved as Hawke stood inside the doors, letting his eyes adjust from the blinding whiteness of the snow outside to the indoor lighting.

He nodded and walked over to the table. A man who appeared to be in his sixties, like Herb, extended his hand.

"Chuck Sampson," he said, shaking hands.

"Trooper Hawke. You can call me Hawke." He sat down across from the man. "I hope Herb didn't tell you stories about why I wanted to talk to you," Hawke said.

The man glanced at Herb, who laughed.

"He's pulling your leg, Chuck," Herb said.

"I've never sat down and had a meal with a law officer before," Chuck said. "Not sure how to act."

"Just act normal. This is just a friendly lunch with friends," Hawke said as his favorite waitress at High Mountain came over. "Desiree, you're working days now?"

She smiled and blushed, holding out her left hand. He noticed a shiny ring on her ring finger. "Lucas and I are engaged. That's my boss's son. He told his dad he didn't want me working nights. Didn't like me driving home late or having to break up drunken brawls."

Hawke nodded. "I'd say he's a keeper."

Her grin grew. "I'd love to have you meet him. He's off getting supplies in Boise today. Maybe he'll be here the next time you come in."

"I'd be honored to meet the guy who captured your heart." Hawke meant it. Desiree and her family were some of the first people he'd helped when he transferred to Wallowa County and the Fish and Wildlife job almost twenty years ago. He'd enjoyed watching her and her brothers grow up into responsible adults. He knew it pleased their parents that the oldest boy had taken over the ranch and the younger boy was working full time at the bank.

"What do you want to drink, and are you ready to order?" she asked Herb and Chuck.

They both ordered their meal and drinks.

Desiree returned her attention to Hawke. "Are you having your usual?"

He grinned. "I might as well."

She took the menus and walked away.

"How often do you eat in here?" Chuck asked.

"Enough to know the people who work here and

the owner well." Hawke waited until Desiree delivered their drinks, and then he asked Chuck, "What can you tell me about the Whitbys?"

"You have to remember this was back when I was a kid. James was close to my age, and Brenda was younger by six or seven years. I think she was just starting school when the mill closed and they moved away." He sipped his beer.

"Do you remember if the brother and sister were close?" Hawke suspected they hadn't been from the start, and the tension from the grandmother's inheritance hadn't improved the relationship between the cousins.

"James was tolerant of his little sister, but he tried to get away from her all the time. She followed us around when we were outside playing. And her mom would make him allow Brenda to play the board games with us. But she was so young, she didn't know the rules and just did what she wanted. That would make him mad, and then I'd get sent home."

Desiree brought their meals over.

Hawke thanked Desiree and picked up one half of his Reuben sandwich and took a big bite. He didn't know what High Mountain put in their sauce, but they served the best Reuben in the county. After they had sated their hungers, Hawke asked, "Did you see or talk to Brenda when she was married to Jack Tabor?"

"I heard she'd moved back and married a rancher, but we didn't move in the same circles. Her kids attended schools in Eagle, and ours were at Alder schools." Chuck took a bite, chewed, and washed it down with his beer. He wiped his mouth and said, "I heard she ran off and left Jack with the boy and took the girl. Is that true?"

"From what I've discovered so far, it is."

"Huh, I wonder if Jack was mean to her? Can't think of any other reason a woman would leave an established ranch and take her daughter." Chuck finished off his beer and leaned back in his chair.

"We have no idea why she ran away with her daughter," Hawke said, to keep rumors from flying around that might rile up Ivan, whom he needed to talk to again. This time, he'd have him brought in to the Sheriff's Office to make it clear the conversation was serious. He finished his meal and reached for his wallet.

Herb put a hand on his arm. "I've got this. Go on back to work."

Hawke shook his hand. "Thanks. I'll return the favor next time." He extended his hand to Chuck. "Thank you for visiting with me."

Chuck shook hands. "This have anything to do with the woman killed during the dog races?"

Hawke glanced at Herb.

He shook his head.

Hawke took that to mean he didn't say anything about it. "It's just an inquiry for an investigation I'm conducting." Leaving the restaurant, Hawke's phone buzzed. It was Darlene.

*I have information for you that I got from Mildred about the Tabors.*

*I'll drop by on my way home from work*, he texted back and headed to talk to the EMTs. He needed their information to finish the report on the vehicle accident. Once he'd learned that the women didn't require medical care, he headed back to the office in Winslow to keep digging into his suspects.

## Chapter Eighteen

This time when he entered the office, it was bustling. Spruel was in his office on the phone. Ivy was sitting at a computer typing. The patrol sergeant, Mike Buckman, was in the conference room working on the patrol schedule.

Hawke walked over to his computer and sat. He pushed the button to turn the monitor on and waited for the screen to open. The email at the top of his inbox was from forensics.

"How's your investigation going?" Ivy asked.

"Slow. I can't find information for the next of kin for the second victim. I don't think Unity Allard is her name." Hawke double-clicked the email from forensics.

"Unity is an unusual first name. Did you try just putting that in to see if a different surname comes up?" Ivy suggested.

"I've tried that. I've checked all the surrounding states and Wyoming because someone said she talked about it like she'd lived there once. But nothing." His eyes scanned the email, and then he latched onto a sentence. *According to DNA from both victims, they are related.*

Hawke leaned back in his chair and stared at the sentence. Bobbi and Unity were related. He continued reading the reasoning behind the DNA makeup that established the connection between them.

"No wonder I can't find a Unity Allard. She's Brenda Whitby Tabor." He stood up and walked around the office area. What did this mean to his investigation?

"What are you mumbling about?" Spruel asked, walking into the open area.

"Forensics ran a DNA test on my two victims, and they're related. The second one is the aunt of the first one." Hawke stood in the middle of the room, still trying to wrap his head around what it meant. If Ivan killed them, he not only killed his cousin, he killed his mother. Did he know she was his mother? Was that why he killed her? Or had it been because she had been his accomplice in killing Bobbi?

Spruel placed his hands on Hawke's desk and leaned down to read the email. When he finished, he straightened and peered into Hawke's eyes. "Now you know who the next of kin are."

"Yeah. At least I know where to find the son and husband. But where is the daughter?" Hawke sighed. "I'll have to start looking into marriages from Oregon, Washington, Idaho, and Wyoming to see if Brenda Whitby Tabor married someone after she left Jack. If she's been using the name Unity Allard since she left, I would think she would have used the same last name for her daughter when registering her for school. School records might be more useful. But that isn't all on computers and could take way too long to discover."

Nathan clamped him on the shoulder. "Good luck finding the daughter. Make finding the killer your main priority. The daughter will come out of the woodwork when the press gets hold of this unique double homicide."

Hawke agreed.

He called Sheriff Rafe Lindsey and asked him to send a deputy out in the morning to bring in Ivan Tabor for questioning. Then he contacted the Washington State Officer who'd gathered the information on Elston and his kennel, and asked him if he was equipped to question Elston while Hawke watched on a live stream. The officer said he could do that at the state police headquarters in his district.

"Can you schedule it for tomorrow afternoon?" Hawke asked.

"I can try. It will depend on how cooperative Mr. Elston is."

That wasn't what Hawke wanted to hear. He needed to get answers from Elston. "Make sure he understands this is to learn more about what happened and not that we think he's a suspect. I need to know exactly what Unity Allard did for him and if he knew her true identity, Brenda Whitby Tabor. I need to see his reaction to those questions and be patched into you so I can give you questions to ask based upon his reactions." Hawke hated that he couldn't be there himself to do the interview.

"Understood," replied the Washington State Trooper.

They ended the call with Hawke sending the trooper his report on the homicides.

It was nearing 5 o'clock. If he didn't hear from Sheri Nichols by six, he would try her again. She should have had a break sometime between when he left the message and now to call.

He sat for a few more minutes, digesting the fact that Bobbi and Unity were related and that neither of them seemed to know. Surely, Bobbi's last name would have given her aunt an idea of who she was. Why hadn't the aunt acknowledged her? It was clear that Bobbi wouldn't have had the slightest idea that Unity was related. The different last names, her brashness, and her sleeping around. Bobbi had been small when her aunt left, taking her cousin. There was no way she would have realized the connection.

But Unity… Why would she keep who she was from her niece? Shame? Anger? Revenge? He could sit here and play the what-if game all night and not get any closer to figuring out who killed both women.

He thought of Beverly and picked up the phone. No, the next of kin were Unity's husband and son in Promise. But he didn't want to tell them now. He wanted it to come out in the interview with Ivan tomorrow. After he talked to Ivan, he'd let Beverly know what he'd discovered.

Hawke walked out of the office and headed home. He remembered Darlene wanted to talk to him. He turned in before his driveway and parked in front of Herb and Darlene's house. The lights were on, making it look inviting. He'd just stepped onto the front porch when the door opened. The aromas made his mouth water.

"Do you have time for dinner?" Darlene asked.

"I think Dani will have something ready for me

when I get there. But it smells delicious." Hawke wiped his feet on the doormat and stepped inside.

"How about some cookies and coffee while we talk?" Darlene asked, leading the way into the kitchen.

"I never turn down your cookies." Hawke sat at the kitchen table.

Darlene placed a cup of coffee in front of him and a plate piled with chocolate chip and oatmeal cookies within reach.

Hawke narrowed his eyes. "How is it you have mine and Dani's favorite cookies baked fresh?"

"I plan on sending them home with you." Darlene smiled and sat with a cup of tea. "Mildred says that Brenda was caught twice fooling around with other men. When Jack confronted her about it in church, Brenda was gone the next day, along with the daughter. Mildred said the woman was so embarrassed she turned red, hid her face, and left the church before the service even started." Darlene sipped her tea and continued. "Mildred also said that Brenda had been friends with Judy Meyers, who told Mildred that Brenda lived with several men but never remarried because Jack refused to give her a divorce. Brenda didn't have any more children, raising Raina as a single mother." Darlene smiled and her eyes twinkled.

"What are you leaving out?" Hawke picked up another cookie.

"Judy said that Brenda bragged about changing her name all the time because she liked pretending she was anyone but the woman who had been humiliated in church. She believes that Brenda also changed Raina's name. But she couldn't remember what she changed it to."

Hawke nodded. "Any idea where the two were living?"

"Wyoming, Colorado, and recently, Judy said the number Brenda called from was in Washington."

Hawke grinned. "Thank you. Now maybe I can get some answers." He stood.

"Don't forget the cookies." Darlene slid the cookies from the plate into a large Ziplock bag.

"Thanks for the cookies and the information."

"You're welcome."

Chances were that Dani would have fed the horses already, but he felt a need to sit with them for a bit. Jack, his older gelding, always had a way of making him see what was right in front of him.

He parked in his usual spot. By the time he closed the vehicle door, Dog was by his side. "Hey boy, you have a good day lying by the fire and dreaming?" He scratched behind Dog's ears and glanced at the house. "Where's Dani?" Only the light they left on during the winter gave off its faint glow in the front window.

They crunched through six inches of snow to the barn. His two geldings and mule were in the corral just behind the barn. Dani's string of horses for the hunting lodge were out in the closest pasture. When the snow melted, maybe by April if it was a warm year, they'd be moved to the far pasture. Hawke hoped he'd be able to take time off when they trailed the string of horses to the lodge in the Wallowa Mountains after the snow receded. He enjoyed working alongside Dani's wrangler, Tuck Kimbal, and his family. They would all be moving back up to the lodge for the summer and most of the fall.

Dot nickered as Hawke and Dog stepped through the smaller door on the front of the barn. Hawke breathed in the scent of hay, horse, and dust. It was a comforting fragrance. He flicked on the lights and opened the tack room door. He scooped grain and walked to the three stalls, pouring a portion in each wooden feeder along the wall. Then he walked over and opened the gate leading from the barn to the corral. Jack and Dot headed to their stalls and started munching on the grain. Horse, the mule, walked over to the tack room door.

"You don't get more to eat than the rest, get in your stall." Hawke grabbed the mule by the mane and led him into his stall. After he closed the gates on the stalls, he forked grass hay into their metal feeders hanging from wood stall partitions. Once he'd taken care of the food, Hawke walked into Jack's stall and brushed him.

"How was your day?" he asked, not expecting a reply.

Jack snorted, and Hawke laughed. "That good, huh?"

Dog sat on the ground next to Jack's front legs. Jack put his head down and sniffed Dog. Their friendship began when Hawke brought Dog home as an 18-month-old from Justine's dog kennel.

Hawke told Jack about Ivan, then he moved over into Dot's stall and brushed him, giving him the lowdown on the DNA discovery.

Finally, Hawke entered Horse's stall as the animal started eating his hay. The mule had one ear cocked backwards as if intensely listening to Hawke lay out his plans for the next day and his interview with Ivan.

The front door to the barn opened, and Dani

walked over to the stalls. "I figured you were in here with the boys when I saw your vehicle here and no one was in the house." She placed her hand on Horse's back. "Are they helping you with your investigation?"

Hawke grinned and faced her. "They always have a way of helping me figure things out. How was your day?"

"I crunched numbers to see if there was a chance of building a barbecue pit behind the lodge. It turns out that if I don't have any large expenses with my airplane and helicopter, I can make it work. But then there's the logistics of getting all the bricks and paving stones hauled up and the thing built before the first guests start arriving." She sighed.

"You are the one who wanted to make Charlie's Hunting Lodge 'the place' to go to get away from it all." He put an arm around her shoulders and pulled her close. She smelled of fresh air, dog, and cooking grease. "Did you go see Justine today and stop off somewhere to pick up dinner?"

She pulled out of the one-arm embrace and stared at him. "How did you know that?"

"You smell of dog and cooking grease." He walked to the stall gate and motioned for her to step through. He closed the gate and returned the brush to the tack room. He closed the door, and then they walked to the front of the barn. Hawke flicked the light switch and closed the door.

They walked to the house.

When Hawke entered the back mud room, he sniffed. "You smelled of cooking grease. How come the house smells like my favorite Chinese restaurant?"

Dani grinned. "You thought you were getting

burgers from the Rusty Nail, didn't you?"

"Yeah. Did you drive to Eagle just so I'd have Chinese food?" Hawke was thinking this night couldn't get any better.

"No, I drove to Eagle to talk to a mason about how hard it would be for Tuck and me to lay the paving stones for the patio at the lodge. And since I was in Eagle, I dropped by and ordered our favorites from the Bamboo Garden." Dani had her coat off and was washing her hands.

Hawke washed his hands and sat down at the counter. Dani set a plate in front of him and one in her spot. He pulled containers of food out of the bag.

Once they had filled their plates and were eating, Hawke's phone rang. He glanced at the name. No name but it was from Washington.

"Trooper Hawke," he answered.

"This is Sheri Nichols. I received your message, and then when I arrived home, my husband said you wanted to talk to me."

He could tell she didn't want to make the call and her husband was most likely listening in. "Yes, Mrs. Nichols, thank you for calling me back." He pulled his notebook out of his pocket, and Dani slid a pen over to him. "I wanted to know how well you knew Bobbi Whitby and Unity Allard."

The woman took her time replying. "Bobbi was a musher whom I've talked to a couple of times at races. She also held a class here at my husband's kennels."

"Were you friends? Did she visit and tell you things about her life?" Hawke asked to try and get the woman to open up more.

"No. We only talked about the health of her dogs at

races. When she was here, I was working as a vet tech at a race." There was a hint of bitterness in her tone.

"I see. And what about Unity? Where did you meet, and were you friends?"

Sheri made a strange sound and said, "We met through the dog races. And no, we were not friends. That woman was always throwing herself at the men. All they had to do was say something nice and she was all over them. She was pitiful."

"While you were at Ollokot, did you notice anyone paying extra attention to Bobbi or Unity?"

"Not more than normal. Bobbi always has a man or two during each race who takes a shine to her, but she never reciprocates their attention. She treated them like a friend or acquaintance. Unity, most men who had been at races with her before, kept their distance if they could. Poor Dr. McPherson had to take care of one of her dogs. After that, she thought he was being nice because he wanted her." Sheri laughed. "It was like watching a love-sick cartoon character trying to capture the advances of someone out of their league. Sad, and yet you couldn't stop watching the woman make a fool of herself."

"And where were you Thursday of the race from one a.m. to four a.m.? Hawke asked.

There wasn't a sound for a few minutes, and then she said, "I was in my tent resting. I'd been helping all day Wednesday with the wellness checks, and Thursday, after the start of the race, we were hauled to Ollokot and I began helping again. When I couldn't keep my eyes open, Dr. McPherson told me to go take a nap. I think that was about twelve-twenty. I returned to the vet tent around four, I think it was."

"Were you sleeping in the volunteer tent?" Hawke asked, thinking that if so, she would have an alibi.

"No. I took my own tent. I knew that I'd only get small intervals to sleep and wanted to make sure I'd be alone so I could."

"Then no one can vouch that you were in your tent from twelve-twenty to four?" He made a note of this, even though she wasn't a suspect, other than the fact that she was married to the man who would inherit from Bobbi's death.

"I guess not." She said as if she had just realized the same thing.

"And Saturday, when did you pack up and leave Ollokot?"

"We waited until the last of the dogs were gone, that would have been the new girl with her dogs. She insisted on being the last one out, watching until they put Bobbi's dogs in the box sled and hauled them down."

A thought struck Hawke. He made a note to contact the person in charge of the box sled and see if Unity's dogs had been on it. Tearing down her sled would have been easy enough to do and conceal with other items that went into the storage sheds.

"Anyway," Sheri continued, "once she'd left, we loaded the veterinary supplies into the sled behind a snowmobile, and it left. Then we helped with other tents that needed to be emptied as the snowmobiles came and picked people up to shuttle them to Salt Creek and the van waiting to take people back to Race Central."

"Did you see Unity while you were hauling boxes to the sleds?" Hawke asked.

"No. She would have left with the rest of the mushers during the night."

That was something that had been nagging at his brain. She didn't leave that night. She was scratched from the race. Who scratched her, and was it before or after she was killed?

## Chapter Nineteen

Hawke ended his call with Sheri Nichols and looked over at his cold meal.

Dani stood. "I'll nuke it and it will be almost as good as it was."

He nodded, jotting ideas down in his book.

Setting the warmed-up food in front of him, Dani asked, "Was the call helpful?"

"Yes and no. I came up with more questions that aren't answered and a possible suspect." He went on to tell Dani everything that Sheri said and what he'd learned today.

"It sounds like you have a puzzle of an investigation to untangle," Dani said, clearing away the packaging and her dishes.

"I want to be at the interview my Washington counterpart is conducting tomorrow, but I have to stay here. I hope he doesn't interview at the same time I'm in with Ivan." Hawke felt like he was being pulled in too many directions to give this investigation a complete evaluation.

"You can always stop the interview here and do the Zoom one. You never know, it might give you more to ask Ivan." Dani whisked his empty plate away, and Hawke headed down the hall to take a shower. Yeah, he was worrying too much when he needed to be following the information.

Hawke drove straight to the Wallowa County Sheriff's Office the next morning. He wanted to be ready when Ivan was brought in. He'd talked to the Washington State Trooper and Elston was coming in for the interview at one in the afternoon. Hawke thanked him, ending the call as Deputy Novak walked in behind Ivan Tabor.

"Good morning, Ivan," Hawke said. "Thank you for coming in to speak with me."

The young man snorted and said, "Don't thank me. The deputy made it sound like I didn't have a choice."

"Are you in handcuffs?" Hawke asked.

Ivan's forehead wrinkled. "No."

"Then you came of your own free will, and I appreciate all the help you can give me." Hawke motioned for Ivan to follow him. Novak walked down the hall behind Ivan. Hawke thought it was a nice touch.

Once he and Ivan were settled in the small interview room, Hawke motioned to the two cups of coffee sitting in the middle of the table. "One of those is for you. The jailer should be bringing us some donuts here pretty soon."

Ivan slowly dragged a cup of coffee toward him,

his brow still wrinkled as if he were puzzling over what was going on.

Hawke snatched the other cup and took a sip. He'd picked up the coffee from the Toasty Bean drive-through in Alder before coming to the Sheriff's Office. The donuts were an afterthought. He'd caught the jailhouse deputy going off duty and asked him to bring back half a dozen and get some for himself.

"What are you waiting for?" Ivan asked.

"The donuts. I don't like to work on an empty stomach." He grinned, slowly pulled his notebook out of his pocket, and clicked the pen to make it ready to write.

A knock on the door meant the food had arrived. "Come in," Hawke said, watching Ivan settle himself after jumping at the knock on the door.

The deputy handed Hawke a bag from the bakery. "Thank you." He opened the bag, peered in, and tipped the bag toward Ivan. "Take two if you want."

Hawke slid a napkin across the table to Ivan and watched the man put the two largest donuts in the bag onto the napkin.

He plucked a chocolate-coated cake donut. Holding it in front of his face, he asked Ivan, "When did you find out Unity Allard was your mother?"

Ivan's eyes widened and he started choking on the bite in his mouth. Hawke dropped his donut and moved behind Ivan, pounding on his back. The chewed-up dough flew halfway across the table.

Hawke returned to his seat and studied the man sitting across from him, wiping his mouth with the back of his hand. Tears glistened in his eyes. Hawke wondered if it was for his mom or because he nearly choked.

"What did you say about Unity?" Ivan asked in a cautious voice.

"We learned yesterday, through DNA, that Unity was Brenda Whitby Tabor, your mother and Bobbi's aunt." Hawke narrowed his eyes. "I don't think it's a coincidence that two family members were murdered on the same weekend at the same event. And since you were related to both of them, I'd like to know more about your relationship with them."

"I had no relationship with them. My mother took my older sister and left when I was two. I never saw either of them again. They never came back to the ranch, and Dad never made an attempt to find them. He figured if they didn't want to be there, he couldn't make them stay. I couldn't even tell you what my mother looked like. Dad threw all the photos of her and Sharon away."

"How does it feel to know you killed your mom and cousin?" Hawke watched as the horror of the thought chased across his mind.

"I didn't kill them. Why do you think I did? Killing either of them accomplishes nothing for me."

"Why do you say that?" Hawke asked.

"I haven't seen my mom since I was two. I got over hating her a long time ago. She left. Dad took care of me. Did he rant over the years about her leaving until sometimes I wanted to scream? Yes! But I wouldn't kill her because of that. In some ways, I can see why she left. Dad isn't the easiest person to live with. He has bouts of depression, and then he's filled with energy and everyone has to work as hard as he does when he gets in those moods. It can be exhausting. I don't blame her for leaving or leaving me. I'm sure it was hard to get along as a single parent. Do I wish I'd had known she was my mother? Maybe. I didn't see much of her, but what I did see, I'm not sure I want to be associated with her."

Hawke could see the man was telling the truth. He felt nothing for his mom. Yet, he was embarrassed over the woman she'd become. "What about Bobbi? You resented her getting your grandmother's money."

Ivan's hands shook as he raised the cup of coffee to his lips. He drank. The way he stared up at the ceiling, Hawke could tell he was formulating what to say.

"Just tell me the truth, not something you make up," Hawke said.

Ivan's gaze flicked from the ceiling to him. "What makes you think I won't tell you the truth?"

"You're looking at the ceiling and putting together what you think will be a good story."

The young man's eyes narrowed as he continued to look at Hawke. "The last time I saw Bobbi was when our grandmother's will was read. She at least apologized for Grandmother leaving us less than she did the twins. Beverly, just grinned and walked out of the attorney's office with her head high, not even acknowledging me."

"Was Sharon there?" Hawke asked.

"I told you. I haven't seen her since Mom took her and left Promise. So, no. She did collect the money and stocks, but didn't collect the little bit of things Grandmother left to us, the attorney gave them to me. It wasn't worth anything; they were mostly heirlooms. I sold them to an antique store in the Tri-Cities."

"Have you seen Beverly since the will was read?"

Hawke asked, thinking it was odd that she hadn't mentioned much about it other than what everyone received.

"I went to her gallery in Seattle a few years ago. She acted like she didn't know who I was and fobbed me off onto an assistant. I went there to talk to her to see if she wanted to invest in the ranch. It's falling apart. Dad insists there isn't any money to put into fixing it up. I can't think of anywhere else I want to live, but if we can't get more crops growing or fix up the place, we're going to have to sell it, and it won't go for what it's worth the shape it's in."

"You need money. Did you think that Bobbi wouldn't have a will, so knock her off and you could get your hands on some money?" Hawke saw the way the young man flinched.

"No! I didn't kill her either!" Ivan slammed a hand down on the table.

The door flew open, and Deputy Novak looked in.

"It's okay. Ivan is just blowing off steam," Hawke said, motioning for the door to be closed. When the deputy disappeared behind the closed door, Hawke asked, "If you didn't kill Bobbi or Unity, then do you know who did?"

Ivan's hands started shaking, and his knee bounced under the table. The motion made the floor vibrate under Hawke's feet.

"Who are you scared of?" Hawke asked.

Ivan leaned forward. "Think about it. My mom and my cousin are dead. That leaves me, Sharon, and Beverly if it's someone after the money, as you keep saying. They're going to bump us all off until they get the money."

Hawke studied Ivan. No, his fear was deeper than thinking his family was going to be killed. He knew too much. Perhaps like his mom. He was fearful that he would be next.

"Who told you to dump Unity's body? Was it the same person who had you shove Bobbi's body in the kennel sled?"

Ivan's body shook. Was he remembering how he'd had to break bones to make Bobbi, his cousin, fit in the dog kennel? Or maybe he realized that he'd killed his mother because someone told him to. Whatever it was, his lips were in a tight, straight line. Until Hawke could get some physical evidence on him, he couldn't lock Ivan up. He needed a warrant to have Ivan's snowmobile checked by forensics. Maybe they could find DNA from Unity on the machine. Or Bobbi's DNA on Ivan's snowmobile clothing.

"Sit tight. I have some calls to make." Hawke shoved the rest of the donuts toward Ivan and left the room.

"Did you get anything?" Rafe asked, meeting Hawke in the hallway outside the room.

"Not really. I need a warrant to have forensics go over the snowmobile and Ivan's riding gear."

"Good luck with that when you have nothing but your gut to go on," Rafe said, continuing down the hall.

"Yeah," Hawke muttered and pulled out his phone to call D.A. Lange.

"Hawke, you don't have enough evidence for me to write out a warrant to seize his clothing or snowmobile," D.A. Lange said, sitting across the desk from Hawke.

He'd been able to get an in-person interview with the D.A., hoping he could persuade the man to write out the warrant.

"I know he's involved in some way, but without a chance to check his belongings and snowmobile for DNA, I don't have anything." Hawke hadn't come in here confident, but he'd hoped his experience with Lange in the past would sway him.

"I'm sorry. You know the law as well as I do. You aren't bringing me enough. My hands are tied." Lange leaned back in his chair. "Tell me more about this case. Maybe I can come up with something else that will work."

Hawke told him everything.

Lange whistled when Hawke recounted finding out the victims were related. "That's quite the twist to this. And they didn't know each other?"

"I'm sure the aunt knew who the niece was, but the first victim had never seen her aunt so she wouldn't have known what she looked like." Hawke thought about that for the millionth time. Why hadn't Unity told Bobbi who she was? "I think the second victim was helping to get rid of the first victim. I'm not sure why, but I'm certain she helped cover up the crime by picking up the impostor who drove the first victim's sled and dogs out of Ollokot." He studied Lange. "Her sled and dogs are missing. I need to find them so forensics can see if they can find any other DNA on her things than her own." He stood, knowing that he had to go through the containers at Ollokot and see if the sled was in there. He also needed to ask about the dogs being transported from Ollokot in the kennel sled.

"Do you still need that warrant?" Lange asked.

"I could use it, but if I can't get it, I'll go a different direction."

"If you can come up with evidence that connects Tabor to the crime, other than speculations, I'll sign the warrant."

"I hope I can find it before he gets smart and washes the snowmobile and his clothing." Hawke left the courthouse, walked into the Sheriff's Office, and told them to let Ivan go, then he pulled out his phone and called Justine.

"Hey, Hawke, I'm in the middle of the breakfast rush," she answered.

"Who do I talk to about getting into the storage containers at Ollokot?" he asked, proving to her he wasn't in the mood for chatting.

"That would be the race coordinator. Roger Duggan. His number should be on the website."

"Thanks." Hawke slid into his work vehicle, opened his laptop, and pulled up the Eagle Cap Extreme Sled Dog Race website. He clicked and scrolled until he found the phone number for Roger Duggan.

He dialed the number.

"Hello?" answered a man with a deep voice.

"Roger Duggan?" Hawke asked.

"Yes."

"I'm Trooper Hawke. I'm investigating the events that happened at the sled dog race this past weekend. I need to have access to your storage containers at Ollokot."

"I'm tied up and can't go with you. My niece is getting married this weekend, and my sister will have my hide if I don't show up."

"I'd like to get your keys. I'll take a snowmobile

up there today and check it out. I believe there may be evidence in a container." Hawke needed to find Unity's sled. "Also, were Unity Allard's dogs transported by kennel sled to Race Central? And who picked them up?"

"I guess you can have the keys. You'll have to come by my work. It's Duggan Printing, two blocks off Main. The only dogs shipped out on the last day were Bobbi's. The others were taken down as soon as the storm cleared."

"Who would I talk to about the dogs?" Hawke had to find the dogs.

"Delbert Winn stores the sled in between the races each year. He'd know when it was ready for him to take."

"Thanks." Hawke looked up Delbert's home address. He lived in Prairie Creek. Hawke decided to go grab the keys to the containers from Roger and call Spruel to get a snowmobile released to him, go pick it up, and stop at Delbert's house on his way to Salt Creek.

## Chapter Twenty

At the Winslow OSP office, Spruel reminded Hawke that he wanted to sit in on the Elston interview.

"I'll get the key from Duggan and talk to Delbert Winn. Then I'll go to the Sheriff's Office to be part of the interview." Hawke slowed his thoughts down. He needed to prepare for the interview with Elston.

After getting the keys and learning from Delbert that the kennels were empty when they returned from Ollokot, he settled himself in an office at the Sheriff's Office. He synced into the Washington State Police interview room, where the detective he'd sent the reports to was waiting to start the interview.

The Detective started by stating his name, Washington State Detective Thomas Volle and he asked Elston to state his name.

"Cameron Elston. Why am I here?"

Hawke stared at the belligerent set to the man's face and the lowered eyelids. Elston was hiding his emotions behind the mask of belligerence.

"We are questioning you for the Oregon State Police in regards to the deaths of Bobbi Whitby and Unity Allard," Volle said.

Elston's eyebrows shot up at the mention of Unity. "Is that why my dogs haven't been returned? Because she's dead?"

Hawke texted Volle. *Ask him why she had his dogs.*

The State Trooper barely glanced at his phone and asked, "Why did the victim have your dogs at the race?"

"She works for my kennel. She was working with them and suggested she could run them in the race and give them more trail time." Elston didn't look at the detective when he replied.

Hawke texted. *What is her job description?*

Volle asked, "What exactly did she do for your kennel?"

"She cleaned kennels and worked with the dogs, training them for racing." Again, Elston didn't look at the detective.

It was clear to Hawke that he was hiding something. There was something more to Unity working at his kennel.

*Ask him why he had his kennel manager at the race if Unity was the only one racing?*

The trooper asked the question.

Elston stared at Volle with his mouth open.

"Do I need to repeat the question?" Volle asked.

"No. I thought it would be a good way for her to see the other side of racing. She is usually mushing our team, and I wanted her to see what being a Race Marshal was like."

Hawke snorted and texted. *Then why was she in Prairie Creek while you were at Ollokot?*

"You were at Ollokot all weekend and she was staying in Prairie Creek. How could she be learning anything sitting in a motel room?" Volle asked.

A snicker slipped from Hawke's lips. He glanced around to make sure he was the only one in the room. It was unprofessional of him to be delighted at the way the trooper phrased his question. The expression on Elston's face said he was getting flustered.

Elston ran a hand over his eyes and his bravado slipped away. "I planned to take Melanie to the camp with me, but when Unity saw her at the vet checks and smiled, I knew she'd mention something to my wife. I decided that Melanie would stay in town."

Hawke raised an eyebrow, his mind spinning. *Ask him if Unity was blackmailing him about Melanie.*

"Was Unity blackmailing you over your affair?" Volle asked.

Elston's gaze drilled into the trooper. "Why would you ask that?"

"Because you didn't want Unity to see you with Melanie. And if she was using your sled dogs for the race, wouldn't you have known she would be there? Maybe you brought Melanie along to help you get rid of your blackmailer?" Volle leaned back and crossed his arms, staring at Elston.

Hawke squirmed in his seat. Volle was doing a good job, but he wished he was there to ask more questions.

"I see what you're doing. You're trying to say I killed Unity. No, she wasn't blackmailing me. I just didn't want her to know I was stepping out on my wife.

Melanie and I have been careful to make sure my wife doesn't find out. I don't want to lose my wife, and Melanie doesn't want to marry me."

"It's a good thing I had her brought in to question, too. This way we can see who is telling the truth." Volle started pushing his papers together as if to leave.

Hawke texted *Ask him why Bobbi Whitby would put him in her will.*

A quick flick of the trooper's eyes to the phone, and he asked, "Why were you named in Bobbi Whitby's will?"

Elston was a poor actor. "I was? Wow, that was nice of her. The only thing I can think of is that I helped her purchase her first sled dogs and gave her some of my old sleds and gear to get started. I guess she remembered my generosity."

That couldn't be right. Justine had told Hawke that when Bobbi received her inheritance, she went out and purchased dogs and equipment. She would have gone for the newest and best with the money she had. He might have helped with dogs, but not gear. Hawke texted *Press him. I don't think that's it.*

"What kind of gear did you give her?" Volle held a pen as if to write it down.

"I can't remember. It was a few years back."

"What about the dogs. Which ones did you sell her?" Volle pressed.

"I'd need access to our records to find out. What does it matter?" Elston came back.

"Because I don't believe that's why you are in her will. Was she one of your conquests? Maybe she is paying you back for more than kindness?" Volle hit the nail with that comment.

Elston's face reddened. His gaze dropped to the table.

"I think you have been unfaithful to your wife for a long time. Because you come across to me as a philanderer."

Hawke texted. *Was he a lover during or after her marriage?*

"Were you a lover during or after her marriage?" Volle stared at Elston.

"Why? What difference does it make?" Elston was evading the question with a question.

"Which was it?" the detective insisted.

"After her marriage broke up. She was torn up, scared her husband would find her. I came across her at a race. She was frightened. Said she thought she saw her ex-husband, and she was scared of him. I took her to my tent and we talked. She told me about her ex and how she'd come into some money and had started sled dog racing, hoping to fill a void in her life. One thing led to another and we had sex and hooked up a couple of times at later races. Then at a race, she told me she'd fallen in love with someone else and thanked me for being there when she needed someone. I'm guessing she put me in the will after dumping me."

Hawke texted *Did she say who it was she fell in love with?*

"Did she mention who she fell in love with?" Volle asked.

"No. And when I asked around, no one seemed to know. She seemed more confident and not scared when I saw her at races. The racing world has lost a good person."

That was the first sincere thing the man had said

during the whole interview. Hawke wondered who the mysterious person was that she had fallen in love with. It was obvious she kept it a secret from everyone. Even Justine, who everyone told their life to, didn't know who it could be.

*Ask him again about Unity,* Hawke texted.

"Tell me more about your connection to Unity Allard," Volle said.

Elston narrowed his eyes. "She was just a woman I employed to help with the dogs. Why are you hounding me about her?"

"How is it she had your dogs at the race and you didn't know about it?" Volle asked.

Elston closed his lips and shook his head.

"Are you refusing to answer my questions?" Volle asked.

Elston crossed his arms and stared at the wall.

*Ask him how he pays his employees,* Hawke texted, thinking his tax evasion should get him talking.

"How do you pay your employees?" Volle asked, again picking up his pen as if getting ready to write.

Elston's arms swung apart. He stared at the detective. "W-what do you mean?"

"We're trying to find information about Unity Allard, who was working for you. We'd like her information from your tax forms to try and piece together more about her."

"I don't have to give you anything like that without a warrant." Elston said it as if he wasn't sure about the legalities.

"We'll get a warrant and we'll bring the IRS into this as well." Volle held his gaze on Elston.

Hawke watched as a flurry of emotions raced

across Elston's face.

"I want to talk to my lawyer before I say anything." Elston crossed his arms.

*Let him go*, Hawke texted. If nothing else, they could sic the IRS on him for evading taxes.

When Elston left the room, Hawke called Volle. "Thank you for letting me sit in on the interview."

"I'm afraid I didn't get much out of him," Volle replied.

"You wiggled enough out of him to give me some other leads. Thanks again. Did you have Melanie brought in, too?" He admired the man thinking ahead.

"No. She arrived here minutes after Elston arrived. I've had someone taking notes on what she had to say. I'll send them to you as soon as I get hold of them."

"Thanks. She may give us something to prove Elston was in on at least one of the homicides." Hawke ended the call and leaned back in his chair, taking a look at the notes he had written. He was positive that Unity and Elston were up to something, possibly killing Bobbi. Then Elston decided Unity knew too much and killed her, too. But putting all the pieces together to prove it was going to be hard. Mushing was a sport where everyone wore gloves and lots of clothing. This made prints or DNA transfer hard to use as evidence.

His phone dinged. It was a text from Volle. It was photos of the notes another trooper took of Melanie's account of the weekend. It appeared she had come to the race to learn more about other opportunities to be a part of the sport than mushing. But when Cam saw someone he knew at the vet checks, he told her to stay in town. He didn't want that person to see them together. She never did find out who the person was, but she had a feeling it was a woman he was sleeping with. Mrs. Elston had asked Melanie to keep an eye on her husband since she was going to the race as well. Only she couldn't keep an eye on him when she was stuck in a motel room. When she was asked about Unity, she said she'd seen Cam and Unity huddling near the dogs and talking several times in the last few months. She didn't know what about, but they appeared not to care for one another when people were watching. And yes, Cam told Unity to use some of their dogs for the race. Which was unusual. Especially since they had been five of their best dogs. But Unity had been training them with her dogs for the last month. She hoped they got them all back.

Hawke stopped reading and studied the pages. Cam and Unity had been up to something. Could that have been killing Bobbi to make them both rich?

## Chapter Twenty-one

Hawke stood at Ollokot camp in front of the container, holding the key that Roger had given him. The world around him was white. The blue sky above showcased a sun that was moving toward the top of Mount Howard. He slid the key in and popped the lock open. Pulling up on the metal handle, he opened the door, which groaned in protest.

The equipment was all piled to one side, making it easy to walk in and see what was stored together. The tents were the first thing he walked by. He pulled out a flashlight as he went farther back in the container. He didn't see anything that looked like a sled with the tables, folding chairs, or kitchen items.

He'd asked Justine if she remembered what color the sled was. She said the sled bag was forest green, which seemed odd for a flamboyant woman like Unity to have such a reserved color. He didn't see green anywhere. Could he be wrong? Had the person mushed the sled off along with the dogs?

Could Unity have scratched her team and then mushed off to meet up with whoever killed her? That was a possibility, but he was going to dig deeper. Hawke started one-by-one packing the tents out of the container. That's when he spotted green. The sled had been wedged against the wall behind the tents.

He stepped out of the container and texted Spruel to send up a forensic team to gather the sled.

Scanning the area around Ollokot, he listened. What happened to Unity's dogs? He had three hours to wait for the forensic team, hoping they'd get there before dark. Hawke replaced the tents and locked the door. He wouldn't be able to hear anything with the rumble of the snowmobile, but he'd cover more ground. Swinging a leg over the machine, he settled on the seat and started the engine. The dogs had to be somewhere that anyone leaving Ollokot wouldn't find them. Hawke set out in the opposite direction of Salt Creek and the groomed trail to the finish line.

Every fifteen minutes, he'd stop, turn off the engine, and listen. The second time, he cocked his head. A mournful howl, so sad, it made his heart squeeze. He headed the snowmobile in the direction of the sound. He came upon the dogs, tethered between two trees.

Anger roiled in his belly and burned his temples. How could anyone involved in a sport that uses dogs do this to these animals?

He stopped a bit from the dogs. Some looked at him, others yelped with happiness. Slowly, he approached, walking through the deep snow. He cursed not bringing snowshoes, but he hadn't thought he'd be in the deep snow looking for dogs. Empty food dishes were scattered around. Whoever left them here had planned to come back. He'd bet his finding Unity's body so soon had kept whoever it was away for fear they'd be seen up here.

He walked down the line, approaching each dog slow and easy as he petted them and told them he'd get them out of here. He used the satellite radio to contact Spruel, asking him to have a deputy bring the box sled up to Ollokot. He'd found the missing dogs.

"You've had a busy day. Over." Spruel replied.

"I'm going to bag the dishes I found with the dogs and give them to forensics. They might have prints, but I doubt it. Whoever left them here would have been wearing gloves, but I want everything checked. Over."

"Sounds logical. I'll contact Rafe and get the deputy up there as soon as I can. Over."

"These dogs are hungry. Have him bring food and water. Over." Hawke ended the call. He didn't want to leave the dogs, but didn't know how well they'd be able to travel having been without food for days. He unchained one end of the tether from a tree and attached it to the snowmobile. Then he unchained the other end and attached it to the snowmobile. "I'm going to go slow. I know you haven't had anything to eat for days."

Hawke started the snowmobile and idled forward. Before he could turn his head to see how the dogs were handling it, there were five on one side of him and five on the other, walking as best they could on top of the crusty snow. Every once in a while, one would break through. The pull of the others and its own footing would get it back up on top.

It was a slow trip until Hawke found the groomed trail. Then the dogs trotted alongside him as he sped up a bit. They reached Ollokot only minutes before Deputy Alden arrived with the box sled, food, and water.

Hawke had the dogs tethered between two trees. They were eating snow when Dave idled up next to Hawke's snowmobile.

"Where were they?" Dave asked as Hawke reached into one of the kennels and pulled out food. There were even bowls. He handed the food to Dave, who poured the food while Hawke handed out the bowls to the hungry dogs.

After all the dogs had food, Hawke said, "About three miles southeast of here, tied just like this. Whoever left them intended to go back for them. I think the investigation heated up faster than they thought it would. There were empty dishes that I bagged for forensics to take with them. They're coming to get the sled I found buried behind the tents in the container. They should be showing up in another hour. I'd like them to see if there are any fingerprints on the dogs' collars or harnesses."

"Who do you think did this?" Dave asked as they sat on their snowmobiles watching the dogs finish the food.

Hawke rose and poured the water Dave brought into the bowls when the dogs finished. "I've been thinking about that the whole time I was looking for them. It had to be someone who knew his or her way around the camp and the logistics of when things were torn down and people left."

"Someone who was up here working or someone who had worked the event before?" Dave asked.

"Exactly."

Dave laughed and said, "You didn't answer my

question."

"Because it could be either one. It would make more sense that whoever killed both women and tried to decoy us away from the bodies wasn't here working but was here wandering around, having access to everything and everyone. There is only one person who would know if someone wasn't supposed to be here. The camp coordinator would have the list of everyone signed up to work. If the volunteers see a familiar face, they just think it's a volunteer they've worked with before." Hawke dug in his daypack and pulled out a package of jerky. He held it out to Dave. "Thanks, Dave. You've given me another avenue to investigate."

They finished off the jerky as the sound of several snowmobiles rumbled through the trees.

"What do I do with the dogs when I get them down to Prairie Creek?" Dave asked.

"If they are Unity's, they need to go to family, but if they aren't, as some have suggested, they need to go to the real owner. Give Justine a call and see if she can put them up for a couple of days while we sort it out." Hawke gave her number to Dave. "She raises sled dogs and knows how to handle them." He had another thought. "I noticed on Justine's that the dog's name and her kennel name were on the collars. I wonder if all mushers do that."

He and Dave walked over to the first dog. Hawke talked to the dog, walked up, and patted the animal's head. He reached down, grasped the collar, and read; Happy, Razor Ridge Runners Kennel. Moving down the line, the dogs were a mix of dogs from Razor Ridge and Unity's.

"Part of these dogs go to a kennel in Washington.

But don't call it. I want to wait until we have gathered more evidence here." Hawke walked back to the snowmobiles.

"I'll deliver the dogs to Justine. Do you want me to tell her not to call the kennel?"

"Yes. Tell her I asked that they aren't contacted yet. She'll understand."

The forensic team on two snowmobiles, one pulling a sled, stopped next to Hawke.

"What are we looking for?" A woman in her thirties asked, pulling on gloves.

"There's a dog sled frame beneath the tents in this container. You need to check it for any fingerprints or DNA that doesn't match the second victim who was sent over from here." He waved to the dogs. "I'd like you to see if there are any prints or DNA on their collars and harnesses."

She frowned. "Can you take them off and put them in a bag for us as you put them in the kennels?"

Hawke thought about it. Would the dogs be easy to handle without their usual collar to control them? Better not risk it. "Okay. We'll take off the harnesses as we load them. Leave the collars on for control."

Hawke walked over to the container, unlocked the door, and opened it. "The sled is behind the last two tents there." He pointed to the last tents before the kitchen supplies.

When he finished showing them, he joined Dave by the dogs. "Move the box sled closer to the line of dogs." When the kennels were closer, Hawke unhooked a dog from the tether line and led it to an open kennel door. Wearing gloves, he took off the harness and urged the dog into the kennel.

"That one went better than I expected," Hawke said, walking over to the next dog. They went through the same routine on four more dogs. The sixth dog curled his lips back and snarled at Hawke when he approached. "Let's skip him for now." Hawke started on the other end of the line, and they loaded the rest of the dogs. The snarling one had lain down, ignoring them until Hawke walked toward him again. The lip curled, his eyes narrowed, and a low, angry growl escaped.

"What are you going to do with that one? We don't have any way to sedate him." Dave pointed at the growling dog.

"He didn't give me any trouble when I came upon them, led them back, and when I checked his collar." He remembered the name Thor and that the dog belonged to Unity. "I think he doesn't like the kennel. I'll see if he lets me unhook him from the tether line. If I can't, you'll have to lead him back."

Dave shook his head. "I'm not a dog person. He's going to sense my fear. You'll have to bring him back."

Hawke peered into the dog's eyes. Yes, this animal would get the better of Dave. "Okay. We'll leave him be, and I'll bring him along when forensics finishes. You take off so Justine can get ready for the extra dogs before it gets too late." The sun had set in the last thirty minutes.

The forensic team had turned on battery-powered lights that shone into the container.

Dave waved, started up the snowmobile, and drove away, the box sled swaying behind the machine.

Hawke sighed, sat down on the snowmobile, and pulled out a sandwich he'd made, knowing he might be up here a while.

Thor's ears perked up as he watched Hawke eat. He tossed the dog a piece of crust. The animal pounced on it and licked its lips after swallowing the small offering.

"Well, we know you are food motivated." Hawke broke off pieces of the other half of his sandwich, tossing them to the animal. Then he walked toward the dog, talking to him in a soft tone and tossing small bites of the sandwich. Hawke walked up to Thor and patted his head. "Is this your stomach letting me get close, or did you just not want to go into a kennel?" Hawke asked, petting the dog.

He heard a commotion in the container and looked that way. The forensic team was working to put the sled in two large evidence bags. He walked over. "Did you happen to find the contents of the sled in there? Clothing, dog food, safety equipment?"

"There was a garbage bag with a green canvas bag with that type of stuff under the sled itself. Is that something you want analyzed, too?" one of the forensic team asked.

"Yes. I believe that sled carried someone who might be an accomplice to the two homicides." Hawke could have stomped a merry grass dance, knowing they had the contents of the sled as well.

It was dark with a sliver of moon and multitudes of stars in the sky when the team had everything bagged, tagged, and loaded into the sled behind one of the snowmobiles. They said good-bye and headed back toward Salt Creek summit.

Hawke made sure the container was locked, unhooked the tether line from the trees, and walked over to the snowmobile. He attached the lead from the tether on Thor's collar to the handle of the snowmobile and then put the tether line into his daypack. Once he was settled on the snowmobile, he patted the seat in front of him. "Come on, boy. There's no need for you to run if you'll ride here."

The dog sniffed the seat.

Hawke scratched behind the dog's ears, ran his hand down the animal's back, and then put an arm around the hind end and lifted him onto the seat. Hawke continued scratching the animal until he relaxed. Holding Thor's collar, Hawke started the snowmobile. The engine purred, and Thor stiffened.

"You like the way the wind hits you as you run. You're going to like this," Hawke said, easing the snowmobile forward. He lowered his arm, holding the animal around the chest. As the dog relaxed, Hawke eased the machine to go a little faster. He managed to get the snowmobile up to half the speed he'd driven out. It was better than traveling slower to allow the dog to run alongside the machine.

The ski lift area was dark and quiet when he arrived. Everyone had left for the night. His pickup sat by itself in the plowed parking area. Hawke drove to the vehicle, released Thor, and swung his leg over to stand next to the machine. He led the dog over to the vehicle, opened the back door, and Thor jumped in.

Hawke sat back on the snowmobile and drove it up onto the trailer. Once it was tied down, he slid behind the wheel of his vehicle and called Dani to tell her he had to run a dog to Justine and then he'd be home.

"How about we meet at the Blue Elk for dinner after you drop off the dog. Invite Justine to come along."

Hawke had planned on following up leads, but he hadn't spent a lot of time with Dani since the call about a missing musher. "Ok. I'll see if Justine wants to join us."

## Chapter Twenty-two

Hawke only stayed at Justine's long enough to drop off Thor, ask her if she noticed that half the dogs belonged to Razor Ridge, and invite her to join him and Dani for dinner.

"I don't want to impose. You've been busy with the case. I'm sure Dani wants alone time with you," Justine said, closing the door to the kennel and following him to his vehicle.

"It was her idea to ask you. If you don't have anything to do, follow me back to Winslow. I have some more questions to ask you." He had thought of more things as he'd driven from Fergie to Justine's. But he didn't want to keep Dani waiting by asking them now.

"If Dani invited me, I'll come. I have to change. I'll be right behind you." She headed to her house.

Hawke got into his vehicle and headed down Jim Town Road toward Winslow. Knowing that the Blue

Elk was one of Dani's favorites, he was sure she was happy he'd been driving all the way to Winslow so she could suggest dinner there.

He pulled up to the front of the bar and restaurant, smiling. Dani sat at her favorite table. It was on the far side of the room, with a great view of the five-point elk mount that had been spray-painted blue with some shimmers here and there.

Before getting into his vehicle at the ski area, he'd shimmied out of his snow bibs and swapped his snow boots for his regulation boots. Now he left his hat, heavy coat, and duty belt in the pickup. Heads turned when he walked in wearing just his uniform, not all the gear.

"You must be off duty," Archie, the town drunk, said as Hawke passed his table.

"I can still write you up and haul you in for driving drunk or disorderly conduct," Hawke said, smiling.

He sat at Dani's table where he could see everyone in the room and the door. "I'm not surprised to see you at this table."

She smiled. "I don't know why this shimmery blue elk makes me happy, but it does." She picked up a menu. "Is Justine coming?"

"Yeah, but only because you invited her. She didn't want to be a third wheel if I was asking." Hawke glanced at Dani's beer and wished he could have one, but he was driving the state vehicle.

Val, the new waitress, walked up to the table. "What would you like to drink?"

"I'd like a beer, but I'm still in work clothes and vehicle. I'll have iced tea, please."

She smiled. "Are you ready to order?"

"We're waiting for one more," Dani said. "But you can bring the sampler appetizer, please."

"I'll bring the tea and get that order placed." Val spun around and headed to the kitchen door behind the bar.

Dani sipped her drink and asked, "Did you learn anything today?"

Hawke sighed and said, "Yes and no. We found the sled and dogs from the second victim. Forensics took the sled and the dogs' collars and harnesses to check. One of the dogs refused to go in the kennel on the sled, so I brought him back with my snowmobile. That's why I had to go to Justine's. Deputy Alden took all the other dogs there."

Dani nodded. "She has the best facility in the county to hold that many dogs."

Val brought Hawke his iced tea as Justine walked into the establishment. She smiled and walked up to the table.

"Thank you for inviting me. I haven't had time to go to the store since I returned from the race." Justine took the seat opposite Dani.

Val hadn't left and asked, "What would you like to drink?"

"I'll have a hot chocolate with Bailey's."

Hawke studied her. He hadn't known her to order an alcoholic drink. "Is this investigation getting to you?"

Her forehead wrinkled as she stared at him. "No. Why would you ask?"

"Because you don't usually order that strong of a drink."

Justine shot a glance at Dani.

She laughed and said, "You don't hang out with us much, do you? Justine always has one drink and I have two when we have dinner. We know our limits, but it's nice to have something to relax with as we visit."

Justine nodded. "And after seeing a friend, like I did, and taking care of so many dogs, I need a bit of relaxation."

Val returned with Justine's drink and took their orders. When she left, Hawke pulled out his notebook.

"Tell me everything you know about Razor Ridge Runners," he said to Justine.

"The kennel where half of Unity's dogs are from?" she asked.

"Yes."

"There was a team of dogs from that kennel in the last race I ran in Washington. They weren't any of the ones that Unity was using." Justine sipped her drink.

"Who raced them?" Hawke asked, picking up his drink and sipping.

"Melanie. She's the trainer for Razor Ridge. I liked how she took care of the dogs. That's about all I know."

"But you know who owns the kennel," Hawke stated, because she'd known Bobbi had given Cam money. He also wondered why Melanie would decide to see the workings of a race rather than race.

Justine nodded. "I've only seen dogs from there a few times. Usually Cam or Melanie raced. This was the first time I'd seen Cam as a race marshal. Why are you asking about his kennel? Is it important?"

"Did Bobbi ever mention the kennel?" He wondered if Bobbi had mentioned Cam and maybe alluded to the affair. Had she moved on to Nichols? Was he the person she'd fallen in love with? Or was he another shoulder to cry on until she did fall in love? At least Nichols admitted he and Bobbi had been intimate, which made sense of why she left him something. She obviously had feelings for him that couldn't be returned because of his wife.

"Only the one time she said something about giving Cam some money to help him out. Why?"

Hawke shook his head. "I'm not at liberty to say at the moment. Had she ever mentioned Sawtooth Sliders or Russell Nichols?"

"Yes. She had been working with that kennel, teaching mushing to the owner and to some of the people who had purchased dogs from him." Justine smiled. "Bobbi loved teaching others about mushing and sharing the love of dogs and the outdoors."

Writing in his notebook, Hawke asked, "What will happen to Bobbi's dogs?"

"I talked to her sister, Beverly, today. She told me to keep the dogs. She doesn't want them nor would she know what to do with them. I told her if she wants them sold, I could do that for her. She said only if they went as a team. That Bobbi had told her they were the best bunch of dogs she'd had, and she didn't think they would work well with any other dogs." Justine looked up from staring at her drink. Her gaze latched onto Hawke's. "She'd been moving dogs around and putting in different ones the last two years, making the perfect team. She would have gone to the Iditarod with this team. I'm guessing she would have done well. It's so sad."

"Will you use the team to do the Iditarod?" Hawke asked. He didn't think she would go that far away and take that much time off.

"I was thinking about that today, and yes, I will do the qualifying races next year with Bobbi's team, and when I finish the Iditarod, it will be for Bobbi."

Justine had a spark in her eyes that Hawke had never seen. She'd found her calling.

"If you need help for any of the races or the Iditarod, I'll go with you," Dani said.

"That would be awesome. My brain kept saying it wasn't safe for me to travel around by myself. I could use someone to help with driving and the logistics of taking care of the dogs." Justine reached across the table and grasped Dani's hand.

Val arrived with their meals.

The two women leaned back, a new glow in both their eyes.

Hawke knew Dani was an adrenaline junkie and had been feeling like she was boring. He could see she was looking forward to a new adventure. That's why she made such a good pilot for the Air Force. She was ready for anything they asked her to do. And Justine had lived her whole life doing for others. It was time she spread her wings and did what she wanted.

"You two will have a great time at the races," Hawke said, picking up his knife and fork to cut into his steak.

"You don't mind?" Dani asked.

"Nope. Not if the thought of doing it puts that much of a light in your eyes." He cut the bite of steak and popped it in his mouth. Delicious!

Hawke waited until they were finished eating before he asked Justine some more questions. "You're sure that Bobbi didn't know Unity other than from races?"

Justine nodded. "Bobbi thought Unity was a fool the way she carried on around the men and was reckless with her dogs."

He was pretty sure that Bobbi had no clue who Unity really was. But he wondered why the older woman had become a musher when it was clear she wasn't good at it and why she hadn't told her niece who she was.

"Why do you keep bringing up whether Bobbi knew Unity?" Justine asked.

Ignoring her question, Hawke asked, "Do you know Ivan Tabor?"

"Yeah, he and his dad come into the Rusty Nail a couple times a month. What about him?" Justine's tone said she was frustrated with him not answering her questions.

"Did Bobbi ever mention him?"

"Why would she? She lived in Idaho." Justine narrowed her eyes. "Would you just tell me what you're fishing about?"

"Ivan Tabor is Bobbi's cousin, and Unity Allard was his mom." Hawke watched as disbelief and horror crossed her face.

"You're saying that Bobbi *and* her aunt were killed? Do you need to call Beverly and warn her?" Justine leaned forward. "Is someone killing off the family?"

Hawke shook his head. "I don't know what's going on. Ivan was one of the volunteer snowmobile drivers. He was one of the sweepers who found Bobbi's sled and dogs. He stayed there looking for her while the other driver went back to Ollokot and told everyone what had happened." Hawke lowered his voice. "He was a cousin who received considerably less from their grandmother's inheritance. He and his sister, whom he says he hasn't seen since his mom left, could be looking to get more."

Justine shook her head. "I don't remember seeing Ivan at all. Even after Bobbi's body was found. And Unity was his mom? How did he not know she was there?"

"He insists he didn't even know what his mom looked like. That he was two when she left with his sister, and his dad didn't keep any photos."

"That makes sense to me," Dani said.

Hawke nodded in agreement. "I'm not sure if this was a murder of two family members or Bobbi was the intended victim and Unity saw something or was an accomplice and was killed to keep her quiet."

"Either way, it's horrible," Justine said and finished off her hot chocolate.

"I agree. There is never any reason to take a life unless yours is threatened." Hawke shoved his plate to the center of the table. "Dessert?"

Dani groaned. "I can't eat another bite, but if you want to get some, I don't care. I can wait while you eat."

Justine slid from the chair and stood. "I'm tired and want to get home. Thank you for inviting me." She pulled a twenty out of her pocket.

"This is on me," Dani said. "You've been through a lot the last week. Go get some sleep."

Justine walked around the table and hugged Dani. "Thank you! You know you two are the only family I have, and I appreciate you."

Hawke patted Justine's back. "We're here for you."

Justine pulled out of Dani's hug and said, "Thanks." She walked to the door and disappeared into the darkness.

"I don't know what it would feel like to be so alone," Dani said softly. "We have extended family and each other. She has no one."

"That's why I've been her friend. Everyone needs someone." Hawke smiled as Val walked over. "I'll have a piece of apple pie with ice cream, please."

The waitress smiled. "Coming right up."

## Chapter Twenty-three

Hawke invited Dani along for his trip to Ontario and his visit with Russell Nichols. They picked up coffee and donuts on their way out of the county. It was a three-hour drive that they filled with conversation and ideas for trips they'd like to take together.

"I'd like to attend my cousin's wedding in May in Lapwai," Dani said. "I'd like you to go with me."

Hawke nodded and said, "I'll put in for time off. Text me the dates." He glanced over at her. "Are you going to be able to take the time away from the lodge then? That's when most things go wrong after everything sits all winter."

"Tuck, Sage, and Kitree can run the lodge for four days. I already ended registrations for that time, so there will only be five parties there the weekend I'll be gone. I'll fly a party in, pick up the outgoing party, then pick you up at the airport, and fly us to Lapwai for the four days.”

“It sounds like you have it all planned,” Hawke said, wondering if he’d be able to connect with his aunt from his dad’s side while he was there. They’d met briefly last summer. He’d talked her into coming to Tamkaliks Powwow and reuniting with his mom.

“I’m actually looking forward to it. I haven’t said that about going to Lapwai since I graduated and left.”

He glanced over at Dani. She was staring out the window. He knew she’d not had a good experience at the school on the reservation because her father was Nez Perce and her mother was Caucasian. Knowing she could pass more for a White girl than an Indigenous girl, they had moved from the reservation. She continued her education in Boise and went on to join the Air Force, where she became a pilot.

Hawke pulled off Interstate 84 and down into Ontario. He found the restaurant and parked. “Do you want to come in or wander around town?” he asked Dani.

“What do you think is best?” she asked.

“Since it isn’t an official meeting, you could sit in if you want. But I’m not sure how Russell will feel about it.” Hawke had looked up the man on Idaho’s DMV and knew what he looked like. There were four cars with Idaho license plates in the parking lot.

“I’ll walk in with you. If he doesn’t seem upset, I’ll stay. If he asks what I’m doing there, I’ll say I’m going shopping.” Dani slid out of her side of the pickup.

“Works for me.” Hawke slid out and locked the doors. They walked into the restaurant together. Hawke scanned the people at the tables and spotted Russell.

He led the way to the table with Dani in his wake.

"Russell Nichols? I'm Trooper Hawke. We spoke on the phone." Hawke held out his hand.

They shook hands, and Russell's gaze landed on Dani as Hawke held out a chair for her. "This is my partner, Dani."

Russell's gaze darted back and forth. "Neither one of you are in uniform."

Hawke pulled on the chain around his neck and dug out the badge dangling from it. "She's my partner in real life, not my work."

"If you don't want me here, I'll go shopping," Dani said, not sitting in the chair where Hawke's hands rested.

"I don't mind if you stay. I do have some things to say that may need to be followed up on, but I didn't kill anyone." Russell put his hands around a cup of coffee.

Dani sat in the chair, and Hawke took the one across the table from Russell. "I'll be taking notes." He pulled out his notebook and a pen.

"That's fine. Like I said. I didn't kill anyone, but I have a feeling I might know who could be a part of it." Russell sipped his coffee as the waitress came over.

"We'll have two coffees," Hawke said and faced Dani. "You want anything to eat?"

"Could you bring me some toast, please?" Dani asked.

"I'm good," Hawke said as the waitress turned over the cups on the table and filled them with coffee from the pot she held.

"I'll get that toast started," the waitress said before walking away.

"Who do you suspect of helping to kill Bobbi?" Hawke asked.

"I thought about that name you said. Unity something? I saw it on the return address of a letter my wife, Sheri, received right after we married."

"When did you two marry?" Hawke asked.

"Five years ago. We met through sled dog racing. I had a team at a race here in Idaho and she was a volunteer vet tech. We got to talking. One thing led to another, and the next thing I know, I'm standing in front of a Justice of the Peace and we're married." He had a puzzled expression. As if he still didn't know what happened.

"Was it love at first sight?" Dani asked.

"That's it. I never loved her, and I still don't. Like I said, I don't remember much besides meeting her and then getting married. I can tell you she hasn't been faithful. She doesn't even hide her affairs. Our marriage is just something made legal by a Justice of the Peace. The woman I love, loved, was Bobbi. We discussed my getting a divorce so we could get married and travel to races. But then Sheri started threatening to do something to Bobbi if I divorced her. I told Bobbi we'd have to be more secretive and not tell anyone about us. We would meet when Sheri was volunteering at races that Bobbi wasn't entered in." He took a sip of coffee and said, "I wouldn't put it past Sheri to have killed Bobbi just to show me she could."

"Is she strong enough to physically strangle someone?" Hawke asked.

"If she were mad, I believe she could do anything." The finality in his voice said he did believe it.

"I know she doesn't have an alibi for the time of Bobbi's murder and the sled leaving Ollokot camp. But I haven't been able to find out if she was really where she said she was when Unity went missing and was killed." Hawke scribbled some notes and asked, "Did you ever ask her about the Unity person?"

"I did, and she told me it was an old acquaintance who heard about our wedding."

"Where did your wife grow up?" Hawke asked.

"Wyoming. She was in high school at Casper and attended Eastern Wyoming College in Torrington for vet tech."

Hawke grinned. Now he was getting somewhere. Unity talked about living in Wyoming. Either they knew each other there or…could Sheri be Raina?

"Has your wife ever mentioned someone named Raina?" Hawke asked.

Russell sucked in air and said, "Her full name is Sharon Raina Tabor Nichols. She prefers to go by Sheri."

This was pulling lots of pieces together for an unofficial meeting. "I hate to ask this, but when I get this all written up, I'd like you to go to the nearest police station and sign it. You're helping me put things together. Your answers have filled in several holes."

"Sure, I can do that. But am I living with a murderer?" He asked as if he wanted it to be true, but feared the truth.

"I'm uncertain at the moment. If you could make an excuse to not go home, it might be a good idea." Hawke didn't want to say, yes, you are married to a murderer when he wasn't sure if she did it or pulled the strings to have it done.

"I've been talking with Justine Bartley about purchasing one of her dogs. I think I'll call Sheri and tell her I'm going to check on a dog I've had my eye on." He blushed and said, "I already have a packed bag in my Bronco. I didn't know what you were going to tell me. Deep down, I hadn't planned on going home until I knew what happened to Bobbi. Sheri can be vicious if she doesn't get her way."

"What about your dogs?" Hawke asked.

"She'll take care of them. That's the one thing that never changes. She treats animals better than she does people." Russell tipped his cup up as if to drink and put it back down.

Dani said, "It will be good for Justine to have you visit and check on the dog. She was close to Bobbi."

"Don't tell Sheri where you are. If she killed Bobbi, she might go after Justine," Hawke warned.

Russell nodded. "I never told her what dog. I'm always talking about looking at dogs from other kennels to improve my line."

"You go on ahead. We're going to get some lunch and do some shopping," Hawke said.

Russell stood and held out his hand.

Hawke shook hands.

"Thank you for contacting me. When I found out about Bobbi, I couldn't believe she was gone. We were just starting to figure out a future." He nodded to Dani and walked out of the restaurant.

Hawke faced Dani. "Do you want to eat here or go shopping and find somewhere else to eat?"

She studied him. "Are you sure you don't want to jump on a computer and learn more about Sheri Raina?"

He shook his head. "I've neglected you enough for a week. I'm all yours today."

Dani smiled. "Then I want to go to the Cultural

Center, see a movie, and then get dinner that isn't fast food."

Back in Wallowa County later that night, Hawke did open up his computer while Dani was showering. He typed up what he'd learned from Russell. He also texted the man and said he could come into the Winslow State Police Office in the morning and sign the official statement. Russell agreed to do that.

Now that he had a connection between Elston, Unity, and Sheri, Hawke wanted to figure out if they were the perpetrators of Bobbi's death.

It was clear that Sheri had it out for Bobbi because of her husband. But did she know Bobbi was also the cousin who became wealthy from their grandmother's inheritance? If so, when did she learn this, and why did she wait until now to strike?

How did Elston fit in? Was Unity or Sheri blackmailing him? Hawke thought about Russell's comment about his wife being unfaithful. Could Elston have been one of her lovers? Or still her lover? Had they discovered they would both benefit from the will and colluded to do away with Bobbi?

And what about Unity? How did she get a job with Razor Ridge? Was it through her daughter? Or did she know about the affair and use it to get a job there? But why?

So many questions.

He remembered that the attorney hadn't replied with the names of people who had access to Bobbi's will at his law firm. That was a person he needed to contact. He had to find out who knew about the will to start pulling all the pieces together. He also needed to know if forensics found anything interesting on the sled or the items in the garbage bag. They had to find physical evidence before he could formally bring anyone in and question them.

He made a list of people to call. People from the race who might have seen Elston or Sheri at the time of the murder and disappearance. Also, to call the attorney and ask Russell a couple more questions that might help narrow down how Elston and Sheri knew one another.

It was too late tonight to call people. He hoped his list would shed light on who might have seen the three people during the time of Bobbi's death and disappearance. Once he figured that out, the person responsible for Unity's death would become clear.

## Chapter Twenty-four

"It's Sunday, why are you going into work?" Dani asked as Hawke put on his uniform.

"Russell is coming in to sign his statement from yesterday, and I have a couple more questions to ask him, as well as a bunch of calls to make." Hawke hugged her. "This shouldn't take more than the morning. Figure out something fun to do this afternoon."

"I was thinking we could ride Jack and Dot through the snowy fields." She studied him.

"Sounds good. I'll let you know when I'm headed home." He kissed her temple, whistled for Dog, and headed out the door.

Since he was just going in to follow some leads, he decided Dog could go along. The animal became mopey in the winter when he didn't get to ride along with Hawke as much.

Dog ran over to the work vehicle and stood by the

door, his tail wagging.

Hawke patted his head and opened the door.

Dog jumped over the console and sat in the passenger seat, his mouth open and tongue hanging out. He was happy to be going along.

Settled behind the steering wheel, Hawke started up the diesel pickup and idled down the driveway to the highway. He made a right and headed toward Winslow. The road was quiet for a Sunday morning when people would be heading to church. There had been enough sun and traffic on the roads that they were down to the pavement with only icy patches where the sun didn't hit.

Cars had begun to fill the parking lot of the Presbyterian church. Hawke drove on by, parking in the back of the OSP building. If he were lucky, he'd be the only person in the office this morning, and he could make his calls without interruptions.

"Come on," Hawke said, motioning for Dog to hop out of the vehicle. At the door, he punched in the code, and the door clicked. The bottom level was dark. Rarely did someone from Fish and Wildlife work on a weekend. He climbed the stairs behind Dog. No lights were on other than the low-wattage ones that remained on all the time.

He flicked the switch to light up the main room. One long desk ran across the back wall with four computers spaced out across it. "Lay down," Hawke said to Dog as he settled onto the chair in front of his computer. Dog curled up under the desk and the computer to the right of Hawke.

He printed out the information he'd gathered from Russell Nichols the day before. After collecting the papers from the printer in the conference room, he sat back down.

Hawke went through his notebook and wrote down the names and phone numbers he had. He used DMV to look up phone numbers for the people he didn't have. Once he had all the information he needed, he dialed Roger Duggan, the Ollokot coordinator.

"Hello?" the man answered.

"Mr. Duggan, this is Trooper Hawke. I have some follow-up questions for you. Is now a good time to talk with me?"

"Yes, I guess so. My wife is at church, so we won't be disturbed. How can I help you?"

"Do you remember seeing anyone at Ollokot that wasn't on your volunteer list?" Hawke asked, hoping to find someone who had been fitting in when they weren't supposed to be there."

"You're not asking about mushers? Just volunteers?" Duggan asked.

"What do you mean? Did you see a musher who wasn't signed up for the race?" That would explain someone using Bobbi's team and knowing the routine for checking out of the camp.

"I thought I saw that young woman who raced for Razor Ridge Runners talking to Cam. But when I looked again, she wasn't there."

Hawke circled Melanie's name. "Thanks, that's helpful. What about a volunteer? Did you see anyone who wasn't on your list?"

"No. But if someone was there who wasn't assigned to Ollokot, they could have easily enough stayed away from me. I'm all over the place, but a person could keep out of my way. I didn't even see a couple of the volunteers. They were sleeping when I was checking on something, or cross-country skiing or snowshoeing on their off time."

"Do many of the volunteers bring their skis and snowshoes to the camp?" Snowshoes could have hidden the tracks of the attacker coming and going from the crime scene. Snowshoes or skis could be how the person who drove out of the camp with Bobbi's sled made it back to the camp without being seen.

"Sure. But the only two I saw using them were Neal Preston and Sheri Nichols. Neal was cross-country skiing on Saturday after the snowstorm, and I saw Sheri coming into camp early Friday morning with her snowshoes."

Sheri hadn't mentioned being out snowshoeing early Friday morning when they were looking for Bobbi. "Thank you for the information. I appreciate it."

"Do you need anything more?" Mr. Duggan asked.

"Not at this moment, but I might call back if I think of something."

"I'll help in any way. It is a tragedy what happened to Bobbi."

"Yes, it was." Hawke ended the call and glanced at his list. This new information had him wanting to call Sheri, but he knew he needed as much evidence against her as he could get before confronting the woman.

Next, he dialed Neal Preston.

A woman answered. "Hello?"

"Mrs. Preston?" Hawke asked.

"Yes?"

"I'm Trooper Hawke with the Oregon State Police. I'd like to speak with your husband if he's around."

"Is he in trouble?" the woman's voice wobbled.

"No. I'm talking to the volunteers who helped at Ollokot during the sled dog race. I'm trying to piece together people's movements to help me find out what happened to the murdered musher." He wasn't sure how much Neal had told his wife about the happenings at the race.

"Oh, yes! Neal told me how someone brutally murdered a woman musher. That's terrible. I'm sure Neal will want to help you. I'll call him. He's outside shoveling the sidewalk."

"Thank you," Hawke said, wondering if the wife had any inkling as to how her husband felt about the murder victim.

Heavy footsteps grew closer and a voice said, "Trooper Hawke, how can I help you?"

"I understand you took cross-country skis to Ollokot."

"Yeah. I always do. It gets hectic when racers are leaving and coming at the same time. When I've finished a couple of hours of non-stop holding dogs and moving them to their parking places, I like to ski out through the trees where it's quiet and peaceful."

Hawke nodded, knowing the feeling. "When you were out skiing, did you notice anyone else skiing or snowshoeing?"

There was silence on the other end before Neal said, "Saturday, when I was slipping through the trees, I saw a snowmobile sitting about half a mile from the camp. No one around it. I thought it was strange but figured the driver had to take a leak or ran out of fuel and walked to camp to get it."

"What time was this?" Hawke asked.

"After the storm let up but before the mushers

started heading out. I was only gone about thirty minutes before I headed back. I knew everyone who had been held up by the weather would want to get going."

"Do you remember anything about the snowmobile?"

"It was green and black. Most are usually red, blue, or white. It looked like a sporty model. That's about it."

"If you saw it again, would you recognize it?" Hawke asked.

"The color and model, yeah. The exact one, probably not—" He paused. "There was a sticker on the side. Not the brand or make. It said Grip it and Rip it."

Hawke smiled. That was specific enough to get the county deputies to search the race volunteers' snowmobiles for the make, color, and sticker.

"Thank you. You've been very helpful." Hawke said.

"Have you figured out who killed Bobbi Whitby?" Neal asked.

"I'm working on it. Thanks again." He ended the call and jotted down the information he'd just collected on the snowmobile.

Hawke decided to call Opal King. As he started dialing, his phone dinged. It was a message from Justine.

*I'm outside the building with Russell. He's here to sign the papers.*

*Be right down.* Hawke replied and headed to the stairs.

He hurried down and opened the door. "Sorry about that. I'm the only one in here right now."

"I thought about texting to ask if you were here,

but Justine said you would be here because you never take time off when you're working a case." Russell smiled at Justine.

Hawke was sure she blushed.

"Come on up. I have the papers ready for you to sign." He led the way up to the conference room. He stepped through the door and flipped on the lights. "Take a seat, and I'll get the papers."

Dog stood by the desk, his tail wagging. "Go say hi to Justine. I'll be right in."

Dog trotted across the room and disappeared into the hallway.

Hawke entered the conference room and found both Justine and Russell petting Dog.

"Justine is a good judge of dogs and who she puts them with," Hawke said. "I told her I was looking for a dog and three weeks later she called and said she had the perfect dog for me." Hawke patted Dog's head. "She was right. He helps me when I'm out in the wilderness and has a good nose on him."

"You just need to get better at giving a wonderful creature like this a good name." Justine glanced up at him before resting her gaze on Russell. "He named this intelligent, obedient dog, Dog."

Russell chuckled and said, "That is what he is, I guess."

Hawke sat down and shoved the papers toward Russell. "Read through there and make sure it's what you said. Then sign the line at the bottom and print your name underneath."

As Russell read through the papers, Hawke asked Justine how Bobbi's dogs were doing.

"They keep looking for her, but they are getting

along with my dogs and settling in. When can I get rid of the ones Deputy Alden brought me?"

"I'll be talking to Cam Elston today. I'm hoping he'll come down and get those. Unity's, I'll talk to Ivan and see if he wants them." Hawke hoped to get Cam down here so he could question him.

"This is all so sad and twisted. I never dreamed when I was staring up at the wolf moon and thinking it was a good omen for the race that anyone would be hurt, let alone murdered." Justine swiped at a tear in the corner of her eye.

"The wolf moon is about resilience. In the past, when this moon appeared in the sky, my ancestors heard the wolves howling to show their strength and prosperity through the hard winter. Don't let what happened this year take away the truth of the moon in years to come." Hawke put a hand on Justine's shoulder. "The strongest survive, and you are a survivor." He peered into her eyes and saw the sorrow replaced with determination.

"You're right." She nodded her head toward the man seated on the other side of her. "Russell is going to help me prepare for the Iditarod. He likes my idea of taking Bobbi's team to the race. Of finishing what she wanted to accomplish."

Russell nodded. "I know how hard Bobbi was training and discovering the best combination of dogs for a strong endurance team."

"I think that's a great idea. I'm sure Russell has a lot he can teach you to make your racing safer." Hawke had a feeling the two would be doing more than racing together, but he kept that to himself. He'd discuss it with Dani later.

"Are you having a party up here?" Ivy asked, leaning in the doorway.

"Not now that you spoiled it," Hawke said, standing. He held out his hand to Russell. They shook hands, and he said, "Thank you for the information and for coming in to sign the statement."

"My pleasure. I'll be staying in the county until you get this figured out. If Sheri finds out what I told you, she'll either disappear or come after me. With her, you never know which." Russell maneuvered Justine out of the room and down the stairs.

Hawke stood at the top, making sure the door locked behind them. When he turned, Ivy stood in the hallway watching him.

"What did he mean about Sheri? Who is Sheri?"

Hawke motioned to the main room. He sat down in his chair, Dog sat at his feet, and he told Ivy what he'd learned so far.

"You have an interesting investigation going on. I just came in to check something on the computer, then I'll get back out, keeping the roads safe." She sat down at the computer on the end and started tapping on the keyboard.

## Chapter Twenty-five

Hawke decided to call the veterinarian, Ronald McPherson. He might have information about Sheri.

"Hello?" a woman answered.

"Mrs. McPherson?" Hawke asked.

"Yes? Who are you?"

He told her who he was and that he would like to speak to her husband. "It's about the death that occurred at the Eagle Cap Extreme Sled Dog Race."

"Why would he know anything about the death?" she asked in a snooty tone.

"I'd like to ask him about some of the people he worked with. Character reference type of thing," Hawke said, not to get the woman worked up any more than she was.

"Let me see if he's available. What did you say your name was again?"

Hawke repeated his name and title and waited as heels clicked across a hardwood floor. There was an earthy ring to the click, telling him it was wood and not marble she crossed.

He was just beginning to think he'd been forgotten when McPherson asked, "Who are you interested in?"

"Can you tell me if Sheri Nichols was helping with vet checks from midnight Friday to early morning?" Hawke tapped on the notebook with his pen, waiting.

McPherson let out a long breath and said, "I'm not clear on the time, but she was sleepy and I told her to go take a nap. Which was unlike her. She usually stayed up longer than any of the rest of us. What she did after she left the vet tent, I can't tell you. I know I worked through the night and didn't see her again until about eight the next morning. Just about the time everyone was buzzing about the fact Bobbi Whitby's sled had been found."

Hawke jotted all of that down. "And Sunday, during the take-down of the camp, did she help clear out the vet tent?"

There was a pause. "I remember her packing a box of supplies out of the tent, but I don't remember seeing her again until we started getting rides back to Salt Creek." He made a clicking sound and asked, "Is she involved in the deaths?"

"I'm just checking on everyone's whereabouts," Hawke said.

"But you asked me specifically about her and not any of the other vet techs or volunteers. So you do suspect her. Why?"

"I'm sorry. I'm not at liberty to divulge that information. Thank you for your answers." Hawke ended the call. He hoped the vet didn't call Sheri and say the police had been asking questions about her.

His biggest question now was to find out how Sheri or Cam Elston found out about Bobbi's will. That had to be the catalyst that caused the woman's death. But it was Sunday, and he didn't have the attorney's home phone. He'd have to wait until tomorrow.

He glanced down at the other two names on his list. Melanie and Opal King. The first one had been at the camp when she'd said she stayed at the motel in Prairie Creek. Was the green snowmobile one she'd borrowed to get to the camp? He wouldn't know until he asked, but he wanted to talk to her in person. She was in Washington. He sent a text to the Washington State Trooper who helped him with the interview of Elston. Hawke asked if he could set up an interview with Melanie Mirsky the following day. He added, *I'd like to watch on Zoom again.*

After hitting the send icon, he dialed Opal King. The woman had known quite a bit about Bobbi's family. He wondered if she'd known Unity was Bobbi's aunt.

"Hello?" An older woman answered.

"Mrs. King?" Hawke asked.

"It's Ms. King. Who is this?"

"It's Trooper Hawke. We talked at Ollokot."

"Oh, yes. Justine's friend. How are you?" she asked.

"Stumped. I'm talking to people who were at the race and trying to piece together people's movements. Do you mind helping me?"

"If it will help you solve Bobbi's murder, I'd be delighted to help. It hurts my heart every time I think about her not being at the next race."

"Do you remember seeing Melanie Mirsky

volunteering?" Hawke asked.

"I saw her there, but she wasn't volunteering. She wasn't on the list, and she wasn't doing anything but shadowing Cam Elston every chance she got. Though she was trying to stay out of sight of everyone else."

Hawke smiled and asked, "How did you happen to see her?"

The woman chuckled. "I may be getting up there in age for a judge, but I've also been around long enough to not trust some people. One of them is a race marshal who runs all over the place looking like he's taking care of things when he really hasn't a clue what he's doing. I go behind and clean up the misinformation he gives people."

Hawke sat on this a moment before asking, "How does a person become a race marshal?"

"Years of experience as a musher, then a judge, and then they become a race marshal."

"Then why doesn't Cam have a clue about what he's doing?" Hawke asked.

"Because this was his first time at this race. He filled in for the usual race marshal at the last minute. While he knows about mushing, he knew nothing about how the Ollokot stage of the race went." Clinking as if she put a cup on a saucer echoed through the phone. "He has been dodgy even when he was mushing. If he could find a way to do something easier, he'd do it. When he started that kennel, I thought, 'Oh boy, this will be interesting. He doesn't have a good head for business.' Sure enough, his wife bailed him out the first time, but I think after catching him messing around with another woman, she dumped him. He talks like he's still married, but I ran into her at a different dog event and she said she was living in Montana now and raising border collies."

Hawke jotted this down. "Do you happen to know who he's been fooling around with lately?"

"I thought maybe it was that Unity woman, since he gave her a job there, but then I figured out it was Sheri Nichols. She has a perfectly nice husband. I don't understand why she'd be sleeping around with Cam."

This opened the door for Hawke to ask, "Did you happen to be up and about Thursday night into Friday morning?"

"Yes, I was checking the sleds coming and going. In between, I'd walk to the Hilton for a cup of hot coffee to stay warm. Why are you asking?"

"Did you see Sheri, Cam, or Melanie Mirsky wandering around?"

"I saw Melanie earlier following Cam. I wasn't sure if it was because she was his new flavor or she was keeping tabs on him. They only talked twice."

"Was this between midnight and two am?" Hawke asked, working to keep his tone neutral.

"I didn't see Cam during that time. I did see Melanie getting something to drink in the Hilton." The sound of cup and saucer clicking came through the line again, and she said, "I didn't see Sheri all night, which was unusual. She always helps with the vet checks on that first night." The woman squeaked.

Hawke wondered if the woman was in trouble. "Ms. King, are you okay?"

"I'm fine, I just realized something. At the time, I put it off that Bobbi was tired, but when she walked by me and didn't acknowledge me, it wasn't her. I watched her walk over to her dogs and start getting the team ready to go. The dogs weren't enthusiastic, and one lay down, raising its paws, like for a vet check. I bet that was Sheri who took Bobbi's dogs out of Ollokot."

"Are you willing to sign a statement about what you saw?" Hawke asked, feeling he was finally getting some evidence that could stack up to an arrest.

"Yes. Do I need to come to Wallowa County to sign it?" she asked.

"I can have it sent to the nearest police station to you."

"Where I live, it's just as easy to pop back over to Wallowa County. Where is your office?"

Hawke gave her directions to the Winslow office. "When would you be here?"

"I can be there tomorrow mid-afternoon."

"You don't plan to drive back that same day, do you?" he asked, worrying about her being out on the roads at night.

"I'll call one of the volunteers in Alder and spend the night with her. We've become friends over the years."

"That's good. I'll have the statement here at the office for you to sign. I can't guarantee I'll be here." Hawke would be working the following day and unless he had more information to make the D.A. issue an arrest warrant, he'd be out in the field.

"Who do I ask for if you aren't there?" Ms. King asked.

"Sergeant Spruel. He's up to date on the investigation, and I'll place the statement on his desk after I write it up."

"I'm glad I could help this investigation along. Thank you for calling."

"Thank you for being open to talking to me. Safe travels tomorrow."

"Thanks."

Hawke ended the call and immediately typed up the information that Ms. King supplied him with. He had a meeting tomorrow with Melanie via Zoom. He hoped that would give him more information, since she was following Cam around. What they needed now was DNA or fingerprints on Unity's things to find out who took her sled apart and possibly killed her. He also had the information about the snowmobile. Things were coming together.

He sent an email to Sheriff Lindsey asking him to have his deputies check out the following list of people to see what make, model, and color of snowmobile they used while volunteering at the sled dog race. He posted the list to the other OSP officers in Wallowa County.

He glanced at his watch. One o'clock. He texted Dani. *Writing up a report. Should be home by two.*

Hawke sat atop Dot, his young gelding, enjoying the crisp air, the way the saddle creaked under him, and the glitter of snow that the horses' hooves kicked up as they walked through the foot of snow.

"Thank you for doing this with me," Dani said. "I've always enjoyed riding in the snow." She and Jack had become a good duo. The older gelding was bomb proof and didn't have to prance and dance to get where he wanted to go. Just the right energy for someone who hadn't ridden as much as Hawke.

"I enjoy riding in this weather as well. It sure beats the trip we took to the lodge when you broke your leg." He'd let his emotions for Dani keep him from seeing the criminal in their midst, but they had prevailed and found the killer with a little help from Dani's uncle in owl form. He didn't dwell on what happened on the mountain. He was just grateful the creature had given him the strength to continue and not die lying in the snow.

"You haven't said much about your investigation. Are you getting closer to discovering who killed Justine's friend?" Dani asked.

"I've been building a case against someone or ones. I've known all along that the crimes involved more than one person in attempting both homicides. However, identifying the suspects has been slow. Because of the weather, there is little DNA transfer, but I hope forensics will find something useful to make an arrest, especially if I can't get another statement about seeing my main suspect when she said she was sleeping."

"Russell's wife?" Dani asked.

He nodded and decided to change the subject. "Did you know Russell is planning to help Justine prepare for the Iditarod?"

"I haven't talked to her today. Is that what she told you?" Dani stopped Jack and shifted in the saddle to face him.

Hawke stopped, nodded, and looked her in the eyes. "The way Justine was blushing, she may be falling for him."

Dani did one quick dip of her chin and said, "She could do worse."

*Especially since they both will be inheriting money from Bobbi*, Hawke thought.

## Chapter Twenty-six

Monday, Hawke went to the office early. He had received a text from the Washington State Trooper saying he would be interviewing Melanie Mirsky at nine. Hawke wanted to be at his desk and prepared when the Trooper called him for the interview.

Sergeant Spruel stopped him on his way in. "I found the statement from Ms. Opal King. This could be important to the case."

"I agree. Over the weekend, I've slowly discovered bits and pieces that I'll take to Lange this afternoon to see about getting an arrest warrant." Hawke was feeling confident about his investigation. "I have a Zoom interview at nine with the Washington State Police and Melanie Mirsky, the trainer for Cameron Elston, the race marshal, who I believe is mixed up in this as well."

"It's good to get this homicide cleared up so you can get back to doing your Fish and Wildlife job."

Spruel waved him away.

Hawke got the hint. He'd like nothing more than to be driving around checking on trappers, fishermen, and the elk refuge.

Turning on his monitor, he grabbed a cup of coffee out of the conference room and sat back down. There was an email from forensics. He opened it as he sipped his coffee.

*There weren't any fingerprints found on the sled or the items in the bag. However, we did find two different colors of hair with follicles. They are with the DNA division. One set of hair was bleached. The other was chestnut brown.*

Hawke knew the bleached hair was Unity's. He tried to remember what color Sheri's hair was. The one time he saw her, she had on a stocking cap. And Melanie's was strawberry blonde.

He printed out the report, picked it up from the printer, and added it to the case file. It was nearing time to log into the interview. Once logged in, he waited for the screen to come to life.

It did when Trooper Volle turned on the video camera for the interview. Hawke studied Melanie. She appeared nervous, jittery.

Volle stated who he was and asked her to state her name and where she lived and worked. The addresses were, as Hawke had found, the Razor Ridge Runners Kennel.

"Were you at the Eagle Cap Extreme Sled Dog Race two weekends ago?" the trooper asked.

"I planned to attend but stayed in a motel room in Prairie Creek instead," Melanie said.

Hawke texted Volle. *She was seen multiple times at*

*the Ollokot checkpoint, following Cam Elston around.*

"Witnesses have stated that you were not in Prairie Creek but at the Ollokot race check-in," Volle said, his pen poised over a notebook.

The woman squirmed. "They must be mistaken."

"No, they said it was you, following Cam Elston." Volle leaned back in his chair. "There are more people who saw you there than at the motel. Care to explain that?"

Hawke thought that was a nice touch. He studied the woman. She was agitated. She wanted to say something, but fear was holding her back. He texted, *She's scared. Ask her about her relationship with Elston.*

"How is it you are living and working at the Razor Ridge Runners Kennel?" Volle asked.

"I'm the trainer. It is best if I'm there all the time to take care of the dogs. The owner is busy, and his wife left him, so he has other obligations to take care of." She twisted her fingers together and didn't make eye contact.

*Ask how long his wife has been gone and why he hired Unity.*

"Did his wife leave when you moved in?" Volle asked.

The woman's head came up and she glared at Volle. "No! She left him after Unity was hired. I'm not sure what Unity said or did, but Mrs. Elston packed her bags and left the day after Unity arrived."

"What was Unity's job description?" Volle asked.

"She was supposed to help me, but she just took care of her own dogs and borrowed from the kennel. I could tell that Cam didn't like her, but he wouldn't send her away." Melanie's face screwed up in distaste.

*Ask if any women stayed the night with Elston.* Hawke texted.

"Did your boss have any lady friends who spent the night?" the trooper asked.

"He was always dragging someone home when he'd come back from a race. But the vet tech, Sheri, she came home with him more than anyone else." The woman shuddered.

*Ask her why she doesn't like Sheri.* Hawke texted.

"Why don't you like Sheri?" Volle asked.

Melanie pressed her lips together and stared at her hands.

"Did she threaten you? Did you see something, and she told you to keep your mouth shut?" Volle pressed. "If she threatened you and you did see something, we can make sure she doesn't know you gave us any information. What you tell us could put her in jail, where she can't hurt you."

Melanie's face slowly raised and she studied the trooper's face. "She's evil. I don't know if you or anyone can stop her."

"If you give us information that we can use to put her in jail, she can't hurt anyone again." Volle leaned forward. "You could be saving not only your life but possibly your boss's and anyone who gets between Sheri and what she wants."

Melanie's eyes glistened with tears as she contemplated what Volle had said.

Hawke silently willed her to tell them about Sheri. *Ask her why she believes Sheri is evil. Maybe that will get her talking,* he texted.

Volle loosened his sitting position and said, "Why

do you believe Sheri is evil?" His tone was softer, approachable.

Melanie glanced up at the trooper and swiped at the tear slipping from the corner of her eye. "I watched her kick a dog when she was mad at Cam. Anyone who would take their anger out on a dog is not fit to be a human."

"Do you know what they were fighting about?" Volle asked.

Melanie sat up in her chair. "Yeah. She'd learned that Bobbi had been seen with her husband when Sheri was away at a sled dog race. She said something about 'she took my money and now she thinks she can take my husband.'"

Hawke leaped to his feet. That was the catalyst. Learning that her husband was sleeping with the cousin who got everything. *Ask her if she ever overheard Sheri and Unity talking*, Hawke texted.

Volle asked. "Did Cam know what she was talking about when she said 'took my money'?"

Melanie nodded. "He said something like, I'm sure there are ways to get it back."

Hawke wrote all of this down in his book. Cam had to have known the two were cousins and that Sheri felt wronged by receiving small things from their grandmother.

"Did you ever overhear Unity and Sheri talking?" Volle asked.

"Yeah, when those two started going at each other, they never saw anyone else. I'd walk into a room where they'd be arguing and could stand there and listen. Though I never stood in full sight. I didn't like the vicious side of Sheri."

"What did they argue about?" Volle asked.

"Unity usually asked, 'When will we get the money' and Sheri usually said, 'When I get things figured out.' Then Unity would say 'Hurry up, she needed the money' and Sheri would say 'You should have done your part to keep us in good graces with dear old grandmother. If you had done that, we wouldn't have had to be homeless and laughed at.'"

Hawke could see there was a lot of hostility between mother and daughter. He was betting that Sheri killed her and not Ivan. He'd looked genuinely surprised to hear she was his mom and horrified that he'd been mentioned as her killer.

"So the two of them didn't get along?" Volle said.

"Not at all. But I think Unity had something on Cam. That's the only reason she was there and could do whatever she wanted with the dogs." Melanie wasn't looking as scared as she revealed what she knew about the two women.

Hawke texted, *Did Bobbi ever come there when Unity or Sheri were there?*

Volle asked the question.

Melanie shook her head. "I thought Bobbi only knew Cam through mushing. I never saw her at the kennels, only at races. She was nice to me when I started mushing and learning to train dogs." The woman stopped and thought. "Russell, Sheri's husband, was the one who introduced me to Bobbi."

Hawke's fingers flew over his phone's keyboard. *Ask her when that was.*

"Do you remember how long ago that was?" Volle asked.

"Three years ago. And a year after that, Cam asked

me if I wanted to work at his kennel. At first, I thought he liked my training. I soon learned he was trying to make me a conquest, and when that didn't work, he used me to keep things from his wife. Like Sheri and the other women he'd bring here when his wife was gone for work."

Hawke contemplated how long Russell and Bobbi's affair had been going on under Sheri's nose without her finding out. *Ask her when Sheri had the blow-up about finding out Bobbi was sleeping with Russell and who told her*. Hawke texted.

Volle asked the question.

"It was last summer. I don't remember the exact date. I remember I'd just come back from taking the team on a run with the ATV, and I heard shouting. I slowed down and listened. That's when I heard Sheri going off about Russell and Bobbi."

*When did Cam get the call about being race marshal for the Eagle Cap Extreme?* He texted.

Volle frowned when he read the message, but asked, "When did Cam learn he was going to be the race marshal this year for the Eagle Cap Extreme?"

Melanie's brow furrowed. "I don't understand. He didn't get a call. As far as I know, he was the planned marshal all along. He kept saying he was going to be the Eagle Cap race marshal. That I couldn't enter the race because it would look bad if I won. Then I learned Unity would be in the race, and that's why I followed him around. I figured he was up to something."

Hawke had been scribbling in his notebook. Now he sat up and texted, *This is what I've been wanting to know. Can she tell you what Cam was doing from midnight to 4 am on Friday of the race and Sunday after the racers all left Ollokot?*

"While you were following Cam, did you see what he was doing from midnight to four a.m. on Friday?" Volle asked.

Melanie started looking scared again.

"It's okay. What you say will remain confidential," Volle said.

"He caught me following him and told me to get the hell out of the camp or he'd tell Roger I wasn't supposed to be there and have me hauled off by the police." She crossed her arms. "But I pretended to leave and circled back. Later, probably about midnight, that's when I saw him and Sheri talking by her tent. She was dressed in snow bibs, a stocking cap, and carrying snowshoes. I ducked back when they headed toward where the teams were bedded down."

Hawke could now place Sheri and Cam going toward Bobbi's sled and team. He had Opal's recollection that a vet tech had been getting the dogs ready because of their behavior. That should be enough to get Lange to bring in Sheri. That, and the conversation Melanie overheard.

"Did you see Cam after he and Sheri walked to the teams?" Volle asked.

"Yeah, he was there when Unity headed out. That was about fifteen, twenty minutes after the person they thought was Bobbi left." Melanie twisted her fingers.

Hawke found it interesting that the man would see Unity off and not the impersonator. Had Unity been part of the scheme, or had she seen Sheri walking back, and the other two framed her to keep her quiet? When that didn't work, someone silenced her.

"When did you leave the camp?" Volle asked.

"I left Saturday. right before the storm," Melainie said, but she didn't look at Volle.

"How did you leave? Did one of the snowmobile volunteers take you?" the trooper asked.

"I took one of the snowmobiles. I don't know whose it was, but I just wanted out of there. I hated that I had to wait around for Cam to be finished with the race to leave, but we'd driven up together."

Hawke started texting. *Why did they drive up together if Cam didn't want her there? And who took care of the kennel while they were both gone since the wife had left?*

"Let's back up. You said Cam didn't want you there, but you rode up with him? That's not making sense," Volle said, tapping his notebook with his pen.

The woman's face flushed. "He asked me to go along and watch Unity to make sure she took good care of the kennel's dogs. I did keep an eye on her when she was there. But after it felt like Cam and Sheri were up to something and then Bobbi was missing, I decided I didn't want any part of any of it, but I couldn't get away since I'd ridden up with Cam."

"Who was watching the kennel and other dogs while you and Cam were here?" Volle asked.

"A musher who keeps dogs there. He lives a few miles down the road and comes over every day to take care of his dogs anyway. Cam gives him free months for watching the kennel when we go to races." She became calmer when she talked about the dogs, kennel, and racing. Hawke felt she was a younger version of Justine.

"I'll get this all written up and then have you sign it," Volle said as he typed on his phone to Hawke,

*Anything else you want asked?*

*No, that's good. Thanks. Just send the typed-up interview to me so I can show it to the D.A.*

*Copy.*

Hawke closed out of the Zoom, hopeful that they would have Sheri in for questioning soon.

## Chapter Twenty-seven

*The Will.* That kept banging around in Hawke's head. The knowledge of who knew the contents of the will would help him gather more fuel to get the arrest warrant. He picked up the phone and called Mr. Stevens' office.

The receptionist told him to wait, and eventually, the attorney came on the line.

"Sorry to keep you waiting. I was in a meeting. You wanted to know who might have been in this office who could have been in contact with Cameron Elston or Russell Nichols. I haven't come up with anyone connected to either of them."

Hawke decided to go on a hunch. "What about Unity Allard?"

"That name rings a bell. Hold on."

Hawke waited about five minutes and was beginning to think he'd been forgotten when the line clicked and heavy breathing rasped in the phone.

"Sorry that took so long. I had to ask my secretary where I knew the name from, and then we dived into the records to get all the information about her we could." Mr. Stevens cleared his throat and said, "Unity Allard was hired to clean our office three years ago. My secretary caught her going through the file cabinets, and she was fired on the spot."

"Were any of the files she was going through near Bobbi's will?" Hawke asked.

"Not when she was caught, but who knows how many files she'd gone through before my secretary came upon her." The disgust in the man's voice could have peeled paint.

"How did she come to be hired?" Hawke asked, wondering how she knew that Bobbi had a will on file there—or if it had just been a lucky coincidence.

"I had mentioned to a colleague that I needed a reliable person to do the cleaning. My receptionist, secretary, and paralegal were too busy to keep up with it. About two weeks later, he called and recommended this Unity person." Throat clearing ensued, and then he said, "I gave him a piece of my mind when we caught her going through files. He apologized and said she came with excellent references from a friend."

"I'd like the name of the lawyer and his friend if you don't mind." Hawke needed to find all the connections.

"I can help you with the person I talked to, but you'll have to ask him about the other person." Mr. Stevens recited the man's name and his phone number.

"Thank you. One more question. When will the recipients of Bobbi's will find out what they received?"

"We have the letters written up, but are awaiting

the findings from the police since it is a homicide. As you may know, if one of the recipients is the killer, they would forfeit their inheritance." The man said it in a tone that said he believed it was a beneficiary.

"What leads you to think someone who would profit from her death killed her?" Hawke asked.

"My receptionist said she's had a man call in twice asking how long it took to receive money from an inheritance. She couldn't get him to leave a name or number." He cleared his throat. "That has happened twice since Bobbi's death. We've never had calls like that at any other time. My receptionist brought it to my attention because she'd never encountered it before."

"That is interesting," Hawke said. "Someone is anxious to get their hands on the money. I'll look into who needs it the worst and talk with that person. Thank you for all the information."

"My pleasure. Get the miscreant who did this." The line went silent.

Hawke immediately dialed the number of the person who had recommended Unity.

"Offices of Peterson, Rancher, and Skully," answered a female voice.

"I'm Oregon Senior Trooper Hawke. I'd like to visit with Mr. Peterson, please."

"I'll see if he's available. Can I tell him what this is about?" she asked.

"I'm doing a reference check on someone he knew." Hawke decided not to go into any more detail than that.

"Please hold."

Hawke waited as classical music played. It wasn't bad, but he preferred Native flute music. It was more soothing.

The music clicked off, and the woman said, "Mr. Peterson is busy at the moment. He can call you back in an hour."

Hawke left his cell phone number and looked at his email. Volle had sent him a copy of Melanie's statement. He called the D.A.'s office.

"District Attorney's office, how may I help you?"

"Hi, Terri. It's Hawke. Is there a chance I can get in and talk to Lange today? I need to get an arrest warrant for the murders that happened during the sled dog race."

"Hi, Hawke. He has an hour at four, or you can try to catch him at lunch. He's having lunch with Judge Vickers at twelve-thirty at Treetop Café."

"Thanks, I'll try to catch him there. But pencil me in for the four o'clock opening in case I miss him."

"You're down."

"Thanks."

He glanced at his watch. He had an hour and a half until the lunch between the D.A. and the Judge. Hawke decided it would be interesting to find out from the race coordinator when Cam was picked for race marshal and why.

The phone number and address for Roger Duggan were in his notes. Rather than talk about this over the phone, he decided to visit the man at his place of business.

As he left the building, Justine texted him. *Sheri has been texting Russell, asking him who he's been talking to. What have you been up to?*

Hawke shook his head. Cam must have called her and told her the questions he'd asked. Or he'd discovered Melanie was brought in and told Sheri. They had to move faster to get this solved before Sheri disappeared. She'd learned from her mom how to stay under the radar.

*I had a Washington State Trooper pull Cam in and ask questions. I also sat in on an interview with Elston's trainer. She filled in a lot of interesting information. Tell Russell that if he can stay away from his wife, it would be good. It sounds like she has a short fuse.*

*I'll relay the message to him when he comes this afternoon. He went to La Grande to buy some more clothing. He hadn't realized he'd be staying this long.*

Hawke worried that Justine might be getting too close to the man. There could be some fallout when his wife was arrested for murder. *Where has he been staying?* Hawke texted.

*In my spare bedroom. I didn't think he needed to spend money when he's been told to stay away from his volatile wife.*

He could hear the reproach in her words as clearly as if she'd uttered them.

*Didn't mean to get you riled up. Just asking.*

*Have you learned anymore?*

*I'm working on a meeting to talk to the D.A. about an arrest warrant.*

*Is it Sheri?*

*I'm not at liberty to say. Have a good day.*

He went out of messaging, walked over to his work vehicle, and slid in. Roger Duggan's stationery store was in Alder. The same place he had to be to meet up with D.A. Lange.

Driving from Winslow to Alder, Hawke stared up at the Wallowa Mountains. He couldn't wait for the snow to melt, when he and Dog could be up there patrolling again. He didn't mind the cold winters with snow, but he lived for the days of riding in the mountains and being a part of nature.

Entering Alder, he pulled onto Main Street, drove two blocks, and parked directly in front of the store. He exited the vehicle and held the door for a woman who had her hands full with boxes of stationery items.

Inside, he adjusted his eyes to a dimmer light than staring at the snow all the way to town.

"Can I help you?" a man in his fifties asked.

"I'm looking for Roger Duggan. I'm Trooper Hawke."

"We spoke on the phone. What can I help you with? Is this still about Bobbi's death?" He patted his wide chest. "Sorry, I'm Roger."

Hawke smiled. "I figured that out. Yes, I need to ask you a couple more questions."

"Anything to help find her killer. I can't believe that happened with so many people coming and going." The man shook his bald head.

"They picked the best time. Everyone was coming and going and tired from a long day."
Hawke realized he'd said they, but Roger was just nodding his head.

"Can you tell me who was going to be the race marshal before Cam Elston?" Hawke asked, pulling out his notebook.

"Marsha Collins. She's been the race marshal here for nearly ten years."

"What happened that she couldn't make it this year?" Hawke asked.

"She took a bad fall about three weeks ago. She

broke an arm and a leg. She called and said what happened and that she wouldn't be able to officiate, but that Cam Elston would be available. So I called him and he said he'd do it." Roger shrugged as if that was it.

"Marsha suggested Cam?"

"Yes. Why is there a problem with that?" Roger studied him.

"No. I just want to get all the facts straight. Do you have Marsha's phone number handy?"

"Yeah, it's on my phone. Just a minute." Roger pulled his phone out of his pocket and started scrolling. "Here it is." He recited the number to Hawke, who wrote it down in his notebook.

"Thanks. Can you tell me what you thought of Cam's ability to be a race marshal?"

Roger's gaze remained on his phone. "He did okay for not having been to the race before."

"Why hadn't he been to the Eagle Cap Extreme before?" Hawke asked.

"His dogs don't usually do well. They get tired. Not enough training. The Eagle Cap is grueling. That's why it's a qualifier for the Iditarod." Roger smiled with pride.

"Do you think Cam followed protocol when Bobbi's sled was found?" Hawke wanted to discover all he could about the man's not following through on a missing musher. That was part of getting him as an accomplice.

"He should have called SAR in right away and not just when we pushed that a storm was coming." He sighed. "Though now we know that she wasn't out there, but it was still protocol."

*Exactly*, Hawke thought. Cam had known Bobbi

wasn't out there. That's why he'd dragged his feet about calling in Search and Rescue.

"Thank you for the information." Hawke walked out of the establishment and blinked at the piles of white snow piled along the street. He slid into his vehicle and pulled out his phone and notebook.

He dialed Marsha Collins. The phone rang several times before a female voice said, "Hello?"

"Ms. Collins, I'm Oregon State Senior Trooper Hawke. I'd like to ask you some questions to help me tie up some loose ends on a murder investigation."

The woman gasped. "I don't know how I can help."

He wondered how she hadn't heard about Bobbi. "I'm investigating the death of Bobbi Whitby at the Eagle Cap Extreme."

"Bobbi? Oh my, that's horrible!" Her voice trembled.

"Ms. Collins, why did you suggest Cam Elston take your place after your accident?"

"I-I can't say." She sounded like she was close to tears.

"Why not? Did someone threaten you if you didn't suggest him?" Hawke asked.

The woman broke down sobbing. All Hawke could hear on the other side were sobs, sniffles, and blubbering.

"Calm down, please. Just tell me what happened. It could help me put away the person you're afraid of." He tried to get through to the woman.

She snuffled and blubbered some more.

"Ms. Collins. Could I come around and talk to you?" he finally asked.

"Y-yes," she said coherently.

"Where do you live?" he asked. He hadn't taken the time to look it up.

"I live in Sweet Home."

That was almost eight hours away. He couldn't waste that much time on the road to talk to her.

"I didn't realize how far from me you are. Could I send another State Detective to talk to you? Would you be comfortable doing that?"

"I guess. But am I safe?" she asked.

"As long as you don't talk to anyone else about any of this, you should be fine." Even as he said it, he decided to see if the county could run a deputy by her house every hour or so. If Sheri was the one who forced her to suggest Cam for race marshal, she might be trying to tie up loose ends.

"Okay. I'll look for a trooper to come see me tomorrow."

Hawke ended the call, looked up Sweet Home and the county it was in, then he called the Linn County Sheriff. After explaining his concerns, he then called his Lieutenant in La Grande and asked that he put in a request for a senior trooper or detective to interview Ms. Collins. But to call him first to know what to ask.

A glance at his watch said he would be at the restaurant a bit after the D.A. and Judge arrived.

## Chapter Twenty-eight

Hawke walked into the Treetop Café and spotted the D.A. and Judge right off. They were sitting at their usual table in the corner. He wondered if this was an everyday event or a weekly meeting.

"Hawke, Terri said you might show up," D.A. Lange said.

Hawke nodded to him and then to Judge Vickers. "Sir, I hope you don't mind if I talk a bit of shop with D.A. Lange."

"I'm curious to see where you're at with the latest homicides in our county," the judge said.

Hawke took a seat. The waitress brought him a menu and a cup of coffee. "Thank you."

When the waitress walked back to the counter, he said, "I have evidence that I believe will give you enough cause to write up an arrest warrant."

"Let's hear what you have," Lange said, leaning back in his chair.

Hawke pulled out his notebook and started reading all the pieces he'd circled as crucial to the investigation. When he finished, the waitress arrived to deliver food to the judge and D.A. and take his to-go order.

Lange waited for the waitress to move out of earshot and asked, "Who is all this evidence against?"

"A vet tech who works the Extreme race and others every year. She goes by Sheri Nichols, her shortened first and married name. I've been looking for her as Raina Tabor. She is the first victim's cousin and the daughter of the second victim."

Judge Vickers whistled and said, "That is taking family rivalry a bit too far."

"This suspect has threatened two women, one of whom has told us incriminating evidence and the other I'm having interviewed tomorrow in Sweet Home. I have reason to believe my suspect had an accomplice, one of the beneficiaries of the first victim's will."

Lange ate the sandwich he'd ordered as he listened. He put a half down, wiped his mouth, and said, "If you get strong evidence tomorrow from the other witness, I'll write up the arrest warrant for the suspect. What do you have on the accomplice?"

Hawke told him what he'd learned so far about Cam Elston.

Lange nodded. "Your evidence does stack up against him as the accomplice with the one witness statement and what you get tomorrow. I'll get these drafted up, and when you have the statement from the woman in Sweet Home, call and tell me what she had to say. If it locks down the case against the suspect, I'll issue the warrant."

Hawke leaned back as the waitress placed a bag in

front of him.

"Do you need anything else?" the waitress asked.

"No, this will do," Hawke said, handing her money to pay for the meal and her tip.

The waitress left.

He stood and said, "Thank you. I'll be in contact tomorrow."

As he walked to his vehicle, his phone buzzed. It was the attorney who had recommended Unity.

"Oregon State Trooper Hawke," he answered.

"Trooper Hawke, my receptionist left a message to call you. What is this about?"

"Mr. Peterson, could you tell me how you knew Unity Allard?" He waited as the man sputtered.

"Why are you asking me this?"

"She and her niece were murdered over a week ago. I'm trying to make a connection that will help me find their killer." Hawke felt that was all the man needed.

"What led you to me?" The lawyer was stalling.

"I discovered that Ms. Allard cleaned a law firm that represented her niece. I believe the niece was killed so that Ms. Allard's daughter would inherit a large sum of money through her husband, who was named in the will. I believe Ms. Allard relayed that information to her daughter, who killed the niece and then her mother."

The man gasped and then said, "Are you trying to make me an accessory?"

"No, I'm trying to build my case against my suspect. How did you know Ms. Allard, and why did you recommend her to Mr. Stevens?" Hawke had his notebook sitting on the armrest between the driver and passenger seats.

"Ms. Allard had come to my office to contest a will. She was out of money and living in her van. When people asked if I knew anyone who could clean or do odd jobs, I'd give out her name."

Hawke asked, "Was the will she wanted to contest in favor of Bobbi and Beverly Whitby?"

The man harrumphed and finally said, "Yes. She felt her mother should have left her and her daughter something."

"I'm guessing it was an air-tight bequest."

"Yes, there wasn't anything they could do about it. She was mad. I never met her daughter. Are you saying they killed the niece to get their hands on the money?"

"That's what it looks like they had planned. But the daughter turned on the mother. I guess she wanted it all. Thank you for calling me back." He hung up and shook his head. How the generous actions of one could have led to two deaths boggled the mind.

He had a couple more hours to do his job. He hoped the trooper who was being sent to interview Ms. Collins would contact him soon.

Hawke drove out Highway 3 to check out the Wenaha Wildlife Refuge. The elk were fed there during the winter. Knowing the animals gathered in the area, attracted poachers and antler hunters. The animals were not to be disturbed, so they would stay in the area and avoid the ranchers' haystacks.

He didn't find any recent tire or footprints in the obvious places where people parked and walked into the refuge. As he started winding his way back to Eagle on the snow-rutted gravel backroads, he decided to stop in Promise and have a chat with Ivan and his dad.

It was dark when Hawke found the driveway to the Tabor Ranch. He drove in, noticing the house had more lights on than the last time he'd arrived. Drawing closer to the house, his headlights swung across the front of the barn. A flash of green caught Hawke's attention.

He remembered that no one had reported back to him about having come across the green and black snowmobile that Neal had reported seeing on Saturday afternoon. His first instinct was to drive up to the barn and check it out. But he decided against it. He parked in front of the house and walked up onto the porch, knocking on the door to talk to the father and son.

"Hold your horses," called a gruff voice from inside.

The sound of wheels rolling over uneven wood filtered through the door. The sound grew louder and closer. The door swung open, and Hawke peered down at a thinner version of Ivan sitting in a wheelchair.

"Mr. Tabor?" Hawke asked.

"Yeah. You here about my son?" the man asked.

"In a way. I came to talk to you and your son. Where is he?"

The man slammed a hand down on the arm of the wheelchair. "I called the Sheriff's Office an hour ago and no one has come to ask me questions. I thought that's what you were here for." The man rolled his wheelchair backward and stopped in the living room. "Well, shut the door and listen."

Hawke shut the door and pulled his notebook out of his shirt. "Is your son missing?"

"Yes. He's always home before dark to feed the cattle and chickens and get me dinner. He took off this morning, saying he'd figured things out and he'd be back with money by dark." The man's eyes grew watery. "He had to have done something foolish."

Hawke pulled a chair up in front of the man. "Did he say where he was going?"

Mr. Tabor shook his head. "He's been jumpy ever since he learned his mom and cousin were killed. He kept saying he had an idea. I asked him about what, and he said how to make some money. I got a bad feeling he tried to blackmail whoever killed Brenda and Bobbi."

"What was he driving when he left?" Hawke asked.

"A two-thousand and four Chevy Silverado fifteen hundred. It's a faded blue."

"What's the license plate?"

The man recited the plate.

Hawke wrote it all down. "I'll get the county and the state police looking for it." Hawke saw the man's hands shaking. "Do you want me to find you something to eat or maybe get you a cup of coffee?"

"I've had too much coffee waiting for that fool to come home. But I could use something to soak up the caffeine in my stomach."

"I'll go see what I can find in your kitchen." Hawke slipped the notebook back in his pocket and headed out into the hall that split the house. He found the kitchen at the back of the house. Most of the old farmhouses were set up the same way.

He noticed as he walked down the hall that there was a bathroom and bedroom on the left side of the hall and a dining room on the right. The kitchen had a small table where it looked like the two men took their meals.

In the kitchen, he looked for bread and found half a loaf in a bread box that sat too far back from the edge of the counter for the man in the wheelchair to reach.

He pulled it forward and took out two slices. After looking through the refrigerator and not finding anything to make a sandwich out of, he opened the cupboard doors.

"If you're looking for the peanut butter, it's the next door," Mr. Tabor said from behind him.

"Thanks. You didn't have anything in the fridge to make a sandwich out of." Hawke grabbed the peanut butter jar. Since the man was in the kitchen, Hawke placed two slices of bread on a plate. He set that, the peanut butter, and a knife, on the table where it appeared to be his spot because there wasn't a chair.

The man rolled up to it and started spreading peanut butter on a slice of bread. "We don't keep many perishables. It's a waste of money."

"How long ago did you have your accident?" Hawke asked.

"Right after Ivan graduated from high school. That boy had to take over running the ranch. He isn't good at it. But it was all I had to give him." The man slapped the two pieces of bread together and took a bite. His eyes closed as if he hadn't had anything to eat all day.

"From what you said, you heard your wife and niece were killed during the sled dog race."

The man nodded and kept chewing.

"Were you surprised to discover your wife was in the county?" Hawke sat down and placed his notebook on the table.

"Not really. Every once in a while, someone would say they saw her here. But she never made the effort to come see us. Once she left, she was dead to me. Left me here tending a ranch and a toddler all alone. I told Ivan to stay away from the Whitby women. They were nothing but trouble."

"Are you talking about Beverly and Bobbi?" Hawke asked.

The man nodded. "And my wife and daughter. They all have a mean streak in them."

"From what I've been told about Bobbi, she didn't have a mean streak. I can't vouch for Beverly, but she seemed upset about her sister's death. Now, your wife…there has been a lot said about her and your daughter. None of it was complimentary."

"Well, maybe they took after Brenda's mom and not the Whitby side. That old lady, Brenda's mom, was a dragon. She blew flames and puffed smoke out of her nose as she dictated how we should live our lives. She was unhappy that Brenda married me, a rancher, someone who would always be dirty and sweaty because I did manual labor." He motioned to the sink. "Could you get me a glass of water?"

Hawke walked over to the sink and came back with a tall glass filled with water. He placed it next to Mr. Tabor's hand.

"Can you think of anything that Ivan talked about after the race that would give me an idea of where he went?" Hawke asked, returning to his seat and notebook.

"When he first came back, he said that Bobbi was killed. He was shaken up about that. Said he'd talked to her to see if she'd be willing to help us with the ranch. She said, if he could get her the county assessors' figures and the books for what we've done the last five years, she'd consider it. Knowing he lost that backing, he knew we couldn't keep this ranch. It was breaking his heart. He didn't have the skill or knowledge to keep it running, and as you can see, I could tell him what I thought needed to be done, but he'd barely listen to me even though I'd been turning a profit on the land ever since my daddy gave it to me."

Hawke nodded. The offspring didn't always carry the love of the land that their ancestors had. "You said you tried calling him. What's his number?"

Mr. Tabor took his phone out of his shirt pocket and scrolled through it to his call list. He turned the phone toward Hawke.

He found Ivan's number, put it in his phone, and dialed. The phone rang four times and went to voicemail. He left a message for Ivan to call his dad, he was worried about him. What he really wanted was the number to see what calls he'd made.

Hawke stood. "I'm going to call his vehicle in to the authorities and get them looking for him. I pulled the bread box closer to the edge of the counter. Leave the peanut butter on the table. I'll come by or have a deputy come by tomorrow and check on you. We'll let you know when we hear something about Ivan."

"Thank you. He's all I've got. If not for him sticking around, I'd have ended up in a nursing home." Mr. Tabor's eyes were watering.

"We'll do what we can to find him." Hawke let himself out.

He glanced at the barn. Since he was here, he decided to check out the shiny green he'd seen as he drove up. The door was open enough for a snowmobile to fit through. And that's what he found. A green and black snowmobile with the *Grip it and Rip it* sticker. What was Ivan's snowmobile doing sitting half a mile away from the camp on Sunday when they were tearing down? A question to ask him when they found him.

As soon as Hawke started down the road, he radioed dispatch to put out an all-points on Ivan's vehicle. When he was on Highway 82 headed to Eagle, his phone dinged. The OSP Detective had tried to call him. Hawke pulled over in Eagle, texted Dani he was eating in Eagle, and exited his vehicle at Al's Café.

"Hawke, it's been a while," Lacie, the co-owner of the café, said, walking toward him with a coffee pot and menu.

"I'm just ordering to go." He walked up to the cash register, placed his order, and paid. Hawke nodded toward his vehicle parked outside. "I'll be sitting in there when it's ready."

"I'll bring it out." Lacie tucked the tip he gave her in her pocket and placed his order on the string in the window between the seating area and the kitchen.

"Thanks." He returned to his vehicle and called the OSP Detective back.

"Detective Ward."

"Detective, this is Senior Trooper Hawke, I put in the request to have Marsha Collins in Sweet Home interviewed."

"Yes, I was calling to find out what you needed to know."

Hawke told him about the double homicide and what he needed to know from Marsha. "I can send you the case number, and you can review what I have so far if that would help you do the interview. But what I need to know from talking to her on the phone is who she is scared of. I have a feeling the broken bones she suffered to take her out of being the race marshal were inflicted by my main suspect. The woman you'll be interviewing was scared to talk. But I think she is also angry and wants justice."

"Send me the number. I'll review it tonight and be prepared for tomorrow."

"Thanks. I'll send it now."

A knock on the window pulled Hawke away from the phone. He rolled down the window, thanked Lacie, and rolled the window back up. As soon as his hands were free, he picked up the phone and sent the case number to the detective. He texted, *Call me as soon as you finish talking to Marsha. Her statement will help me get the arrest warrant.*

*Copy.*

Hawke pulled out his laptop and sent a request to get a readout of the calls Ivan had made since Sunday. When he couldn't think of anything else he could do at the moment for the case, he dug into his bag and started eating the fries. As he ate, his thoughts went to Ivan. What could he have seen or heard that would put him on the trail of the killer?

# Chapter Twenty-nine

Tuesday morning, Hawke went straight to the office to see if Ivan had been found or if his phone records had been sent.

Spruel stopped him as he topped the stairs. "How's the investigation going?"

"I have a detective talking to someone who may have been threatened to recommend a replacement for her as race marshal. Ivan Tabor is missing. His crippled father is worried about him. I put out an APB on his vehicle last night. He owns the snowmobile we've been looking for. His dad said Ivan was talking about getting money because he knew something about the deaths. I hope he has the wrong person because if he goes after Sheri, he may end up another victim."

Spruel nodded. "I agree. We need to find him and bring him in for questioning. How did the talk with Lange go?"

"He was making up an arrest warrant for both Sheri

and Elston, but he wanted the information from Ms. Collins before he gave it to me." Hawke was feeling frustrated. Nothing seemed to be coming together on this, even though he was pretty sure he knew the killers.

"I'm going to stick around close and wait for Detective Ward to call me. As soon as I get that, I'll contact Lange." Hawke clicked on his monitor and discovered another email from forensics.

He clicked on the email and read it.

*The bleached hair found on the sled matched that of the second victim. The brown hair follicle was from a male. No relation to either victim.*

Hawke whooped and jumped to his feet.

Spruel hurried into the main room. "What's up?"

"Forensics confirmed the hair found on the sled in the container was from our second victim and a male. That would have to be Elston. While Sheri was killing her mom, he was disposing of her sled and dogs. This is more proof for Lange."

His phone buzzed. It was Detective Ward.

"Hawke."

"This is Detective Ward. I just completed the interview with Marsha Collins and thought you'd like to hear this before I wrote the report up."

"Yes, I'd like to hear what she had to say," Hawke said, keeping his tone as neutral as he could, imagining having the arrest warrant in his hand.

"She said that a woman called and told her that if she didn't pull out as the race marshal for the Eagle Cap Extreme by two weeks before the race, she would come to harm. When she didn't call and pull out by the date, the next day she was hit by a car while crossing the street. She broke her arm and a leg. The next day, when she was home, she received a phone call from the same person, saying to pull out and recommend Cameron Elston, or something else could happen to her. That's when she called and recommended Elston."

Hawke's mind was flying. "Did she receive the calls on her home phone?"

"Yes. And she gave me her bill that has the number on it." Detective Ward read off the number. "It belongs to Sheri Nichols."

Hawke grinned. "We've got her. Thanks. I'll contact the District Attorney and get the arrests going."

"I haven't seen you smiling this much since you caught the wolverine poacher," Nathan said.

"We've got her. Sheri called and threatened the person who was supposed to be the race marshal to drop out. When she didn't, a car ran her over, and Sheri called her back. Both those calls show up on the woman's phone bill." Hawke picked up his cell phone and scrolled through contacts for the D.A.'s office.

Terri answered. "Yes, he's been expecting a call from you. I'll put you through."

"Hawke, what did you get?" Lange asked.

Hawke told the D.A. about the hair on the sled and the phone number that incriminated Sheri in threatening the race marshal.

"Come get your warrants," Lange said.

"I need the one for Elston sent to Detective Volle of the Washington State Police in District Six. I'll make the drive to Idaho to pick up Sheri."

"Be sure to contact the local police for backup," Lange said.

"I will. I'll swing by and get that warrant in thirty minutes." Hawke ended the call and contacted the

Idaho State Police, requesting backup to help serve an arrest warrant.

"Give us the name and we'll keep an eye on the suspect until you arrive. It would be a waste of time if you come over and she's not here."

Hawke agreed. He gave her name, address, and where she worked so they could see if she was at work.

"I'm going to stop by the house, pack my overnight bag, and pick up the warrant. Then I'll set out for Idaho," Hawke told Spruel.

"Be careful. This woman sounds dangerous."

"I will. I've already called for backup." Hawke gathered his hat and coat and headed down the stairs and out to his work vehicle.

When he stopped at home, he told Dani what he was headed to do.

"I'm going to go visit Justine and invite her and Russell over for dinner. I want to get a feel for whether they are friends or heading to something more," Dani said.

"That's fine. I want her happy. I don't want her to be with someone who won't let Justine be herself. She's been a free spirit for a long time and shouldn't have her wings clipped." Hawke had found Justine's resilience in bouncing back from adversity to be her strength, but she didn't need any more adversity in her life.

"I agree. That's why I want to meet the man." Dani kissed his cheek. "I love how you care about everyone. Today, think about yourself and stay safe."

"I will. See you tomorrow." Hawke had an eight-hour drive to make.

He pulled up to the courthouse in Alder a little over thirty minutes later. As he approached the District

Attorney's office, his phone buzzed.

"Hawke."

"This is Trooper Perez with the Idaho State Police. No one has seen your suspect for two days. It wouldn't be worth your time to come over here with the warrant. I'll keep asking around and see if I can find her."

"Thanks." Hawke ended the call and thought about Ivan trying to get money out of the killer. Had he put things together and called Sheri? Could she be in Wallowa County right now? He walked into the D.A.'s office.

Terri smiled and held up an envelope. "Here's your warrant."

He took the envelope and stared at it.

"What's the matter? I thought you'd be happy to get this?" Terry said.

"I am, but it seems the person it's for has disappeared." Hawke tapped the envelope in his other hand as he thought. "I need to make a few phone calls. Thanks."

He spun around, walked down the stairs, and out onto the street. He called Detective Volle first.

"Trooper Hawke, I received the arrest warrant and I'm headed to the kennel to arrest Elston."

"Good. But be careful. The woman I believe is behind the killings can't be found. She could be there with Elston. Let me know one way or the other."

"Copy."

Hawke ended the call and dialed Detective Ward.

"Ward," the detective answered.

"This is Hawke. The woman who threatened Ms. Collins is unaccounted for. It would be a good idea to have someone keep an eye on Ms. Collins."

"Copy. I'll send someone right over. Let me know when the suspect is apprehended."

"I will." Hawke ended that call and called Spruel.

"What's up, Hawke? I thought you were headed to Idaho."

"The Idaho State Police can't find her. I'm staying here and concentrating on finding Ivan. He may have called her, threatening to spill what he knew if she didn't cut him in on the inheritance. That means she could be here. Has anything come back on the APB I sent out? And could you see if you can speed up the trace on the calls Ivan made the last few days? Specifically, to see if he did call Sheri Nichols."

"I can take care of that. Negative on the APB. No one has seen the vehicle. What do you plan to do?"

"Drive back out to the Tabor Ranch and see if I can find anything that might give me an idea of where they might be meeting up."

"Be careful and call for backup if you find them."

"I will. Thanks." Hawke ended that call and texted Dani. *Change of plans, I'm in the county today. Will be home for dinner with Justine and Russell tonight unless my suspect is caught.*

Dani sent, *Okay.*

Hawke slid into his vehicle and headed out of Alder, keeping his eyes peeled for a blue 2004 Chevy Silverado.

Hawke drove up the road to the Tabor Ranch slowly. He didn't want any surprises. The door to the barn was open, and he didn't see the snowmobile. He also didn't see the Chevy Silverado.

He parked, scanned the area that he could see, and

then slid out of the vehicle and walked up to the door. He knocked and listened for the sound of the wheelchair.

Nothing.

He knocked louder and called out, "Mr. Tabor, it's Trooper Hawke." He listened.

Nothing.

Grasping the door handle, he turned it and walked in. The home was cold. "Mr. Tabor? Are you here?" He walked through the house, peering into all the rooms. The backroom that he'd thought was the bedroom for Mr. Tabor had the door closed.

Hawke opened it and found Mr. Tabor tied to his chair, his mouth gagged. His skin was blue.

Hurrying to the man, he pulled the gag off and checked for a pulse. There was a weak one. Using the radio on his shoulder, he called for an ambulance and backup. They needed to go through this house and the barn to see if they could figure out where Ivan was and what happened to Mr. Tabor.

Why would his son tie him up? And if not his son, then it had to be his daughter. Sheri had to have been here.

Hawke untied the man and wrapped him in a blanket, then pushed the wheelchair out into the living room. He found some wood and started a fire in the woodstove. He left the door ajar on the stove to hasten the flames.

While he waited for the ambulance to arrive, Hawke searched downstairs for anything that might give him an idea of where Ivan might be. An hour after Hawke's arrival, the ambulance pulled up to the front.

He met Roxy and told her what he'd found. She

and Bonnie put Mr. Tabor on the gurney and rolled him out of the house as Ivy and Deputy Alden pulled up in their vehicles.

Hawke quickly told them that he believed his murder suspect, Sheri Nichols, was in the county and may have Ivan Tabor. "I searched downstairs and didn't find anything. Dave, you and Ivy look in and around the barn for anything to show someone has been here recently. There was a snowmobile in there last night when I was here. It's gone now. I'll finish searching the house."

The deputy and state trooper headed to the barn, and Hawke re-entered the house. He went up the creaky staircase to the second floor. It was easy to see which room was Ivan's. It had a path cleared in the dust from the top of the stairs to one door.

Hawke opened the door and found a tidy room with ledgers spread out on a desk, a bed with a worn-out quilt, and maps of the Wallowa Mountains tacked to the walls. There were circles around the better trapping areas. He knew Ivan was a trapper. This showed he was methodical and kept records.

Scanning the ledgers, he noticed it wasn't just how many pelts he trapped and the price he was paid. He also kept track of where and the quality of the pelt. He was a businessman at heart, not a farmer. Hawke raised the hand he'd been leaning on as he read the ledger. A paper stuck to his hand. It had a phone number. One that looked familiar.

He put it into his phone and Sheri's name came up.

Ivan had contacted his sister. How many times? Had they been working on this together? He had thought the young man was innocent; now he was wondering if the man was as accomplished a liar as his sister and mother.

He put the paper in an evidence bag and continued looking through his drawers and closet. He wasn't running. A suitcase sat on the floor and all his clothes seemed to be accounted for.

Hawke ran his gloved hands into the pockets of the jackets. He came up with gum wrappers, gas receipts, and lint. Nothing that would help the investigation.

When he'd exhausted the search in the room, he stepped back out into the hallway. He grabbed the flashlight on his duty belt and flashed it up and down the hall. Someone had entered another room.

He walked down the hall and turned the knob on the room. It was decked out in dusty pink. The color had been bright once, but the thick layer of dust said it hadn't been used in decades. Which fit the timeline when Brenda took Raina away. He used the flashlight to see where the person had stepped. The footprints moved across the room to the closet. Dust was displaced as if someone had knelt to get something from the bottom of the wardrobe.

Hawke beamed the light around the floor and saw where a board had been pulled back. He pried the board up with his knife and found a cookie tin. Reaching in, he pulled the tin out and set his phone on the floor to use both hands to pry the lid off the box. Inside were birthday cards from Beverly and Bobbi to Raina. There were some small toys and a hard piece of unchewed gum. What had been in here that made someone, either Raina or Ivan, come in here and get into the box?

"Hawke!" Ivy called from downstairs.

"Yeah, coming." He put the lid on the box and took

it with him.

At the bottom of the stairs, he asked, "Did you find anything?"

"It looks like a snowmobile did leave here in the last twenty-four hours. But we didn't find anything else."

"Which direction was it headed?" Hawke asked, tucking the tin under his arm.

Ivy's gaze was on the tin as she said, "East."

"Ivan has Sheri's number. I don't know if he recently found it or if he's been in touch with her all along. We need to check his phone records and find out. And we need to put out an APB on Sheri Nichols." He walked out of the house.

Ivy followed, closing the door behind her.

"I'm going to cover some of the back roads from here to Eagle and see if I can find the tracks," he told Dave and Ivy. "You two go about your business but keep an ear out if I call for backup. It will mean I found either Sheri or Ivan or both."

They both nodded and entered their vehicles. Hawke waited for them to leave before heading to the barn and checking out the tracks from the snowmobile. Ivy had been right. The tracks were headed east. That meant the person was using Powwatka Ridge to get back to Eagle. He pulled out his phone and brought up the photos he'd taken on Ferguson Ridge, where a snowmobile had carried Unity to her death. The marks were the same. Damn, he'd hoped he'd been right about Ivan.

## Chapter Thirty

Zig-zagging over snow-rutted roads, Hawke made his way over to Powwatka Ridge Road and kept an eye on the ground for the snowmobile tracks. He finally found them at Whiskey Creek on the outskirts of Eagle. It appeared the snowmobile had run out of fuel, because it was parked at the Nez Perce Homeland grounds, where they conducted the annual Tamkaliks Powwow and held other cultural events throughout the year.

Hawke called in that he'd found the snowmobile and asked that forensics come check it for prints and DNA. Who would Ivan go to for help in Eagle? He wasn't sure, but wondered if Lacie at Al's Café would know who he might meet up with in the café from time to time.

He drove to the café, parked, and entered the building. It was buzzing for a Tuesday midday.

"Hawke, coffee or iced tea?" Lacie asked, clearing a space for him at the counter.

"How about iced tea." He picked up a menu but wasn't really hungry. Not for food anyway. He wanted information.

Lacie set the glass in front of him. "Are you eating?"

"What kind of pie do you have?"

She named them off, and Hawke settled on a chocolate cream.

While she was fussing with putting the whipped cream on the pie, Hawke asked in a quiet voice, "Who do you see in here with Ivan Tabor?"

Lacie placed his pie in front of him and said, "Will Michaels, Jasper Prine, and Nolan Jackson. Is he in trouble?"

"We can't find him, and his dad is in the hospital." Hawke figured that would be a good rumor to go around.

"Oh, that's horrible. I'll keep an eye and ear out to see if I can find out where he is. Those four usually don't come in here but about once or twice a month."

"Thanks." Hawke ate his pie, downed his iced tea, and paid.

When he was settled in his vehicle, he pulled up each of the men on DMV, getting home addresses. They all lived in and around Eagle. One of them lived not far from where the snowmobile was left. Hawke drove there first.

He saw a pickup and a car in the driveway as he parked. A curtain shifted, and Hawke waited to see if anyone came to the door. When they didn't, he exited the vehicle, using caution as he walked up to the front door.

Knocking on the door, he waited, listening for any

sound on the other side of the door.

He knocked again. "It's Trooper Hawke, I'm trying to find Ivan Tabor. His father is in the hospital."

The door opened. Ivan stood in the open doorway, craning his neck to see around Hawke. "How's Dad?"

"He's getting treatment at the hospital. Did you tie him up and leave him in the cold?" Hawke asked, moving into the house, making the younger man back up.

"No! I saw a car coming and headed out to the barn. When I saw who got out of the car, I waited until they were in the house and took off on the snowmobile. It was one cold ride without the proper gear, but it was better than sticking around and ending up like Bobbi and Mom."

"You left your father to your sister's temper?" Hawke wasn't feeling sorry for the man. He'd left his crippled father to deal with a psychopath.

"I figured she'd see he wasn't a threat to her and leave him alone. My pickup wasn't there, so she wouldn't think I would be there."

Hawke glared at the man. "If you didn't think she was a threat and wouldn't know you were there, why did you run?"

Ivan hugged his arms close to his body. "I called her and told her I knew what she'd done. That if she paid me a hundred thousand dollars, I'd forget what I know. It was enough to pay off our loans at the bank." He shook his head. "She agreed, but when she told me where to meet her, I knew she wasn't going to pay. She was going to do to me what she did to Bobbi and Mom. I parked my pickup hours before the meet and then hiked out with snowshoes. I'd only been home long enough to feed Dad and tell him I'd gotten stuck in the pickup when I heard the car pull up."

He ran a hand over his face. "I honestly didn't expect her to go to the house looking for me. Dad always told me to stay away from the Whitby women. That they were mean-spirited. Bobbi wasn't. I'd talked to her over the years. She'd call now and then, asking how Dad and I were doing. That's why I went to her to see if we could get a loan. I wanted to fix the ranch up to sell it."

"Where do you think Sheri will go next?" Hawke asked.

Ivan stared at him. "Who's Sheri?"

"That's the name Raina goes by now," Hawke said. "Do you have any idea where she might go in the county?"

Ivan shrugged. "As far as I know, she doesn't know anyone here. She left in first grade."

"What about people from the Extreme race?" Hawke asked, thinking of Justine, who was friends with Bobbi.

"This was the only year I've ever volunteered. It seemed like a good way to spend more time on my snowmobile. That's the only reason I volunteered. I didn't know Bobbi would be there, or Mom, or Raina."

Hawke hopped on that. "Did you know Sheri Nichols was your sister?"

Ivan shook his head. "I didn't know either of them was my mom and sister. Not until you told me."

"Why was your snowmobile sitting half a mile from Ollokot on Saturday after the storm cleared?" Hawke asked.

Ivan took a step back as if Hawke had hit him.

"How did you know about that?"

"Someone saw it and mentioned it when being questioned." Hawke repeated, "Why was it there?"

"Because the head of the race, Cam, gave me money to have it sitting there. He caught me when I was coming from the Hilton and said he had a hundred bucks for me. All I had to do was leave my snowmobile half a mile west of the camp and pick it up the next morning at the same place." Ivan shrugged. "I could use the money. I thought he was going to use it to check on the sleds. I just did what I was told the whole weekend, and that was the easiest thing I'd been asked to do."

Hawke believed the man. "You need to stay here, where Sheri can't find you. Your dad is at the hospital. I'll make sure they keep him there until you can pick him up."

"Thank you. Did she hurt him?"

"She tied him up and gagged him. Left the house cold. He had hypothermia and is malnourished, according to the EMTs who attended him and took him to the hospital."

"He's better off there until you catch Raina." Ivan plopped onto a chair. "Will won't care if I stay here a while."

"I'll let your dad know you're okay. What did the car look like that Sheri was driving?"

"It was a white Ford Escort. New model."

"Thanks." Hawke left the house and called Ivy and then Dave to let them know he found Ivan and to keep an eye out for a white Ford Escort, newer model with an Idaho license plate. Then he called Spruel, got him up to date, and asked him to pass the word along about the car.

"It sounds like your murder suspect is here in the county. Who do you think she'd be aiming for besides Ivan?" Nathan asked.

"I'm thinking my friend, Justine Bartley. She was friends with Bobbi, and I don't think Sheri knows, but her husband has been staying with Justine since I talked to him because he was afraid to go home."

"That would be more than enough reason for the woman to do both of them harm, I'd think. Check up on Justine, and I'll keep the forces looking for Sheri."

"I will." Hawke ended his call and called Dani.

"Hey, Hawke, will you be able to make it home by six?" she asked.

"I'm not sure. When did you talk to Justine about coming to dinner?"

"It was when I was over there about ten this morning, why?"

He sighed. "My murder suspect is here in the county and may be looking for someone to put her up. I hope she won't go to Justine, but I'm going to drive by there just in case."

"You mean Russell's wife? Oh shit! That would probably send her into killing someone else. I'll head over there—"

"No, you won't! This is a police matter. We're taking all the necessary precautions. You stay there and keep preparing dinner. I'll bring Justine and Russell to our house."

"You make sure she gets here safe and sound." Dani ended the call.

Hawke grinned at the phone. Leave it to Dani to think he could stop a psychopath like Sheri.

Hawke drove up and parked in his usual spot at Justine's. Her vehicle and Russell's were sitting in her driveway. That would be a red flag to Sheri if she pulled into the driveway and saw her husband's pickup sitting there when he'd been gone for a week.

Justine stepped out of the outside dog run and walked toward him.

Hawke exited his vehicle and waited for her to get closer before asking, "Where's Russell?"

"He's cleaning up for our dinner with you and Dani tonight, why?"

"I need him to park his pickup where it can't be seen by anyone coming up your driveway. Then I need the two of you to get in my pickup. I'll take you to our house for dinner."

Justine grabbed his coat sleeve. "What's going on?"

"Sheri is in the county. She tied her father in his wheelchair and gagged him leaving him in a cold house overnight. Ivan ran off when he saw her. He's safe but I have a feeling she's going to come here looking for you. If she sees Russell's pickup, that will only make her madder."

"Why would she be coming after me? Because I was friends with Bobbi? If so, let her come. I'm so angry with her for taking away my friend. I'm pretty sure I'd get the first shot in." Justine's face grew bronzer as her anger flared.

"No, you are both coming with me. We'll have surveillance keeping an eye on your place. Go tell Russell to hurry up." Hawke motioned toward the house.

Justine glared at him and stomped her way to the

house like an angry teenager.

Hawke called Spruel. "Nathan, I'm at Justine Bartley's. I'm taking her and Russell Nichols to my house. We were having them over for dinner tonight. I'm having Russell move his pickup where it can't be seen so easily. It would be a good idea to put some surveillance on the place and we might be able to catch our suspect if she comes to try and take Justine out of the inheritance picture."

"Can you keep the two of them overnight?" Nathan asked.

"Yeah. We have two guest rooms. Justine won't like leaving the dogs for that long, but I'll come over with her in the morning to take care of them."

"Have you heard if Washington has Elston arrested?" Nathan asked.

"No, I've been so focused on our suspect being in the county, I hadn't thought about that. I'll call Detective Volle now." Hawke ended the call and scrolled through his contacts for Volle.

He found it and hit dial.

Volle's voicemail came on.

Hawke left a message. "This is Trooper Hawke, just checking in to see if you have my suspect arrested yet. Call when you get this."

Justine and Russell came out of the house. Justine turned and locked the door while Russell walked over to his vehicle. He drove around to the back of Justine's house. They both arrived at his vehicle at the same time after Justine locked the main gate to the kennels.

"Hop in the back," he said, climbing into the driver's seat. Once everyone was in and buckled up, Hawke started the vehicle and backed out of the driveway.

"What's this you said about Sheri being here?" Russell asked.

Hawke told him what he knew so far and that there was an arrest warrant out for his wife. "We have enough evidence to know that she was in on the homicides of both Bobbi and Unity. We also believe her accomplice in this was Cameron Elston. I sent an arrest warrant to the Washington State Police to pick him up. So far, I haven't heard if they have him. Potentially, both Elston and your wife could be in Wallowa County taking care of loose ends."

"But why is she doing this? Why is she killing people?" Russell asked.

"I'll tell you both at dinner." Hawke drove them around Winslow so no one would see who was in the back seat of his vehicle. He didn't want the locals to start up rumors about Justine being arrested or to have Sheri see her in his vehicle if she happened to be on a side street in Winslow.

# Chapter Thirty-one

Dani greeted them warmly and took them into the kitchen for a before-dinner drink while Hawke went down the hall to the bedroom to change out of his uniform.

Dog sat inside the closed door, his tail thumping on the floor.

"Did you take care of the horses today?" Hawke asked, patting him on the head before taking off his uniform and putting on a pair of jeans and a sweatshirt. He walked back down the hall barefoot.

He returned to the kitchen as Dani was explaining the hunting lodge to Russell. She nodded toward Hawke. "One of these days, I'll get him to retire from the State Police and join me up at the lodge for more than a week here and there."

"I'm not ready to retire yet," he said, walking to the fridge and grabbing the pitcher of iced tea.

"Why are you being a teetotaler when you're

home?" Justine asked.

"I might be called out if there is a visitor at your place tonight," Hawke said, snatching a carrot from the platter of mixed raw vegetables.

"Can we go for a bit not talking about why we know you brought them here tonight?" Dani asked.

Hawke nodded. "Fine by me."

They all helped carry dishes to the dining room table and then sat down, enjoying a dinner of good food and conversation. Hawke looked around the table. A feeling of home came over him. Dani had his heart, and Justine had his respect and gratitude. Russell was coming across as a good guy who found himself married to someone by mistake. And too nice to get out of it. Or too scared since he'd discovered his wife was a dragon in disguise.

When dinner was over and they were sitting in the living room eating the tiny cupcakes Dani had purchased at the bakery, Hawke brought up what Russell and Justine had both asked him.

"The reason Sheri killed Bobbi was to get the inheritance she left in her will to Sawtooth Sliders Kennel. She was able to get Cam Elston to help her because Bobbi also bequeathed money to Razor Ridge Runners Kennel." Hawke studied Justine. "Your kennel is also named in the will."

Justine shook her head. "W-why?"

"I think it was one of the ways she planned to leave a legacy," Hawke said.

"But how did Sheri find out about the will?" Russell asked.

"Unity worked as a cleaner in the law office that drafted Bobbi's will. She was caught snooping in the files and was sacked. She must have come across the will and then told Sheri." Hawke watched Justine and Russell as they took it all in.

Justine set her tea down and stared at Hawke. "She took Bobbi's life to get hold of money?" Tears came to her eyes. "A beautiful soul was taken just so a greedy soul could have money. Monetary gain means nothing. How you live your life helping others is what matters."

Dani sat on the couch next to Justine and put an arm around her. "She'll pay for taking your friend."

Hawke's phone buzzed.

Dog's head came up off his paws, where he lay in front of the fireplace.

Hawke glanced at the number and walked down the hall to the bedroom. "What do you have?" he asked by way of answering.

"Not good news," said Detective Volle. "We found Elston in his car. He'd been asphyxiated by carbon monoxide."

Hawke cursed. He hated it when he couldn't send someone to jail. "Self-inflicted?"

"That is unknown at the moment. Forensics is still working the scene. Thought I'd let you know."

"Thanks. We believe the other suspect is here in Wallowa County. We haven't been able to find her to make an arrest."

"Happy hunting. I'll let you know what we turn up here."

"Thanks." Hawke ended the call and walked out into the living room.

Dani interrupted Russell. "I don't like the look on your face."

Hawke sighed and sat down. He peered at the three

people seated on the couch. "The Washington State Police went to serve the warrant on Cam and found his body in a car filled with carbon monoxide."

"Is he—" Justine asked.

"He's dead. They are determining if it was self-inflicted or if he was murdered."

Justine's eyes were wide, and Russell stared at his hands.

Dani was furious. "We have to stop this woman."

Hawke nodded. "We have all law enforcement in the county looking for her."

"Do you have any idea why she's here?" Russell asked.

"We have some theories." Hawke picked up his cup of coffee.

"And they are?" Justine asked.

He glanced at Dani. She waved a hand as if saying, 'tell them.' He hadn't wanted to tell Justine his thoughts on it. She'd want to go back to her place and face the woman.

Taking another sip of coffee to help him sort out how to say it, he said, "We believe since she has killed so many for the money, she won't stop until you are killed."

Russell shook his head, "But that doesn't make sense. If my kennel inherits from their deaths, she won't get any money. I'm the sole owner of the kennel. I never made her a partner when we married." He glanced at the two women and ducked his head, saying, "I didn't trust her from the beginning. Like I said, I was having a drink with her, and the next thing I knew, I woke up in bed with her, and she said we were married."

"Will she get the kennel if you are killed?" Justine asked.

He shook his head. "I also never changed my will when I married. Everything I own goes to my brother."

Dani threw her hands in the air and said, "She did all of this and still wouldn't have gotten a cent." She nailed Hawke with a glare. "That woman has to be stopped."

"We're working on it. Justine's place is staked out. If she goes there looking for Justine, she'll be arrested." Hawke leaned back in his chair, trying to make the others see he wasn't worried, when his gut was tied in knots and he worried who else the woman was willing to kill over her obsession to get money she would never have.

"Let's play cards," Dani suggested. "It will help us take our minds off that woman."

The others begrudgingly agreed.

Hawke stood and felt his phone buzz. He answered it and walked down the hall to the bedroom. "Hawke."

"It's Volle. From the position of the body in the car and drag marks outside in the dirt, forensics believes the victim was drugged and placed in the car."

"Have everything checked for prints. I'm sure I know who did it and why. We're hoping she's here so we can catch her." Hawke ticked off another crime against Sheri on his mental checklist.

"They have been treating it as a homicide. Good luck catching the suspect."

"Thanks." Hawke ended the call and found Spruel's number. He hit call.

"Hawke, something interesting going on there?" Nathan asked.

"I just heard from the Washington State Police. Elston's death is now a homicide. I'm sure it was Sheri. Has anyone seen her car or movement at Justine's?"

"So far, nothing. I have Ivy and two deputies staking it out."

"I brought Russell and Justine up to date on why they may be targets. Turns out Sheri had been doing this all for nothing. She won't inherit if her husband dies and she isn't a partner in the kennel. We need to catch her before she hurts someone else."

"Those out on patrol are watching for her vehicle. Can you think of anywhere she'd go if not to Justine's?" Nathan asked.

"She might go back to her dad's place. When she was there earlier and tied him up, she took something out of a tin box in her bedroom. She might go there to have a place to stay and not be seen around any of the towns." As Hawke said this, he decided he'd go see. "I think I'll go take a look."

"Take backup. Call Ivy off Justine's or call Steve. Don't go alone," Nathan ordered.

"Understood." Hawke ended the call and started putting his uniform back on.

Dani walked into the bedroom. "I wondered what was taking you so long. Did they find her?"

"Not yet. I'm going on a hunch that she might be hiding out at the Tabor Ranch in Promise."

"That's a long way to go on a hunch," Dani said, handing him his handgun from the safe in his bedside table. "You aren't going alone."

"No, I'm going to call Ivy off watching Justine's. The two deputies there can keep an eye on things." He grasped Dani's shoulders. "I don't care what you have to do, but make sure those two don't go to Justine's until I can go with them in the morning."

Dani nodded, before kissing him and saying, "Be careful."

"I will." He walked down the hall and across to the door.

"Did they find her? Can I go home?" Justine asked.

"We don't have Sheri in custody yet. I'm going on a hunch. You two spend the night. In the morning, I'll take you back to Justine's and hang out while she takes care of the dogs." Hawke put his hand on the doorknob.

"Did you find out what happened to Cam?" Justine asked in a quiet voice.

Facing them, he said, "Homicide. Stay put. If I don't find her on this hunch, we'll bring in more troopers to search the county for her." He opened the door and walked out to his vehicle. Once he started up the cold vehicle, he called Ivy.

"Meet me in Eagle and we'll head to Promise. I want to see if our suspect is hiding in plain sight."

Chapter Thirty-two

Hawke and Ivy stood beside their vehicles at the entrance to the Tabor Ranch. They couldn't be seen from the house since the road wound around a small hill, hiding the house from their view.

"Let's go on foot from here," Hawke said, starting up the road.

"I'm glad the moon is growing again, so we can see without flashlights," Ivy said, walking in the tire tracks rutted in the driveway.

"The full moon during the race was a wolf moon. Indigenous people called it that because the wolves howled the loudest at the moon this time of year to prove they were surviving the winter." Hawke shrugged. "Or you can go with the scientists who say it is called this because when the wolves howl at the moon this time of year, it carries farther and sounds louder."

"I like the first version better," Ivy said as they

caught sight of the house.

Sitting in front of it was a white Ford Escort.

"She's here," Hawke said, grasping the radio mic on his shoulder. "Dispatch, this is Hawke. Do you read me?"

A bit of crackling and "This is Dispatch, go ahead, Hawke."

"We have found the suspect wanted in a double homicide. Send back up to…" He rattled off the address. "Tell them no sirens and proceed with caution."

"Copy."

Hawke dropped his hand from the mic and pressed the release on his holster to pull out his firearm. "I'll go down the right side, you go the left. We're just looking in windows to see what she's doing and if she has a weapon."

Ivy drew her weapon and nodded.

They parted, Hawke staying hidden, going from tree to bush to tree to get to the side of the house. Ivy did the same on the opposite side of the road.

At the front, he peeked in the parlor, but it was dark. Then he started down the side, peeking in each window. When he was at the last window on that side, he peeked into the kitchen and spotted Sheri sitting at the kitchen table, tears trickling down her face, one hand on a bottle of wine and the other on something on the table.

He continued to the back of the house and motioned for Ivy to come to him. He stood up to look in the kitchen window.

Sheri was gone.

Shit, he'd taken his eyes off her for only a few

seconds.

Ivy walked up to him. "Do you smell that?"

Hawke sniffed. *Gasoline*.

He ran to the back door, rammed it with his shoulder, and stopped in the kitchen with Ivy banging against his back.

The smell was strong. Hawke pulled a scarf from his pocket and tied it around his face, to keep the smell from causing him to gag or cough and give them away. He glanced at Ivy as she tied a hand towel around her face.

They walked up the hall, checking each room. Until he heard a woman talking.

"Why did she take me and leave you?"

Hawke peeked into the sitting room and spotted Ivan tied up and gagged sitting in a kitchen chair in the middle of the room. Sheri was pouring gasoline around the chair.

"I hated being with her. We moved all the time. I never had a chance to make friends. She did everything short of selling me to make money so she could entice the men to buy her meals and clothing, while I sat in that crappy van hungry, cold, and lonely." Sheri splashed more gas. "I hated you for being here with Daddy, having friends, food, and his love."

Hawke holstered his gun and motioned for Ivy to stay put. He stepped into the sitting room.

"Sheri, don't do this to Ivan. He was a toddler. He didn't have anything to do with your mom's choices."

The woman whipped around, staring wide-eyed at him. "How did you find me?"

"Process of elimination. You already hurt the person who caused you pain. Don't hurt your little brother. He missed you and wanted you back. So did your dad. All the blame goes on the woman you killed, not on the two who remained behind, wondering what happened to you."

She stared at Ivan. "You missed me? You wondered where I was?"

He nodded, his eyes wide and scared.

"Why didn't Daddy come after me?"

Ivan shrugged. He couldn't talk because of the gag.

"He didn't know where to look. Your mom not only took you and ran away from her husband and son, she also ran away from all of her family. No one knew where she was," Hawke said, taking a couple of steps toward the woman. "Everyone wanted you to come back, but no one knew where to find you."

"She was good at telling lies, changing our names each time she moved us. Why? What was she running from?" The gas can slipped from her hand, sloshing gas on her pants and shoes.

Hawke took a couple more steps.

She shook her head and put up her hands. One held a lighter. She flicked the igniter, causing a spark. "Don't come closer or I'll set all of us on fire." She kicked the gas can toward Hawke, making a trail of gas from her to the gas can in front of him.

"You don't want to hurt your baby brother, Sheri. He is innocent of everything your mom did," Hawke said, trying to keep his tone neutral when he wanted to shout at her to put the lighter away and talk to them.

Her face contorted into ugly anger. She flicked the lighter, making a flame. "He's not innocent! He tried to blackmail me. Said he knew what I'd done. I've done nothing wrong. I've gone after what was rightfully mine. That slut was sleeping with my husband and going to give that fool Cam my money. I was justified in getting back what should have been mine in the first place."

"No, it was given to Bobbi and Beverly by your grandmother. She gave you what she thought you deserved. You claimed the money and stocks. Why didn't you come pick up the personal items?" Hawke asked, hoping Ivy had by now figured out she could get in through the firewood door beside the fireplace. Or at least have a shot at Sheri through the box.

"Why would I go get items to take to a dump when I should have been given my fair share of the money?" Sheri peered at him as if he were stupid and flicked the lighter again.

"You should have been thankful your grandmother even thought of you," Hawke said, wishing he hadn't.

Sheri lunged at him.

It wasn't until he grasped her arms that he realized the lighter had dropped to the floor. A whooshing sound sent flames racing around where she'd spilled gas.

"Get her out of here! You're both covered in gas!" shouted Ivy, running past him toward Ivan.

Hawke wanted to shove Sheri out the door and return to help, but he knew Ivy was right. He grasped Sheri by the arm, dragging her out of the house and handcuffing her to a tree. A deputy ran out from behind a tree. "Watch her!" Hawke yelled and ran back to the front door.

"Ivy! Ivy, where are you?" he shouted, hoping he'd be heard above the roaring of the fire eating up the old dry wood.

Frantic that he'd put two people's lives in danger,

he headed through the door and ran into Ivy, dragging Ivan. Hawke grabbed the man under the arms and Ivy grabbed his feet. They ran as fast as they could away from the burning building. They placed Ivan on the ground as the roof fell in, followed by the second floor, sending sparks scattering across the snow.

Deputy Alden ran over. "I called Eagle Fire and the ambulance."

"By the time the fire department gets here, it will be burned to the ground," Hawke said, glancing at the tree where he'd cuffed Sheri. She stood staring at the house, a smile on her face.

## Epilogue

Hawke smiled as he scanned the faces sitting at his dining room table. He and Dani decided to do a winter barbecue in February and invite the people whom they cherished. Herb and Darlene, Justine, Tuck, Sage, and Kitree. And because Hawke felt for the pair, they'd invited Ivan and his dad. Justine had invited Russell, who had been running back and forth from his kennel to hers.

"We're pleased you could all join us this afternoon for a winter barbecue," Dani said, holding up a glass of wine.

"I think I can say from all of us, we're pleased to be here," Herb said, glancing around the table.

Heads nodded.

"Dig in. The soup has camas I baked in the ground just as our ancestors did. The salmon is also one of our first foods," Dani said, putting a hand on Hawke's shoulder.

He glanced up at her and smiled. She'd attended a first foods gathering last spring that was held in the county and became fascinated with serving and sharing them with others. She had learned how to dry camas. After harvesting some last spring, she'd dried it the traditional way in their backyard. "Dani has a new passion. She's gone from flying fighter jets and helicopters to now foraging and serving first foods." He patted her hand. "I'm proud she's learning and teaching me the ways of our people."

"I'm glad we get to join you in that discovery," Darlene said, before taking a sip of the soup."

They finished the soup and main dish before Justine glanced over at Ivan and his dad. "How are you two getting along without a home?"

Ivan shrugged. "Raina did us a favor by burning down the house. The insurance will help us build a better one that is handicap accessible and have some left over to pay off part of what we owe. That will give me some wiggle room until we can find a way to make the farm profitable."

Mr. Tabor nodded. "I wish I'd known how horrible Brenda was treating little Raina. If I'd thought she was going to live so crazy, I would have tried harder to find them and get Raina back."

"Until they invent a time machine, there is no way any of us can go back in time and fix our biggest mistakes," Hawke said.

Justine asked, "What was your biggest mistake?"

Hawke thought about that a moment and said, "Not staying true to my heritage. I've wandered from it and now I feel the need to embrace it more."

"We're both doing that," Dani said.

"I don't think it was a mistake," Darlene said. "You are going back to it when you should be. Life has a way of doing that. Going in circles but changing."

"Like the moon changes each month," Kitree chimed in.

Hawke smiled at the teenager. "Yes, and every time I see a wolf moon, I'll think of Bobbi Whitby and all the people who helped to solve her murder."

«»«»«»

Thank you for reading *Wolf Moon*. When I heard about the Eagle Cap Extreme Sled Dog Race that is held in Wallowa County every January, I knew I had to write a book using the event. It was the perfect setting for Hawke to do his tracking and sleuthing. Visiting with mushers, race officials, and volunteers was fun. You always learn more about something when to talk to the people who participate.

I hope you enjoyed Hawke's latest adventure. Please leave a review where you purchased the book. You can also leave them at Goodreads and Bookbub, too. Reviews are how an author's book gets seen.

If you would like to stay in contact with me or know more about my books, or even purchase ebook, audio, and print books directly from me, you can go to my website: https://www.patyjager.net or subscribe to my newsletter https://bit.ly/2IhmWcm

**Gabriel Hawke books**
**Murder of Ravens**
Print ISBN 978-1-947983-82-3
**Mouse Trail Ends**
Print ISBN 978-1-947983-96-0
**Rattlesnake Brother**
Print ISBN 978-1-950387-06-9
**Chattering Blue Jay**
Print ISBN 978-1-950387-64-9
**Fox Goes Hunting**
Print ISBN 978-1-952447-07-5
**Turkey's Fiery Demise**
Print ISBN 978-1-952447-48-8
**Stolen Butterfly**
Print ISBN 978-1-952447-77-8
**Churlish Badger**
Print ISBN 978-1-952447-96-9
**Owl's Silent Strike**
Print ISBN 978-1-957638-19-5
**Bear Stalker**
Print ISBN 978-1-957638-64-5
**Damning Firefly**
Print ISBN 978-1-957638-82-9
**Cougar's Cache**
Print ISBN 978-1-962065-49-8
**Wolverine Instincts**
Print ISBN 978-1-962065-89-4

While you're waiting for the next Hawke book, check out my other mystery series: Shandra Higheagle Mystery series, Spotted Pony Casino Mystery series, or The Cuddle Farm Mysteries.

## About the Author

Paty Jager grew up in Wallowa County and has always been amazed by its beauty, history, and ruralness. After doing a ride-along with a Fish and Wildlife State Trooper in Wallowa County, she knew this was where she had to set the Gabriel Hawke series.

Paty is an award-winning author of 64 novels of murder mystery and western romance. All her work has Western or Native American elements in them, along with hints of humor and engaging characters. She and her husband raise alfalfa hay in rural eastern Oregon. Riding horses and battling rattlesnakes, she not only writes the western lifestyle, she lives it.

By following me at one of these places, you will always know when the next book is releasing, if I have any sales, and about the next book:
Website: https://www.patyjager.net
Blog: https://writingintothesunset.net/
FB Page: https://www.facebook.com/PatyJagerAuthor/
Goodreads:
http://www.goodreads.com/author/show/1005334.Paty_Jager
Bookbub - https://www.bookbub.com/authors/paty-jager

If you want to get in on my mug-a-month giveaway, join my monthly newsletter. I not only give one person each month a mug, but I also have free books and short stories from other authors and myself.
https://bit.ly/2IhmWcm

Thank you for purchasing this Windtree Press
publication. For other books of the heart, please visit
our website at www.windtreepress.com.

For questions or more information contact us
at info@windtreepress.com.

Windtree Press
www.windtreepress.com
Corvallis, OR